G.O.G. 666

By
JOHN TAINE

ARMCHAIR FICTION
PO Box 4369, Medford, Oregon 97504

GENETIC'S... HOW FAR IS TOO FAR?

When three Communist scientists arrived in America on an official visit, they brought with them a great, hulking assistant named Gog. U.S. Intelligence believed there was more behind their "visit" than they were claiming, so they enlisted the help of Dr. Clive Chase, who was asked to become a spy. Reluctantly, he accepted the challenge; and in doing so discovered the unthinkable truth behind the visiting scientists' real motives—a truth that could cost him his life.

Here is a terrific science fiction tale about biology run wild, with a good dose of International intrigue thrown in for good measure. According to the author, John Taine, this story may have had some connections to actual real life events. Could G.O.G. 666 have been real? One can only speculate…

CAST OF CHARACTERS

DR. CLIVE CHASE
How had this plant genealogist let himself get talked into spying for the U.S. Military…on Communists no less?

DOROTHY GRANGE
With the tenacity of a redhead she was determined to get what she wanted…revenge.

PROFESSOR BROWN
His genius was in immunology, his serums highly coveted, and the visiting scientists showed deadly interest in them—literally.

G.O.G. 666
Introduced as an "aide" he was hideous and brutal, a barbarian unable to reason, or even speak. What exactly was his purpose?

MR. SERBIN
A true aristocrat from an older generation, it was hard to tell if he was the serious gentleman scientist he alluded to being.

MR. ARKOL
He was a pushy, loutish, all around unpleasant person who knew what he wanted—and would let no man stand in his way.

MR. KOTT
He had absolutely no use at all for the Americans and was noticeably bitter about it.

CHAPTER ONE
Commissioned

"MR. NORTH HAS GIVEN YOU A PRETTY STRONG recommendation." The Secretary glanced over the half dozen cards before him, all stamped "United States Department of Agriculture" in green. "Of course your record is not all on these, Doctor Chase," the Secretary continued, sweeping the cards aside. "Mr. North told me you know how to keep your eyes open and your mouth shut. Is that so?"

Chase reddened uncomfortably, but said nothing. The Secretary continued to scan the face before him. Receiving no answer to his question, he nodded appreciatively. "Your chief was right on one count, anyway. I wouldn't have known how to answer that myself, if you and I had been on opposite sides of the table. You can loosen up a bit now, and answer some straight questions. American stock, aren't you, Doctor Chase?"

"Yes."

"What was your father?"

"Farmer."

"And his father?"

"Farmer."

"And so on. How far back?"

"My mother says clear back to the Mayflower."

"But you have never taken the time to check up. Why not?"

Again Chase reddened with embarrassment. "Till I went to school I was out in the fields from sunup to sundown. After I learned to read I had no time to waste on family records. Anyhow, I hated history."

"Even American history?"

"Yes."

"Well, so did I, till the people who appointed me expected me to begin making it," the Secretary admitted. His tone changed. "These questions are not irrelevant. You see, I must know what you *really* think about your country. So many young men nowadays never give it a serious thought. Do you? I will grant you," he continued, "that creating new species of plants may be more interesting to a modern young man than picking the old Mayflower to pieces. But I will not admit that it is more important."

Chase looked startled. What was the Secretary going to say next? And what on earth had North been telling him? Did the Secretary think he was a subversive dedicated to the cause of overthrowing the government by force and violence? Was all this mysterious third degree the unpleasant preliminary to a curt dismissal or, more disgraceful yet, a loyalty investigation? Although barely twenty-seven, Chase had risen by sheer ability and everlasting hard work in less than three years to the coveted post of chief of the division of plant genetics. He did not want to slip back to the bottom or worse.

"I suppose the Mayflower is still important. But—"

"Exactly," the Secretary snapped. "There must be no 'but' about it, when you stand with your back to a wall before a firing squad for keeping your mouth shut. Have you the nerve to do that?"

"What for?" Chase blurted out.

"For the rest of us."

"I suppose so," Chase hesitated. Fortunately he bit his tongue in time to cut short the very natural 'but' trembling on his lips.

"You must have no reservations. I fully realize what I am asking of you. I do not ask it lightly. You are a young man, with a brilliant career before you. You are in perfect health, and you come from a long line of old New England farmer stock, whose men lived on the average well into the eighties, and whose women often outlived them. In all probability you have fifty full working years in which to do good stuff. You can walk out of this room and go back to your laboratory and fieldwork for the next fifty years, if you wish, and neither I nor anyone else who knows the circumstances will think any the less of you for doing so. Any man, and especially any young man, has a right to live as long as he can. I am seeing the possibilities from your natural point of view.

"Let me put them as strongly as I can. With your scientific endowments and the fine promise you have already given, it is not unlikely that you will make a scientific discovery of the highest practical and human importance before you are thirty. I have gone into your record exhaustively. All the experts in your line agree that you are marked for high and early distinction. By going back to your work now, and leading a decently safe life, you may do more for the human race in the long run than you might accomplish were you to risk your life to help your country in what, we are convinced, is an urgent need.

"Let me put my question abstractly first. When you have answered, I shall know whether or not I need put it more specifically. If you were given the choice between doing something now, for the immediate benefit of your fellowmen, with possibly no more than a fifty-fifty chance of success and at a considerable personal risk, and doing something as good, or almost as good, five, ten, or thirty years hence, with no appreciable risk to yourself, which would you choose?"

Chase laughed outright. "Pardon me," he apologized. "I was not laughing at what may be behind the question, but at the question itself. I suppose it is what lawyers call a hypothetical question. A senator might answer it. No man with scientific training would be rash enough to commit himself. So I shall have to ask for the concrete application of the general proposition. What is it that you want me to do?"

"First, if you refuse, will you give me your word never to refer in any way to this conversation?"

"Yes."

"Very well. Mr. Strong, Admiral Simpson, and I have chosen you as the one man in the United States who has sufficient technical training and the right personal qualifications to carry out a mission of extreme delicacy and great hazard for the government."

"What is this mission?"

"We shall ask you to go as an unaccredited observer to a foreign power, which we distrust and which distrusts us. To put it bluntly, you will be a spy. You will not be recognized by our government, and you must do all your work entirely as a private citizen. If you get into difficulties, we shall be unable to help you. It is just possible that in the event of serious trouble you might escape with your life by betraying us—by reporting this conversation, for instance. Indeed, I think it quite possible that you will be decorated if you prefer babble to bullets. Our ambitious friends have a tremendous secret admiration and envy for some of the things we can do, but not much of any more human feeling toward us. So anything like a little unneighborly espionage that they might catch us at would not be entirely unwelcome. If you agree to go, and if you are trapped, will you see it through to the end without talking?"

"Have I a sporting chance of coming out alive?"

"Provided you hold your tongue and keep your wits about you, yes."

Chase looked the Secretary straight in the eyes. "If you were in my position, would you do it?"

"No," the Secretary answered, without a moment's hesitation.

"Why not?"

"Because I have not your qualifications. This job demands a man with a scientific training of a very definite kind in biology. I have had no such training. And even as a young man, I was never the particular sort of fool who tackles an impossible proposition merely for the fun of making an exhibition of himself."

"But if you had the proper training?"

"To tell you the plain truth, I don't know. I believe I would have been daredevil enough to try it thirty years ago. But that may only be the retrospective self-flattery of middle age. Again, I don't know."

"That seems fair enough. Just one more question. Why did you choose me in preference to Wilton or Alexander, say? Each of them has at least as much on the ball as I have. Your advisers must have looked into their ancestry and their scientific records as thoroughly as they seem to have gone into mine."

"Just as thoroughly. Our Intelligence knows you three better than you know yourselves. The results of the investigation were entirely satisfactory, especially for you. In one or two things, to be frank, Wilton has a slightly higher rating than you, and Alexander stands considerably above you in social finesse—which you will probably need."

"Then why didn't you choose him—Alexander, I mean?"

"For a very simple reason. Our friends across the water *asked for you.*"

"What? *Asked* for a spy?"

"Practically. We are not actually at war with them, of course, but we may be if the international situation deteriorates much further, and we must be prepared for even the remotest contingency. Any gesture of friendliness on our part, provided it commits us to nothing serious, is all to the good. So when they asked a favor of us, we were only too glad to oblige them. In fact they asked two favors of us. One of them happened to be you, and not Wilton or Alexander. They seem to know your work over there almost as well as you know it yourself. Their Intelligence is as good as ours, if not better. For every agent we have in their country they have one or two in ours, some of them in pretty responsible positions. But in your work there are several details that puzzle them, and they have asked the purely scientific courtesy of personal conferences with you here on technical matters in biology, especially genetics. If they can get anything of political or military importance out of what they ask, they are even better than we think they are."

Chase laughed. "What a joke! They have been shouting for years that our science—especially our biology—is all antisocial superstition and theirs the real thing. According to them, genetics, from plants to animals, is all dangerous rubbish."

"Don't take all that nonsense at its face value. It is part of the hundred-year plan to keep their people believing their scientists discovered or invented everything from the wheel to the atomic bomb. The men who really count in their pure and applied science don't believe a word of all this political propaganda against our science. They are as sharp as we are; but to keep healthy and working they have to shout with the politicians while working as they please. Officially nothing of what we are doing passes their frontiers. Unofficially they receive uncensored copies of all our scientific publications. They also get reports on some work that is not published and not likely to be. Our Intelligence knows this. There is no guessing about it."

"Then why are they coming here to us?" Chase demanded.

"Perhaps they have realized their mistake at last, and want to get back in step with the rest of the world. Then they will quietly forget all the nonsense and tell their people the facts."

"You believe that?"

"No. But until our Intelligence turns up something better it will do as well as anything."

"Where does Admiral Simpson come in?"

"He doesn't, yet. Our friends know of him only as the retired chief of our Navy's medical staff. They wish to consult some younger, more highly specialized expert in medicine, and asked whether they might confer with Professor Brown of Johns Hopkins. As Professor Brown is a private citizen, he is free to see anyone he wishes. But I thought it prudent to advise Admiral Simpson of the situation. He agrees that any medical demonstrations our visitors may wish to see had better be done in a naval hospital. In fact it is almost necessary that a government hospital be offered, to avoid legal obstructions. I need not go into this now."

"No. But I don't see why they should ask for me if their problem is medical. I know nothing of medicine. My line is plant genetics."

"Just so. We don't profess to know what they are up to. We are hoping you will find out."

"I may. Though I don't see exactly how, their requests are beginning to dovetail and make some kind of sense. They want to consult Brown, an expert doing research in immunology, and me, a plant geneticist. Diseases and crops. What might that add up to?"

"If you are suggesting biological warfare," the Secretary replied, "I think you are mistaken. Our Intelligence says they are nowhere near ready for that kind of attack yet. We are. We are at least twenty years ahead of them."

"Thanks to them and their historic crusade against genetics. Well, I'll take the job. When do I start work?"

"Tomorrow, at 12:30 sharp. You and our visitors will be Admiral Simpson's guests at lunch."

"And after that? Where am I to go, and how am I to get there?"

"That I don't know. The whole matter will be entirely up to you. Win our visitors' confidence, and get yourself invited to visit their laboratories as a return courtesy for the hospitality shown them in ours. It should be simple enough. Alexander could get himself invited for life."

Chase's eyes snapped. "I'll get an invitation."

"I feel sure you will. Good luck." The Secretary shook hands. "Forget this conversation. You will not hear my name mentioned again in this matter, even by Admiral Simpson. Learn exactly what our friends are doing in your line, and then find out why they are doing it. You will be strictly on your own. Report to Admiral Simpson when and where you can. All our suspicions may be groundless. But we can take no risks. Goodbye and good luck."

CHAPTER TWO
Introductions

WHETHER BY ACCIDENT OR DESIGN, ADMIRAL Simpson was 'unavoidably detained.' At 12:29 he telephoned to the steward at the Cosmopolitan Club, asking that seasoned diplomat to request Doctor Chase to welcome the expected guests and ask them to be so kind as to wait till one o'clock for luncheon. When Chase stepped into the club library exactly at 12:291/2, he found the steward waiting with the Admiral's message.

"All right," he said carelessly, to cover his acute stage fright. "You say those are the guests over there by the fireplace?"

"All except Professor Brown and his assistant. I will show them in when they come. Oh," he added as an afterthought, "the tall gentleman's assistant will not join you at lunch. He is to come later."

"Which will make him just in time to upset us as we sit down," Chase muttered to himself. Then, aloud, "Better see that another place is laid. Our arrangements have all gone haywire."

"I will see to it, Doctor Chase."

The steward went about his business, and Chase sauntered over to the group by the fireplace, cursing the Admiral under his breath for forcing him into this awkward position. Chase hated all social functions and he detested meeting more than one stranger at a time. Now here he was facing an excruciating half-hour as genial deputy host to three distinguished scientists whom he did not know even by sight.

The three by the fireplace were unaware of Chase's approach. Talking freely and excitedly in their own language, and utterly indifferent to the curious stares of the half dozen regular members in odd corners of the large room, they wrangled and gesticulated as if they were enjoying a typical row in their national assembly, confident that in all probability no eavesdropper would understand a word they were saying.

In this they were slightly mistaken. Many scientific terms are recognizable in nearly all civilized languages, and an expert in a particular science usually knows enough of the six or seven major languages to be able to pick up the thread of a technical argument in his own specialty. He will at least know what is the subject of discussion.

Chase recognized the topic instantly. The repeated mention of his own name gave him several more clues. They were freely discussing him and his work. Curiously enough, although he missed nearly all the common, 'kitchen' words, Chase got the strong impression that their allusions to him as a man were harshly uncomplimentary. He slackened his pace. "If I am to be an observer," he thought to himself, "I may as well begin observing here and now. The short fellow with the fuzzy black hair and the fuzzier mustache doesn't seem to have any use for me at all. I'll shine up to the slim one with white hair. Sardonic, youngish-oldish sort of devil, but anyway he seems to have a sense of humor. With his white hair he might be any age from thirty-five to sixty. That fellow has real brains, but God only knows what he does with them. As for the lanky number three, I don't like him any better than he seems to like me. He doesn't shout as loudly as the short fellow, but he says more. "Oh, so that's it, is it?" Chase muttered, coming to a halt by the large table with the periodicals. He had just heard his own name coupled with the offensive epithet 'bourgeois.'

For a moment Chase was tempted to stride up to the somewhat pompous-looking savage—civilization had barely succeeded in veneering the gross, Tartar features with a mask of cunning reserve—who stood with massive legs spread wide apart directly in front of the ruddy log fire, declaiming to his companions the contemptible middleclassness of the distinguished young Doctor Chase whom they were to meet and consult. This half-Europe-anized Mongol was the 'tall gentleman' whose 'assistant', according to the steward, was to join them after lunch.

A second, more vigorous explosion of the offensive epithet, coupled with words that Chase could not understand, almost threw him off his balance. Then, from nowhere in particular, a warning voice echoed through the impetuous young observer's memory. 'Alexander could get himself invited for life.' "Damn Alexander..." Chase breathed softly. His tense lips relaxed into a grin. Instead of striding up to the tall savage with the curiously Chinese beard, and telling that vehement gentleman that farmers' sons are not petty shopkeepers, at least in America, Chase coolly walked up to the speaker and extended his hand.

"Admiral Simpson has been detained. My name is Chase. The Admiral asked me to take care of you till lunchtime. It has been set up half an hour."

The blusterer instantly became civil, not to say oily. His mouth snapped shut, concealing the jagged teeth, his sparse black beard waggled sagely, and his thick lips slowly expanded in a benign, tricky smile. To Chase's surprise the barbaric gentleman replied in perfect English.

"Doctor Clive Chase, the distinguished plant geneticist?"

Chase reddened uncomfortably.

"Chase of the United States Department of Agriculture, Bureau of Plant Genetics," he said drily.

"This is indeed an honor, to meet you in person, Doctor Chase. Let me present these gentlemen. This," he waved to the short, bespectacled specialist with the bush of fuzzy black hair, "is Mr. Kott. Something of a geneticist, like you, Doctor Chase. Only he favors animals rather than plants with his scientific attentions."

"How do you do, Doctor Kott," Chase muttered, shaking hands.

"Mister Kott," the bouncing little fuzzy-wuzzy corrected with an expansive smile, which revealed a battery of strong yellow teeth like a gorilla's. "We have no titles in our country. It is all for one, and one for all. So why draw stupid distinctions?"

"Why indeed?" Chase echoed, with an innocent stare at the oldish-youngish cynic smiling sardonically at the springy, effusive Mr. Kott. This specialist was next introduced.

"Mr. Serbin, formerly the boyish President of our late Imperial Academy of Sciences, at present in charge of the fifty year plan in genetics for our Union," Arkol announced with a flourish.

The white-haired man, who for a moment suddenly looked all of sixty, clicked his heels together and bowed stiffly from the waist. Whatever might have been the social status of his companions in zealous scientific research before the successive purges, which made everybody equal, especially the former upper classes, it was obvious that Serbin was the perfected aristocratic flower of generations of tender nurture and cosmopolitan sophistication. Chase marveled that such a man, fastidious to his fingertips, could stomach two such companions as he had accompanied on a tedious journey half way round the world. One look at the finely modeled features, the tragic dark eyes and the bitter irony playing about the reserved mouth, was enough to give him away to anyone who could read the most elementary signs of character. What could he possibly see in a pair of obvious fanatics like the bushy Kott and the bulky, bearded barbarian, who evidently ran the party, and who had now elected himself master of ceremonies? Was it just possible that the aristocratic, sardonic Serbin believed in the strange new light, which had obscured all his class in outer darkness? Chase decided that this former president of the Imperial Academy of Sciences before it was purged out of existence would repay close study. Serbin had been spared, apparently, for his unique scientific ability.

"And I," the veneered savage concluded, with a touch of childish conceit, "am Commissioner Arkol, Director of the fifty year program in preventive medicine. Pathologist by profession, administrator by force of circumstances, researcher by inclination. Now we all know one another," he concluded with a harsh laugh that was intended to be jovial.

Chase could not deny himself the luxury of one slight pinprick. Looking as stupid as he could, he explored the tallowy expanse of Arkol's flat face. "Not *Mister* Arkol, the famous specialist in pulmonary diseases?" he asked innocently, with a swift, sidelong glance at Serbin and Kott. Serbin got the point; Kott missed it as badly as the conceited Arkol himself.

"No other," the happy pathologist confessed. "Now commissioner over one great sector of the fifty year plan for national defense. Only one sector of the front," he added modestly; "but not an unimportant one."

"National defense?" Chase queried.

"Against disease."

"Oh. Quite dramatic."

"Precisely," Serbin agreed with a peculiar smile. "To cast the glamour of romance over the necessary drudgery—to say nothing of the still more necessary chloride of lime—we have dramatized our plan. The fight against disease is a great battle. Commissioner Arkol is a ruthless Gengis Khan to the germs. When they see him and his hordes of flying horsemen coming they silently fold their tents and steal away to the unsanitary havens of bourgeois respectability."

The obvious sarcasm missed its intended victim completely, and Chase wondered why Serbin should trouble himself to vent it. Then suddenly he felt strangely ill at ease. Were they all that they seemed to be, or were they playing with him like a gullible fish? What would Alexander think of it all? Chase began to long for Admiral Simpson to take the amicable trio off his heavy hands. Glancing absently in Kott's direction he caught a gleam of cold, fanatical hatred in that impulsive little man's eyes just as the strong yellow teeth flashed out in a reassuring smile of cordial friendship. Chase went cold. Turning to Arkol, he ended the awkward pause by enquiring after the missing member of the visitors' party.

"The steward said your assistant will be late. I'm sorry he can't join us."

Arkol exploded in a rude, snickering titter of laughter.

"Sorry? Wait till you see him."

"I shall have to," Chase replied stiffly. "What's the joke?"

"Assistant is hardly the right description," Kott volunteered with a prim smirk.

"My mistake," Chase apologized. "What is his exact title? Mister?"

It was Serbin who greeted this question with a hearty laugh.

The laugh was not feigned. Possibly it was the first real laugh that the cynical aristocrat had enjoyed since he decided to cast in his lot with his masters in order to keep on eating. It came from his diaphragm—to be scientifically exact; the dramatic Arkol would have said from the heart. With a peculiar smile, Serbin set the bewildered Chase right.

"Mister? Socially, you are right. But medically you exaggerate. Commissioner Arkol's assistant is what is technically known as the 'vile body.'"

"I'm afraid I don't get the point, Mr. Serbin."

"Pardon me, Doctor Chase," Serbin begged with evident sincerity. "I fear you must think us rather rude. I forgot for the moment that you specialize in plant genetics, and are not particularly interested in animal experimentation. So naturally you are lot familiar with the jargon of the older animal breeders and the ancient pathologists. Commissioner Arkol has wittily taken over some of the obsolete scientific terms—'vile body', the equivalent of the original Latin, being only one of many. It means simply the living creature, human or animal, in which our Commissioner tries out new antitoxins. His present assistant has volunteered for the experiments Commissioner Arkol is going to carry out, with the generous help of Professor Brown, on certain types of pneumonia."

"I see," said Chase. "So you call this fellow the 'vile body.' Curious how provincial a thing humor is, isn't it?"

"How so?" Kott demanded, somewhat nettled. He seemed to have enjoyed Arkol's twisted joke.

"Well," Chase explained, "I doubt whether most Americans would see the point in Mr. Arkol's little joke, whereas I believe almost any illiterate Chinese would get it at once. Our Congress wouldn't get it at all. In fact they have even missed the point to the extent of giving medals to some of the vile bodies and pensions to their widows."

"Bourgeois superstition!" the impetuous Kott exploded. He was thoroughly angry.

Chase was about to continue the argument when his memory came to his rescue. "Keep your mouth shut," he silently reminded himself, "and let him do the talking." Ignoring Kott's challenge to a verbal duel, he laughed the situation off.

"Give us time, and we'll get over our superstitions. We've done pretty well with some of them since the last depression. Even you must admit that."

Arkol gravely nodded. "Admirably," he agreed with all the pomposity of a Chinese magistrate.

Further hot water was avoided for the moment by the long-overdue diversion caused by the entry of Admiral Simpson. With the Admiral were a middle-aged, professional-looking man and a radiantly alive young woman with provocative red hair and a humorous smile, which she was doing her best to control. The Admiral himself, erect, tall, with neatly trimmed white beard, was the personification of dignity and courtesy. The vital young woman on the other hand seemed to find something irresistibly funny about the proceedings, till the professional man nudged her quite violently in the ribs with his elbow, and her face sobered into a polite, slightly flushed mask of maidenly propriety. She could be as distantly civil as any social refrigerator when she put her mind on it, and kept her eyes off Arkol's remarkable face and Kott's black mop.

Introductions and apologies for the Admiral's unavoidable detention followed. The professional man was Professor Brown. He and Arkol immediately became involved in a sultry debate on the possible number of types of pneumonia and their relative deadliness—a somewhat gruesome appetizer for a formal lunch. But as the Admiral did not even hint at cocktails, the party was forced to find stimulation where it could.

Serbin found his immediately in the redheaded young woman with the unruly smile. She, it appeared, was Brown's assistant, a highly trained bacteriologist and a graduate nurse. When Chase was introduced, he repressed an impulse to ask Arkol whether he would classify Miss Grange as a 'vile body' if she were his assistant instead of Brown's. He barely had a chance to say "how do you do?" to her, before Serbin monopolized her completely.

It did not take a sophisticate like Serbin long to discover Dorothy Grange's secret ambition. Halfway to the blue and gold private luncheon room—the club's best—he was promising, unofficially of course, to see that her ambition was gratified. She should travel and see the world, instead of being forced to content herself with gloating over the colored pictures of outlandish places in the illustrated geographical magazines. Trailing behind her and Serbin with the chattering Kott, Chase kept his mind off her seductive figure and her equally seductive hair, and concentrated his attention on what Serbin was saying.

At first Chase thought it was merely a violent flirtation at first sight. Then a chance half-turn of the white-haired young aristocrat's face put a different slant on the animated conversation. The expression on Serbin's face, which Dorothy, being a good nine inches shorter, could not see without looking up a little too constantly, was one of cool, calculating speculation. Anyone but a saint or a greenhorn would have known after one look at Serbin that he had been no ascetic in his twenties, whatever he might now be. On what would such a man speculate in that cool way, Chase wondered, on meeting a charming young woman whose physical attractions would make any man under ninety turn his head? He failed to guess, for Dorothy suddenly looked up at her companion, and the thoughtful impersonal mask instantly disappeared in a benign smile.

"I am sure I shall be able to arrange it, Miss Grange," Serbin was saying. "Our government will be only too glad to give you a free pass, as a slight return for your promised help to Commissioner Arkol. You are to assist Professor Brown in the experiments, are you not?"

"I always do. That's why he brought me along today, to talk over plans."

"Plans," Serbin smiled, "always plans."

"Why not? You can't accomplish much without planning ahead, can you?"

"I suppose not—"

The rest of Serbin's reply was lost to Chase, for just then the steward hurried up.

"Excuse me, Doctor Chase, but the tall gentleman's assistant has just arrived. Shall I show him into the blue room with you?"

"Better ask Admiral Simpson. Where is the man?"

"I left him in the library." The steward looked back. "Pardon me a moment. I see he has followed me. This is most embarrassing."

Chase turned too. His startled exclamation made them all turn sharply. Arkol and Kott showed unmistakable annoyance. A cynical smile played about Serbin's mouth.

"Commissioner Arkol's assistant," he announced, with a suspicion of irony in his mocking voice. "The 'vile body' for the experiment, which Professor Brown has kindly consented to perform, with the very able assistance of Miss Grange."

Chase, Simpson, Brown, and Dorothy Grange forgot their guests for the moment, fascinated by the grotesque spectacle of Arkol's assistant, standing dumbly apologetic in the middle of the hall.

The admiral recovered his presence of mind first. Hurrying back, he invited the assistant to join them.

"He speaks no English," Arkol almost shouted, his voice harsh with rage or contempt—Chase could not decide which. "Leave him alone. He can take care of himself."

The Admiral flushed. "I'll be damned if I do," he said quietly to himself. Taking the assistant by the arm, he led him to the head of the procession.

"You will have to see that he follows our conversation," he remarked to Arkol. "I can only manage English and a little French myself. Well, here's lunch at last. Sorry I kept you all waiting."

CHAPTER THREE
The Volunteer

CHASE TRIED, BUT FAILED, TO KEEP HIS EYES off Arkol's assistant as the ungainly fellow shuffled his way along with the Admiral to a place near the head of the table. Glancing aside for a moment, his eyes met Dorothy's. She quickly averted her own, as if both had been caught spying on something they had no business witnessing. Why had not Arkol kept him out of sight? Grudgingly Chase admitted that the commissioner had tried his best. Admiral Simpson, with his inexcusable delay was the real culprit.

Arkol had said his assistant spoke no English. The more Chase studied the man, the more he doubted whether he could speak any civilized tongue. Outwardly at least he was more of a brute than a man. But even at that there was something nobler about the patient, uncomplaining stupidity of his short, broad face, sparsely covered with a growth of bristly black hair, than the sneering superiority of the intellectual Serbin's. The assistant was himself, as God or the devil had made him; Serbin's superior sophistication was largely of his own manufacture, an artificial barrier between himself and a new world order, which was too real for his effete intellectualism. Glancing from the assistant's face to Serbin's, Chase longed to kick the contemptuous savant. Why could he not show a little human feeling, and avoid being superior to an unfortunate underling who, after all, was to be the 'vile body' in a dangerous and possibly fatal experiment? If Serbin thought so little of life in general, why did he cling so greedily to the sorry debris of his own? Chase pulled himself up in time. He was commissioned as an observer, not as a critic or a judge. Remembering his orders, he used his eyes and held his tongue.

Arkol's assistant was a curious mixture of appealing simplicity, repulsive ugliness, and more than a suggestion of brutal strength, which might burst from control at any moment to destroy anything within reach. Nearly six feet six, he dominated any ordinary group of normal human beings. He walked with a slouch, his massive head thrust well forward, and his abnormally long arms swinging awkwardly back and forth in front of his body.

Chase was not the only one who furtively studied every movement the strange creature made. Brown was interested in him as the probable battleground between two ruthlessly virulent poisons, one of which might destroy him while the other fought to prevent the destruction. Naturally the massive chest attracted Brown's particular attention. He shook his head. The lung capacity must have been at least double that of a strong athlete. Pneumonia would make short work of such a victim were it once fairly started, unless the entire resistance of the body was on a similar scale, which Brown doubted. He wondered why Arkol had chosen such a subject for his experiments.

A third personally interested spectator of the lumbering assistant's progress was Dorothy Grange. She would have to nurse this monstrosity of a man when his fight with death began. Brown, she knew, would trust him to no one but herself. She had a record with such cases—the natural kind—and knew to a split second when a crisis demanding Brown's attention was at hand. Male nurses also would be in attendance, but the responsibility and the headwork would be hers. She had seen more than one queer case through, but never one in a class with this, and she wondered how she would take it. The others had been all in the day's work, and she had forgotten most of them as soon as the patients left the hospital. But this one, she felt, she would never forget. She was not afraid, but instinctively repelled, and for a moment she thought of asking Brown to find someone to take her place. Then, ashamed of her unscientific prejudice against a man who was probably as harmless as he was brave and repulsive, she decided to stick it. Brown had lavished his own patience and skill on her education, and she would be a little less than yellow to let him down now when he was counting on her. So she silenced her instincts and forgot her half-formed fears in the joyous anticipation of a hearty lunch, for she was as hungry as a bear in spring.

Admiral Simpson took the head of the table, Dorothy the foot, and Serbin the place of honor on Simpson's right. Arkol was satisfied with his equally honorable station at the right of the radiant Dorothy.

At a significant glance from the Admiral, Chase steered the awkward assistant to the place beside Arkol, and seated himself next. Kott and Brown sat facing Chase and the assistant. Just as he was about to sit down, Chase caught sight of the assistant's feet. They were the finishing touch, huge, square, almost clubbed, and shod in massive black leather boxes.

"Oh, by the way, Mr. Arkol," the Admiral observed when they were seated, "I believe you forgot to mention your assistant's name."

Before Arkol could reply, Serbin supplied the desired information.

"Gog," he said with a wry smile.

"Gog?" the Admiral repeated. "What an unusual name."

"It is not his real name," Arkol explained. "What you might call a nickname. His own is unpronounceable, even to us." And for no apparent reason, he burst into a roar of harsh laughter.

The Admiral listened patiently till Arkol's sense of humor was satiated. Then he politely pursued the subject.

"A nickname usually has some aptness about it. I confess I can see none about this one. Our friend no more resembles the traditional Gog than Doctor Chase does."

"Is there a real Gog?" Arkol demanded in unfeigned astonishment.

"Not exactly. All I know about him is his statue. Gog and Magog were stuck up with their clubs above the entrance to the Guildhall in London before it was blitzed out in the last war. That Gog looked nothing like your assistant."

This set all three of the savants off. Whatever the joke might be, they evidently relished it hugely. At last Serbin recovered himself sufficiently to explain.

"You see, Admiral Simpson," he began, "in our country we dramatize everything. Where we lack a good word or a suitable name for anything, we invent the best possible."

"I am still in the dark," the Admiral confessed.

The effervescent Kott took up the parable, effusively. "Just as Mr. Serbin has said, we invent new words to fit our new social order. Some of our best new words come from stringing together the first letters of all the important words in long technical sentences. Just as you might have Pusa in English, for President of the United States of America," he added by way of illustration, evidently quite pleased with his latest invention.

"And what may Gog signify?" Chase demanded.

"General order in genetics," Serbin replied promptly. "Part of Commissioner Arkol's grand offensive. You have 'general orders' in military campaigns, so why not in the war against disease?"

"Genetics?" Chase queried. "I thought all your biologists were against genetics. When did you change sides?"

"We did not have to change sides," Arkol exploded. "Our biologists invented genetics."

"That too?" the Admiral quizzed.

"Yes, that too!" Kott snapped.

"When?" Dorothy asked sweetly.

"In the year 1883," Serbin informed her with a smile that might have been satirical.

"Oh," she exclaimed, as if delighted to have her scientific history set right. "I'm so glad to learn at last who really invented genetics. They taught us in college that it was that Austrian monk, Gregor Mendel, in the 1860s."

Sensing a battle in the offing, Professor Brown hastily changed the subject.

"What has genetics got to do with fighting disease? I have always been under the impression that genetics is a matter of breeding, heredity, and all that sort of thing. You won't get very far with your health program if you start trying to breed everything from common colds to cholera out of wayward humanity. Even the Chinese and the Hindus die like flies when a real plague comes along, and they have had all of three thousand years to develop a resistant strain under the most favorable laboratory conditions— nature's own unadulterated brand of natural selection. Better try something less dramatic, Mr. Arkol. An ounce of castor oil, for instance, might be more effective in certain stubborn cases than the most moving drama ever written."

Arkol did not resent Brown's attack on his dramatic tactics.

"Wait and see," he said, with a cunning, oriental smile. "The East may yet teach the West what true healing is."

"Mysticism?" Brown suggested with open disdain.

This drew a hearty laugh from the grimacing Kott. "Not exactly, Doctor Brown. Quite the contrary. Strictly practical, Commissioner Arkol's prescription."

Anticipating another debate, Dorothy steered the conversation back to names.

"I'm taken with this idea of yours of stringing initials into words. Couldn't you make gorgeous names for your friends that way?"

"And one's enemies, Miss Grange," Serbin added with sly suggestiveness.

"Of course," she agreed lightly. Oh—" she suddenly exploded, "I've thought of a perfectly wonderful one for—" She stopped herself in time, but her involuntary glance at the self-satisfied Arkol drew a sympathetic gleam from Serbin's dark eyes.

"What was it, Miss Grange?" Arkol asked politely.

"Sorry, but it was a flop after all. I put in two letters that don't really belong." Again she caught the flash of Serbin's complete understanding. "I'll have to try again when I'm not so hungry. But now about G.O.G.—'general order in genetics.' I'm curious. Of course I understand that your experiments are all part of some splendid plan—Mr. Serbin gave me a hint before we came in. But don't general orders usually have a letter or a number tacked onto them, to keep different general orders from getting mixed up—this week's with last month's, for instance? What is the number of this particular general order in genetics?"

"Six hundred, sixty six," Serbin answered quietly. "6-6-6."

The Admiral gave him a sharp look. "Is not that the number in the Apocalypse—'the number of the Beast,' as it is called?"

"Possibly," Serbin admitted with mock seriousness. "I do not remember having read the Bible myself. But Mr. Kott used to be very devout, I understand, before he was converted by another general order of our commander in chief. Perhaps he can tell us?"

Kott was bursting to explain his little joke, for it was he who had pointed out to Arkol the wonderful aptness of "G.O.G. 666" as a fitting substitute for their assistant's unpronounceable name. By luck—according to Kott—666 happened to be the correct serial number of the general order on which they were now "heavily engaged on all fronts." What more natural than to confer 666 as a surname on the unsuspecting Gog, whose flaring, flat nostrils, hairy face, hairier body, heavy projecting jaw, and lumbering bulk were more like an awkward beast's than a man's anyway? All this Kott pointed out in detail with ingratiating smirks.

The Admiral suddenly lost his appetite. A fruit cocktail had just been served. He pushed it aside. Chase was about to let out an oath, when he remembered his instructions, and picked up his spoon.

Dorothy looked at her plate with tears in her eyes. Had these savants no decency? Even if their cruel jest did go clean over the head of its butt, who understood not a single word of English, why did they have to degrade themselves by sneering at him? Furtively brushing her eyes, she glanced up at Gog. Their eyes met. What she saw in them startled her. She could have sworn that Gog had understood the drift of the conversation perfectly, although he had not got the meaning of a single word. The expression of the large brown eyes was curious. They were clear and open, but somehow veiled, as if a keen intelligence were struggling desperately to penetrate a fog of superficial stupidity, which baffled and obscured it.

Brown did his best to restore a convivial atmosphere. He too had been nauseated by the savage callousness of the experts, and he could not forgo the pleasure of a dig at Arkol, whom he shrewdly suspected of being an arrant braggart and a coward.

"Well," he said, "we may be slow in getting a joke now and then, but we know guts—pardon me, Dorothy, but you're used to me—when we see them. And I say any man who would volunteer for what is ahead of our friend Gog must have some of his own. How about it, Simpson?"

"Never saw a clearer case in my life," the Admiral snapped. "Wish I had as much myself."

The lunch was not a success. Disaster followed disaster as the unhappy Gog tried to handle the tools of civilized eating. His cocktail went into Chase's lap; his soup into Arkol's. The small steak seemed to sicken him, but he disposed of both Arkol's salad and his own by cramming the green stuff into his mouth with his hairy fingers. For dessert there was the inevitable ice cream. Gog seemed to like it. The resulting mess crowned the debacle.

CHAPTER FOUR
Arkol's Offensive

THE VISITORS HAD BEEN SIGHTSEEING FOR A week, and the time for serious work was at hand.

Gog's zero hour was less than forty minutes distant. At 8 a.m. sharp Arkol would do his best to kill the assistant who had volunteered to risk his life, and Professor Brown, with the help of his skilled nurse and expert bacteriologist, Dorothy Grange, would do everything in his power to prevent the scientific murder. Brown had waged a similar fight over the prostrate bodies of a dozen or more officers and enlisted men of the navy. Sometimes he had won, but the final tally favored the enemy. Nevertheless, Brown counted the losses on the side of victory, for each struggle brought him a stride nearer mastery over the disease he strove to subdue. More to prove to himself that he could take his own medicine than to advance science, he had once substituted for a marine who died of shock before he could contribute any data of value.

All of the men who had risked their lives on less than an even chance had volunteered without coercion of any kind. For each experiment there were at least twice as many volunteers as could be used. The men made no fuss about it; they simply "reported for duty at the hospital." Brown's conscience never troubled him about any of these men, even those who were carried out of the hospital feet first, for they had *volunteered,* and the risks they took had been carefully explained to them, not once but several times, before they were finally accepted.

About Gog however, Brown's conscience was acutely uneasy. He could not believe that anyone so simple as the hulking fellow appeared to be, was capable of understanding what the trivial operation, which was to take place at 8 a.m. sharp, really meant. And if he did not understand what it was all about, in spite of Arkol's protestations to the contrary, no human being had any right to take advantage of his confiding ignorance. Before it might be too late, Brown determined to get the truth out of Arkol.

He found the distinguished pathologist in the bacteriological laboratory entertaining Dorothy with the racy details of the marriage feast among certain half-civilized Mongolian tribes. Dorothy looked quite sick, and was glad of the chance to escape at an order from Brown.

"Go and see that Gog is comfortable," he said, "while I talk over the final details with Mr. Arkol."

Left alone with the wily Arkol, Brown carefully closed the door before trying to get anything out of this oriental diplomat who stood narrowly watching him through slitted eyelids. Arkol's face was a blank mask of impenetrable secrecy. Only the slight trembling of the tip of his wiry black beard betrayed any emotion he might be repressing.

"Arkol," Brown began, "are you sure Gog understands what is likely to happen to him?"

"Why of course, Professor Brown," Arkol purred. "All of us— Kott, Serbin, and myself—have gone over the ground thoroughly with him a hundred times." A trace of a smile flickered at the corners of his mouth. "In fact I fear I must have bored him with my everlasting insistence on the danger. He begged me to desist. Gog is a noble fellow, and a brave soldier of science."

"How does it happen," Brown asked suspiciously, "that all three of you speak practically perfect English, while Gog doesn't understand even a plain yes or no?"

"Ah," said Arkol with a frank smile, "that is easily explained. But I can hardly blame you for being puzzled by Gog's almost total lack of the graces of civilization. His tribe—if I may call it that—is sunk in barbarism. Until our own government took them in hand, they were little better than beasts. Their living conditions had better be left undescribed. "But," he added as a generous concession after a thoughtful pause, "they learn quickly enough under the proper stimulus."

As the time was growing short, Brown did not go into the question of what Arkol might consider a proper stimulus for urging the uncivilized to adopt the 'graces of civilization,' although he was tempted for a moment to follow Arkol's lead and get to the bottom of one or two things that had been puzzling him. He returned to his original question by a roundabout way suited to Arkol's tortuous oriental mind.

"You yourself studied in Vienna and Paris, I understand?"

"And London," Arkol added proudly, "as a postgraduate student after completing my internship at home."

"And Serbin—?"

"Oh, he was a confirmed globetrotter long before he was twelve. That was in the old days, of course. There's a mind for you! Brilliant! A worthy leader in a great campaign. We all are proud to follow him."

"I am not acquainted with his work," Brown replied dryly, "but I understand from our men that it is all you imply, and more too. So Serbin's fluency in all civilized languages is accounted for. Your people are natural born linguists, anyway. What about Kott? Where did he pick up his idiomatic English? There's something queer about it—not ungrammatical, of course—but distinctly foreign. Where did he pick up all he knows?"

Arkol favored his questioner with a sidelong glance of triumphant cunning.

"I forget the exact street, Professor Brown, but I believe it is somewhere in the hundred and thirties, or hundred and forties. Kott lived in that neighborhood till he was sixteen years of age, when he returned home with his exiled father. If you will look up the records you will find his name as one of the youngest matriculants at the College of the City of New York. He entered at the age of fourteen. A keen mind, Kott's, but inferior to Serbin's, I should say. Possibly the equal of my own. 'Know thyself,' as Socrates said. Also, know thy collaborators."

"Exactly what I try to do." Brown glanced at his wristwatch. "Thirty minutes. We still have plenty of time to understand Gog, even if we fail to understand one another. Does his barbarian tribe speak the common language of your country?"

Arkol was caught off his guard. His face went black. Instantly recovering his suavity he tossed the insinuation in Brown's question lightly aside, and concentrated his wily skill on fabricating a plausible equivocation.

"You might call their language a dialect of ours, I suppose. It must be, because they learn ours so quickly. That is," he qualified with a sinister leer, "if we take them in hand long enough."

"How young?"

"Oh, practically infants."

"You caught Gog young, then?"

"Barely weaned."

Brown tried to fix Arkol's eyes. "Look here," he said, drawing a card from his pocket, "either I can't do simple addition and subtraction, or else someone is romancing. By what you have just told me, Gog can only be sixteen or seventeen years old. Certainly not over twenty. He must have been born either during or shortly after your second revolution—the first of the wholesale purges."

"How do you get that?" Arkol fenced warily.

"Easily enough. Your party has been running the country only for about that length of time."

"What of it?" Arkol demanded with a half sneer.

"The old party was not particularly interested in reaching out into the wilds of Asia to civilize barbaric tribes. If Gog was snatched from his mother's breast, it must have been less than twenty years ago."

"Well?"

"Look at that." Brown handed him the card. It was a printed filing card, of the standard form in use in the naval hospital for keeping records of admissions, Gog's name was on it, and opposite the age was written 30 years, 11 months. "Whose handwriting is that?"

"Mine," Arkol admitted. "Surely you remember asking me to fill out the official records, Professor Brown?"

"Perfectly. I just wanted to be sure that you do. Now, what are you going to do about it?"

"About what?"

"Your stories don't check. One may be right. Both cannot possibly be true. Both may be false. How am I to know which one to believe?"

"Believe whichever one you wish, Professor Brown. Or neither, if you prefer."

"So that's it. I refuse to go on with this. Is Serbin about this morning?"

"I believe so," Arkol sneered. "In fact I left him in the lavatory just before I came in here to try to cheer Miss Grange up. She seemed quite nervous about something."

"Fetch him," Brown ordered curtly. "And while you are about it, look for Kott, too. I may as well say what I have to say to all three of you."

Arkol bowed. "With pleasure, Professor Brown."

As soon as Arkol was safely out of earshot—as Brown assured himself by seeing that he was not listening on the other side of the door—he called up the Admiral.

"Admiral Simpson? This is Brown. Can you join me in the hospital laboratory at once? I'm to have a conference presently with our three friends, and I want you to be present if you can."

"I'll be there in five minutes."

The Admiral arrived several minutes before Arkol succeeded in unearthing his collaborators.

"What's up?" he demanded.

"Arkol is lying."

"Of course. Why shouldn't he?"

"About Gog, I mean. There is an irreconcilable discrepancy between Gog's age as stated on the admission card and the story Arkol tells. If he is lying about this, how can we believe anything he says? Or what the other two say?"

"I don't," the Admiral replied simply.

"Then what—?"

"Look here, Brown. We can't be upstage about any of this. These men are important agents of their government. They ask us to help them out on a purely international and impersonal matter—scientific research. There hasn't been an opportunity like this since all the frontiers were closed. With a little patience we can turn them inside out and discover exactly what they are up to. The science may only be a blind—I shouldn't be surprised if it were. So keep your shirt on. Chase is doing nobly with that grinning monkey Kott, and I'm getting a line on Serbin. You dissect Arkol."

"Just what I've been trying to do," Brown answered quietly.

"Then what's wrong?"

"They have probably not told Gog anything of the risk he is taking. If he dies, it will be plain murder."

"Well," the Admiral began, and got no further. Arkol ushered Kott and Serbin into the laboratory.

"Here they are, Professor Brown," he announced. "At your service."

Brown went directly to the heart of the matter. "From an examination of Gog, I agree with Mr. Arkol that men of Gog's race are likely to be particularly susceptible to pulmonary diseases. And I think Mr. Serbin is probably right when he says that if my new inoculation against pneumonia is a success on Gog, it will be a most valuable protection for all the workers in Gog's country."

Serbin nodded. "Without the shadow of a doubt. You are our one hope, Professor Brown," he continued with a touch of his bitter irony. "The men of Gog's tribe are abnormally strong and virile. But as workers they are almost a total loss. Life in the workers' barracks is most uncongenial to those hardy men, used as they are to the glad freedom of life under the open sky. The close air gives them colds. The colds rapidly develop into pneumonia in its deadliest forms. Our own pathologists and bacteriologists have exhausted their skill without halting the devastation. Even Commissioner Arkol is powerless in the face of the enemy. If you will pardon me for making a speech," he conduced with a sardonic smile, "I would say that you, Professor Brown, are the last hope of our government. If your new antitoxin is no better than those developed in our own laboratories under Commissioner Arkol's brilliant leadership, then we may as well retreat and abandon our gains to the enemy."

"They shall not pass!" Arkol burst out dramatically, as if he were the last hero of Thermopylae or Verdun. "Our workers shall not be defrauded of all their gains for a paltry incompetence on our part. We must and shall succeed."

"Bravo!" said Serbin.

"With the brave comrade Gog's patriotic assistance," Kott smirked.

"Not if I know it," Brown interposed quietly. "My new stuff is as strong as the devil and as dangerous as hell. Not for all the workers in the world would I try it out on an ignorant man who has no more idea of what he's going up against than that table has."

"But Gog has volunteered," Kott expostulated, and Serbin seconded him. Arkol said nothing.

"That's curious," Brown remarked. "Mr. Arkol convinced me that Gog knows nothing whatever about the whole business."

"I think you exaggerate, Professor Brown," the wily Arkol objected with oily politeness. He turned to the Admiral. "Admiral Simpson, I shall deem it an honor to convince *you,* as chief in charge of affairs in this matter, that I am speaking the simple truth. Gog knows as well as Professor Brown himself the unseen dangers lurking about his path on his brave reconnaissance into No Man's Land. He has nevertheless, hero that he is, volunteered to dare the enemy in his own front line trenches. In fact—"

Whatever fact Arkol was on the point of divulging will not be known. Dorothy burst into the laboratory, her cap hanging over one ear, her hair disheveled, and her uniform in tatters.

"Come at once," she cried to Brown. "Gog has gone mad. The men can't hold him. I've called help."

Brown grabbed his hypodermic kit and raced after Dorothy.

Arkol turned aside to conceal his emotion. Kott grinned happily. Only the suave Serbin rose superior to the situation.

"Admiral Simpson," he said, "I may finish what Commissioner Arkol was about to tell you. Comrade Gog's impatient heroism would not permit him to wait till the official zero hour. He started on his lonely journey into No Man's Land at one o'clock this morning. To pacify the brave fellow we let him start considerably in advance of the hour agreed upon. He was inoculated at one o'clock this morning."

Arkol himself could not have done it better.

"Who inoculated him?" the Admiral demanded.

"Gog insisted that I do it," Arkol informed him.

"I'm not surprised." The Admiral turned his back on them and walked out.

CHAPTER FIVE
Kott's Campaign

CHASE OF COURSE HAD NOT SHARED ARKOL'S confidence, so he was unaware of what had taken place at one o'clock in the morning. He was to receive Serbin and Kott in his own division of the Department of Agriculture at nine o'clock and show them round. Arkol had planned originally to stay with Brown and watch Gog, and he saw no reason for changing his plans now. If Gog did not need his ministrations he could loaf about and entertain Dorothy when she came off duty. So everything went at Chase's end as it had been planned.

Much of Chase's work was done in a large glasshouse, where the temperature, humidity, and artificial light if necessary, could be delicately controlled. His combined office and study was a somewhat bleak brick box with whitewashed walls and ugly square windows, rather grimy, at the north end of the glasshouse. Plain steel filing cases lined one wall; glassed bookshelves and cabinets filled with neatly labeled specimens of rare or valuable plants ran around the remaining walls. The long worktable down the center of the room was littered with genetic charts like complicated family trees and the desiccated debris of innumerable samples of the experimenter's successes or failures. One handful of dried leaves was all that remained of an unsuccessful attempt to breed a drought-resistant melon; a grayish pinch of chaff was in fact the forgotten monument commemorating a single recess with Mexican alfalfa; and so it went.

Chase looked up from his desk by the north window. The clock above the door had just clicked in response to the daily time signal. He had already put in four hours of hard work. The work of the division must be done on schedule, visitors or no visitors. If intruders, welcome or otherwise, wasted his working day, he got up earlier the following morning. It was now exactly nine o'clock. With a last fascinated look at the chart he had been constructing, and a short sigh of exasperation, he shed his work jacket and reached for his coat.

"Damn it," he muttered, and hurried out to receive his guests. They were on time, waiting for him in the reception room of the administration building.

Serbin bowed with stiff formality; Kott rushed forward to shake hands.

"Shall we go into my office, or would you like to see through the greenhouses first?"

"We are entirely in your hands, Doctor Chase," Serbin said politely.

"All right, then. I'll show you some stuff one of our boys has been doing with sugar cane for the Philippines. You said you were interested in sugar the other day, so we may as well start with that."

Remembering his instructions, Chase strove to make his guests do most of the talking. His own remarks were limited to the brief comments necessary to explain details of the experiments in progress to produce a substantially richer sugar cane. To his chagrin, Kott and Serbin were equally terse. Watching Serbin's eyes, Chase realized that the chief of 'the fifty year plan in genetics' knew his business to the last dot. Serbin never looked at things in the wrong order. As easily and as instinctively as the ordinary man scans the headlines of a newspaper and takes their meaning at a glance, Serbin read the evidence before his eyes and evaluated it instantly. Only once did he ask a question that showed where his mind was. They had emerged from the last glasshouse devoted to the sugar experiment.

"You think the world needs more sugar?" Serbin asked ironically.

"That is hardly my business," Chase parried. "Congress ordered this investigation. The Philippines lobby wanted it done."

"They destroyed—how many million tons of it—in the last five years?" Kott burst out savagely. "And our workers couldn't get enough to sweeten a glass of tea!"

"Did they try?" Serbin asked with cold sarcasm. "Always complaining. Never acting."

"You think of trying sugar in your own country?" Chase asked, more out of politeness than because he was interested. Serbin's nonchalant answer irritated him.

"Possibly, in the south. But I thought I might see something in your experiments to suggest what to do next with bamboo."

Thinking Serbin's remark but another sample of the whitehaired youngish-oldish man's habitual sarcasm, Chase let it pass. What did it matter? This superior savant might sneer as he pleased at Chase's humble efforts to create a better sugar, but in his heart he knew that the work was good and not to be despised. Let him get his spite out of his system in any way he pleased, and be damned to him and his grandiose fifty year plan. They strolled toward Chase's office in silence. Pausing at the door Chase asked whether they would care to see any more of the experimental work.

"Where are the laboratories for animal breeding?" Kott demanded.

"Scattered all over the country. I am not connected with that end of the work in genetics. If you would like to see any of it, I'm sure Admiral Simpson can make the necessary arrangements."

Kott grimaced pleasantly. "Later. And thanks a million—ha? That is the real American, isn't it?"

"Not bad," Chase agreed. "You're learning our lingo at a great rate." He opened the door and ushered them into his office. "Make yourselves at home. Those leather chairs by the desk are comfortable, and there are cigarettes and cigars in easy reach."

"This is the life," Kott sighed as he sank back in the leather air cushions and lit a cigarette. "Quite like old times."

"Yes," said Serbin, "quite like old times. Old, old times. Gone forever. Never to return. Why *will* the world do it?"

"What?" Chase asked.

"Oh, the usual thing. Make a fool of itself."

"In what way?"

"Every way. And if there isn't a way, it will invent one."

Chase imagined he was beginning to see into Serbin's mind, and followed up his lead.

"A revolution, for instance?" he suggested.

"One isn't so bad," Serbin sighed reminiscently. "It was quite exciting while it lasted, I was in love at the time. It cured me. Nothing else could have. But the final revolution—that will be different."

"You think there will be another?"

"Not a doubt. Ask Kott."

Kott nodded vigorously. "We are planning for it."

"Your fifty year plan?" Chase prompted half humorously. Before Kott could reply, Serbin cut in emphatically. It was the first time that Chase had seen him betray any real feeling.

"Exactly," he exclaimed with fierce bitterness. "The curse of brutal drudgery must be lifted from the lives of our workers. And it will be lifted in fifty years, or possibly forty. Even I may live to see the end of human slavery to brute nature. If not—it doesn't matter."

"You seriously think it possible to abolish all drudgery? What about the dirty work? Who is going to do that?"

"The old argument!" Kott exploded. "Always obstruction, no cooperation, no vision."

"Show me the vision, and you'll find us willing enough to cooperate if the vision isn't a pipedream or a nightmare."

"We can't," Serbin admitted with a tinge of sarcasm.

"Why not?" Chase twitted. "Afraid it would vanish in smoke in the cold light of common sense?"

Serbin's cool retort startled Chase and put him on his guard. This man, it seemed, was an adept at reading more than experiments in genetics.

"We are not afraid of any such miracle, Doctor Chase. But we are not yet convinced that you would not share our revelations with Admiral Simpson."

"Why should I—provided you have anything to reveal that you don't want known?"

"Why indeed?" Serbin scoffed. "I am sure I don't know, unless possibly your bourgeois ideal of loyalty might impel you to betray a confidence."

"Really," Chase laughed, "you fellows have been so busy plotting and counterplotting ever since your revolution that you see a spy in every greenhorn you meet. The Admiral, for instance, doesn't give a damn about politics, national or international. All he cares a whoop about is better hospitals for broken-down sailors, and growing prize roses in his ten by twelve hothouse on the roof of his apartment. He never was a fighter in the usual sense, although he retired from the navy with the rank of admiral. He did get a congressional medal, but it wasn't for shooting anyone. It had something to do with yellow fever, if I remember rightly."

"You are slightly mistaken," Serbin remarked quietly. "Admiral Simpson was decorated for his work on dysentery."

Chase stared. "You certainly go to no end of trouble to collect useless information."

"Just a sample, Doctor Chase," Kott smirked. "Your people distrust us."

"Absurdly, irrationally!" Serbin cut in with vehemence. "So why should we take you for granted?"

"You can't help taking me for granted," Chase laughed. "I'm as easily seen through as that window—when it's clean."

Kott peered at the window, as if seeking a light from the cloudy heavens beyond. "How often does the janitor wash your windows?" he asked innocently. Not waiting for a reply, he hurried on. "However much we may think we can get on without it, even the most independent of us must ask our fellow workers for help occasionally. You agree?"

Chase nodded. "I've even asked the janitor for a hand when I've been hard pressed."

"And I," Kott confessed with a grimace that bared all his teeth, "have accepted a handout from an enemy when I was starving. Now, Mr. Serbin and I are going to ask you to put me in the way of another. You can help me without loss to yourself, and by helping me you will help our workers. Our workers? Workers all over the world!"

"How?" Chase asked point blank, cutting short Kott's mounting enthusiasm.

"Our fifty year plan needs the best engineering talent and mechanical skill it can get. Young talent, young skill. Old men have no vitality, no vision. We need both, and we need the best and strongest of both. Your country has them in abundance. You must share your riches! Not so long ago thousands of the men we needed were walking your streets, unable to earn enough to feed themselves. They were living on mouldy handouts, just as I did. They nearly revolted, just as I did. A war gave them the chance to be self-respecting workers. Did you give them the chance? No! There were thousands and thousands too many. You had overproduced. Now you can burn the sugar, the corn and the wheat surplus, and you can let the fruit you can't sell for a profit rot on the ground. You cannot let your young men rot, war or no war."

"Well, what's the answer? We've been looking for it ever since the last war. If you know, tell us, and we'll give you a dozen medals. There may be another depression. We admit that much of your philosophy. What would you do in our situation?"

"Persuade your young talent to work for us. Instead of misrepresenting conditions to them, tell them the truth. We can use thousands for the next fifty years."

"You seriously expect me to do this? What possible opportunity would I have?"

"None. We know you can't."

"Then why talk about it?"

"Because you can persuade Admiral Simpson to give Mr. Kott the opportunity he desires," Serbin replied. "As you saw a while ago, we know all about Admiral Simpson's record. Every American knows and respects him. A word from him to the proper authorities would open the necessary doors."

"What doors?"

"Universities and higher technical schools. With some well-known educator or engineer to travel with Kott and introduce him, we could easily accomplish our aim. And America would gain as much as we would. Perhaps more."

"Why not do it on your own? They won't slam the doors in your faces."

"Won't they?" Kott burst out. "I was a student in your schools while my father was in exile in this country. I know how they feel. I am an American—I was born here. And I don't blame them for feeling the way they do. They don't know. Will you help us—for the good of humanity, and the banishment of drudgery from the world? Put us in the way of a collaborator who will convince your people that Serbin and I are here on a purely technical and scientific mission, and are not a pair of anarchists out to assassinate your President, and we will do the rest. And it will be for the good of the whole human race, I tell you!"

"If you want me to speak to Admiral Simpson, I will. But really, I know him no better than you do—possibly not as well."

"But he believes in you," Serbin pointed out quietly. "He distrusts us. Have we made any impression at all on you?"

"Considerable," Chase admitted. "Speeches always get me. But this fifty year plan of yours. It sounds rather crazy to me, if you don't mind me saying so. Take it from me, you can't save the human race by engineering. And you can't abolish drudgery by machinery. That question of the dirty work sticks in the back of my mind. And who is going to run the machines to do the dirty work? If you think running machines is all a glorious Fourth of July picnic with lots of free beer, take a walk through the industrial section of Pittsburgh. And another thing. What is going to happen to the 'young talent, young skill' that signs up for a spell of your fifty year chore? What's going to become of them when they're not quite so young and virile as they were? Where will they find themselves then? With the unemployed? Or on the scrap heap?"

"Our girls are not so unattractive, Doctor Chase," Serbin replied. "In fact I have known several fully as desirable as Miss Grange."

"Leaving her out of it, if you don't mind, what of it?"

"We plan to offer any who contract with us the privilege of citizenship. Naturally they will marry. There will be children. The skill of the fathers and some of their talent will be multiplied in the second generation."

"So that's your general fifty year plan in genetics," Chase remarked drily. "I should say five hundred years would be a more likely working schedule."

"Only part of our plan," Kott grinned.

"What's the rest of it?"

"We don't quite know ourselves, yet," Serbin confessed.

"Will you ever know?"

"If Gog lives, yes."

"It's too much for me," Chase sighed. "So you want me to speak to Admiral Simpson?"

"Will you?"

"All right. But don't accuse me of betraying state secrets if I do."

CHAPTER SIX
Gog's Defense

GOG PUT UP A TERRIFIC FIGHT, PHYSICALLY and physiologically. A week after his first attack on the two male nurses who bore the brunt of the frenzied onslaught, which sent Dorothy flying for Brown, eight men were still in the hospital, and two were hobbling about on crutches. Wrenched backs, torn ligaments, and vicious bites accounted for most of the casualties, although one man had both arms broken.

Nothing short of a machine gun could have stopped Gog in his first outburst. He was finally subdued with tear gas. Blinded and choking he groped for his enemies, occasionally crushing one in his powerful hands as he made a sudden and unexpected sideward leap in the direction of greatest noise. He fought like a wild beast trapped and fighting for its life, utterly regardless of blows and pain. But the gas was too much for him. Choking his great heart out, he collapsed, and his wary enemies swooped upon him with straps and handcuffs. Securely trussed up, he was carried from the wreckage of what was to have been his sickroom and strapped to a wide bed in the pesthouse, where he could be isolated.

For the first four days and nights of his fever Gog never closed his burning eyes. Apparently realizing that the human odds were against him, he made no further attempt at violence, and the straps were unbuckled. In addition to Dorothy and an assistant who kept an hourly record of his temperature, pulse, and so forth, six strong men were constantly in the room during those first four days, and there was a liberal supply of tear gas handy in case of a fresh outburst.

Gog was probably unaware of his surroundings. He babbled incessantly in some harsh jargon, which Arkol declared was his native language—when he was not coughing and choking from the after-effects of the gas. His blazing eyes were never still, but roved constantly from face to face of his attendants. As the fever rose to one crisis after another, the eyes grew more luminous, only to cloud again as a crisis passed, as if the fever were burning some persistent poison out of his huge frame. His bulk dwindled rapidly. On the morning of the fifth day, when he suddenly passed into a deep sleep, he was little more than a sack of bones in a leather skin.

Dorothy had just taken his temperature. With a startled exclamation she looked again at the thermometer.

"Fetch Professor Brown," she ordered. "Hurry."

An orderly ran from the room, to return in thirty seconds with Brown, who had been dozing in the office next to Gog's room.

"Temperature up?"

"A hundred and twelve. It rose to that within the past hour."

"Something wrong with your thermometer," Brown muttered, bending over the sleeping man to begin an examination. "Send for another."

The orderly brought two. They checked with the first. Brown accepted the brute fact that Gog's temperature was 112.

"Will he live?" Dorothy asked.

"Probably not. So far as I know there is only one other authenticated case of such a temperature on record. A Mexican girl in the Los Angeles County Hospital lived nearly three weeks with a temperature ranging from 110 to 114."

"But she finally died, of course?"

"Yes. The autopsy showed tuberculosis of the lungs. Damn that gas! If they hadn't smothered him in it, this might never have happened. Everything was going along splendidly. Why didn't they fight him like human beings till they got the better of him? It must have been twenty to one before they finally downed him."

One of the men on duty in the room spoke up.

"Try it yourself, Professor, next time he breaks loose. I'd rather tackle a runaway tank myself."

"I suppose you had to do it," Brown conceded with an exasperated sigh. "Still, I wish you hadn't. Well, I see nothing to do but to keep him smothered in ice packs. Hustle."

The men packed him, and Brown left Dorothy in charge for the next six-hour spell. She settled down to her long watch with her fingers on Gog's pulse and her eyes intently fixed on his face. At fifteen minute intervals she took his temperature, and ordered the attendants to see to the ice packs. There was no change as the quarter hours crept by, and she did not summon Brown.

Her watch was nearly up. She had just taken Gog's temperature for the last time on her spell. There was a drop of half a degree. As she was about to send for Brown, Gog's eyes opened. They stared directly into her own. For perhaps three seconds the steady stare was almost supernaturally penetrating. The brilliant, blazing eyes seemed to look into and through her, reading her most secret thoughts. Then, just before they filmed, a look of utter hopelessness passed over them, and all the tragic despair of a frustrated life seemed to accuse her directly of the sufferer's misery.

"Brown, quick!" she cried, just as his eyes closed.

"Is he gone?" Brown asked from the door.

"I don't know. His pulse—I can feel it."

The next four hours were one long, careful, desperate fight with stimulants to keep the shrunken body from lapsing into the rest it craved. Gradually the pulse crept back and the breathing became less labored.

"He will pull through this one," Brown said. "Don't take your eyes off him. I'm going into the office to telephone. Shout if anything happens."

Brown got Admiral Simpson on the telephone. "Gog nearly went four hours ago. He's out of danger for the moment. But if he has another siege like the last, nothing on earth can save him.

Now, if he does die, I am going to ask for a warrant for the arrest of Arkol on a charge of murder."

"You can't do that."

"Why not?"

"Will it do Gog any good?"

"Obviously not. Still, I believe in bringing murderers to book, at least in the medical profession."

"What do you mean?"

"Did Gog volunteer?"

"Arkol and the other two say he did, and we can not prove that he did not."

"Granted that Gog did volunteer, there is still plenty to hold Arkol. He had no authority to do what he did without the supervision of some member of the hospital staff with a recognized medical degree. If they can't exactly hang him, they can give him a long workout in the penitentiary. And I shall do my best to see that he gets what is coming to him, whether Gog dies or not."

"What do you mean?" the Admiral asked, startled.

"Just what I say. I have enough scientific evidence to send Arkol up for life, no matter which way it comes out. And if I don't do it, I deserve something worse than hanging myself."

"You can't. Think of what it means. Hullo? Hullo— Damnation!"

Brown had hung up on the Admiral. Not taking the time to change his lounging jacket, Simpson dashed from his apartment.

"Taxi," he cried to the wondering elevator boy. "Faster, I say, faster!"

"We can't go down any faster, sir. I'll call a cab when we reach the lobby."

The Admiral's luck was with him. In less than ten minutes he was at the hospital. He found Dorothy just going off duty.

"Where's Professor Brown?"

"With Gog."

"Tell him I must see him immediately."

"Bet he has ordered me off duty, and I can't interfere unless it has so nothing to do with the patient."

"It has. Please fetch him at once. You can relieve him for five minutes. I'll promise not to keep him longer."

"Very well," she said. "I shall tell him that you have come on something urgent about Gog."

Dorothy thought Brown unnecessarily irritated by her message. Making allowance for his ragged nerves, she took his sharp rebuke in silence. As Brown made no move to leave the bedside, she quietly repeated her message.

"Admiral Simpson says it is urgent."

"Of course it is—to him," Brown snapped. "And it is just as important to me that you do as I tell you. Now, don't bother me again. This is my watch."

Dorothy was used to Brown's irritability when he was under a prolonged strain, and she thought nothing of it. Brown sometimes remembered to apologize when it was all over; more frequently he forgot. But he had once given her a strict order, when he was feeling himself, to use her head and insist on gaining her point in an emergency, no matter what he might say or do. He knew from experience that her judgment was as good as his own and her nerves considerably better than his. After all he was a research professor, and not a physician, in spite of his M. D. degree.

"Admiral Simpson says it is urgent," she repeated calmly.

"Tell him to go to hell."

Uneasy at the delay, the Admiral had started for the sickroom on his own initiative. He reached the door just in time to get Brown's message.

"Keep your shirt on," he snapped. "Let Miss Grange relieve you for five minutes. I'll not keep you a second longer. Come on now, or I'll camp here till you do."

Brown capitulated. "All right. Five minutes."

"I understand your attitude perfectly," the Admiral began when they were alone in the office. "Please try to understand mine. There is more than a question of professional ethics involved in this. I don't care how irregular Arkol's conduct may have been in proceeding with the inoculation without proper authorization, we've got to stomach it. Chase's latest report shows that we are on the track of something blacker than we suspected. Whatever evidence you might think you have against Arkol must be suppressed."

"Permanently?"

"Till he gets out of the country."

"When it will be too late to do any good. We have no extradition treaty with them," Brown pointed out.

"I see you are set on going through with whatever you may be planning. Now, look here, Brown, you're wrought up. I firmly believe you are imagining things. My advice is to forget it."

"I wonder if you will say that when you have seen the evidence."

"Where is it?"

"Here." Brown walked over to the safe and turned the combination. "You know what pneumonia bacilli look like?"

"I should, I've seen plenty of them."

"Then take a look at what is on that slide." Brown adjusted the slide in the microscope on the center table and waited for the Admiral. "Well, what do you see?"

"Pneumonia. Plain as the nose on your face."

"Plainer. I made those cultures myself from Gog thirty hours after Arkol inoculated him."

"What's wrong, then? Arkol inoculated him with pneumonia, didn't he?"

"Quite evidently he did. Try the highest power lens and see what you get."

Simpson carefully turned the screw, pausing now and then for a closer examination. Presently he stopped with a startled exclamation.

"Something else. What is it?"

"I don't know. But I suspect Arkol does."

"But why on earth should he subject Gog to this unnecessary danger—if it *is* a virulent bacterium—when he wanted him to survive the pneumonia inoculation?"

"I don't know any more than you do what is behind Kott's and Serbin's attempts to make a catspaw of Chase. But I do know that Arkol had no authority to try out anything but pneumonia against my antitoxins. If he is experimenting with two things at once, he is doing so on his own responsibility. And if he has infected Gog with this second thing through carelessness, he is certainly liable to prosecution. If he had waited till eight o'clock, he could at least have done the job cleanly."

"Possibly this new thing is a close relative of pneumonia," Simpson suggested, "and he may have been trying to kill two birds with one stone."

"Not caring whether he missed his mark and killed Gog instead. I shouldn't wonder if the new thing is a rare species of pneumonia, or at least associated with it in certain types. Men of Gog's tribe may always get the disease together—or nearly always. So it may be a case of curing both or neither. If so, Arkol should have told me before we began."

"You've probably hit the nail on the head," the Admiral agreed eagerly, glad of this possible loophole. "Arkol may be guilty of trickiness and secretiveness, but we can't accuse him of anything worse on evidence like this. My five minutes is up. Let matters slide till we see how Gog comes out, will you? Then will be time enough to go into this and make up our minds what to do."

"I'll agree to that. Now I must get back to Gog. Miss Grange needs all the rest she can get."

The Admiral waited for her. When she appeared he asked if he might take her somewhere for a snack.

"Not a snack," she said. "I could eat a horse, but I'm not allowed to leave the buildings. Suppose you take potluck with me in the dining hall? We can have something special. There's always plenty in the kitchen, I'll ask the chef to give us a real feed."

The Admiral accepted with alacrity. "Brown said you needed rest. I won't trespass on your time."

"I'm not a bit tired," she protested. "In fact I was planning to finish a story before going back to work. This case is getting on my nerves, and I've got to have some distraction."

"It must be pretty trying," the Admiral sympathized.

"Oh, the actual work is nothing. The men do all the heavy part. But I can't help thinking about that poor fellow. He is so patient, and his eyes had such a hurt look awhile ago when he seemed to be his real self for a moment. I wish I could understand his language."

"I wonder what he thinks about?" the Admiral mused. "And what he thinks about those queer specimens who brought him here?"

"Not much."

"You mean he never bothers his head about them, but takes them for granted—like laws of nature? Is he that simple?"

"I didn't mean it that way. Once, when Arkol came in to see how things were going, Gog gave him the most awful look I have ever seen. He was out of his head at the time, of course, but he has never looked at any of us as he did at Arkol."

"A murderous look?"

"There was nothing of that in it. The sort of look a faithful dog might give his master who has brutally kicked him for no reason at all. It was as if he couldn't believe what had happened. Well, here we are. Excuse me a moment, please, while I see the chef."

The Admiral spent an uncomfortable five minutes with himself while Dorothy was gone. All the evidence seemed to confirm Brown's suspicions, and his own ethical code as a medical officer urged him to investigate at once. On the other hand, his duty was to learn all that he could of what the real object of the envoys was. To antagonize them now could only frustrate the whole campaign. In a sense he was under orders. If he were that kind of man, he could shift all moral responsibility to his superiors. But he was not, and he determined to face the issue and settle it by himself. If Gog should die, what would he do? Accuse Arkol, and destroy all chance of success in the main objective, or hold his tongue? Fortunately for his peace of mind, the decision was taken out of his jurisdiction, and the matter was settled for him.

Dorothy returned in high spirits. The chef had already put together a masterpiece from what he had in the ovens and on the steam table.

"Do you mind talking shop at meals?" the Admiral asked as they sat down.

"I don't mind anything so long as nobody tries to take my food away from me when I'm hungry. What is it?"

"You are Brown's regular bacteriologist, aren't you?"

"Yes, but he often does part of the routine himself when I'm busy with a patient."

"Have you prepared any of the cultures in Gog's case?"

"All after the first. Professor Brown did that one himself thirty hours after the inoculation. He told me about Arkol taking things into his own hands."

"And you have done all the rest?"

"Yes."

"Did you notice anything unusual about any of them?"

"Not a thing. They were all commonplace. Exactly what we had expected."

"Pardon me, Miss Grange, if I seem to be cross-examining you, but I have reasons for all this. You are always careful to take all the usual precautions in your work, I suppose?"

Dorothy laughed. "If you had ever worked for anyone as fussy as Professor Brown, you wouldn't ask that. Routine and sterilization are his religion. I have seen him take a student's head off, right in the laboratory before the whole class, for some utterly ridiculous slip that couldn't make any difference one way or the other. After three years as his 'right hand'—that's what he calls me—I could make a culture the way he wants it in my sleep. If I had ever fallen down in the least trivial thing in the past three years, I shouldn't be here now."

The Admiral was satisfied. For a moment he was tempted to confide in her, and tell her what he had seen on the slide Brown himself prepared. Then he thought better of it. Until they understood the facts more clearly, there was no point in broadcasting them. So he changed the subject.

Dorothy was not to satisfy her healthy young appetite. The juicy grilled steak, done rare with mushrooms, had just been placed before her when a messenger from the office asked her to go at once to the telephone. She was back in half a minute.

"You will have to excuse me," she said. "Professor Brown wants me in the hospital."

The Admiral jumped up and hurried after her.

"A relapse?"

"I suppose so. He didn't say. Orderly! Drive me to the pesthouse as fast as you can."

The Admiral went with her. They found Brown sitting at the desk in the office. His face was like white paper, and beads of perspiration stood out on his forehead.

"Is he dead?" Dorothy cried.

"No. He will pull out. Take charge, and don't leave him till his temperature is normal. It has dropped to 104. Wire for Miss

Williams to come and relieve you. She should get here in five or six hours. I'm going to bed. I've got a first class case of influenza."

"But—" Dorothy protested.

"Do as I tell you."

"Not till I see you on your way to the hospital."

"I'll take care of him, Miss Grange," the Admiral said. "Better obey orders."

She took off her cape and went quietly into Gog's room, confident that her chief was in the best possible hands.

Gog's convalescence began definitely twelve hours later, when his temperature dropped to normal. Although Miss Williams had arrived fully six hours before, Dorothy remained on duty, obeying Brown's instructions to the letter. The long watch and the lack of food were beginning to tell on even her splendid young vitality, and she was glad enough when the time came that she could be relieved.

The moment she was free she hurried to the main office to learn how Brown was. The man at the switchboard asked her to sit down for a moment. Admiral Simpson would be down presently.

Dorothy sank into a chair, coldly apprehensive. When the Admiral entered she rose slowly, fearing bad news.

"Is he dangerously ill?" she quavered.

"Professor Brown told me to tell you to carry on. He said you would know what he meant. He died half an hour ago. Let me see you to your quarters."

CHAPTER SEVEN
Petition Granted

CHASE WAS FEELING DECIDEDLY RAGGED. It was nine days now since his heart to heart talk with Serbin and Kott, and he had had little sleep since he promised to lay their request before the Admiral. Nevertheless the program of the division of genetics had to go forward as usual, and Chase, feeling as if he had been on a prolonged spree, began his day's work at four in the morning after a catnap of two or three hours. The conferences he was asked to attend began at eight in the evening and lasted till well after midnight. Of all the twenty or more present at the conferences, Admiral Simpson was the only one he knew. The very names of the others were strange to him, and he suspected several of being secret service men. Strong, his own chief in the Department of Agriculture, was never present, nor was his name ever mentioned.

This particular morning, as nine o'clock drew near, Chase was feeling sleepier than usual. His eyes ached, and he had made one blunder after another ever since he started work at four. The early morning's attempt at accomplishing anything was a total loss. He was just about to go out for a cup of black coffee when Strong walked in.

"I came down early," Strong began, "and heard you were already on the job. Don't overdo it. You look a bit done up."

"Oh, I'm all right. I was just going out for a late breakfast. You've had yours?"

"Yes, but I'll join you in a cup of coffee."

They strolled out to seek a lunch counter. Strong passed up several on one pretext or another, till they found a roomy one practically empty. They picked up their coffee as they passed the urn, and Strong led the way to a table at the back of the room where they would not be overheard. Strong sipped his coffee in silence, closely watching Chase, who was too tired to make conversation.

"Better take a layoff," Strong remarked as he pushed his cup aside. "You've been hitting it too hard of late. Your work will suffer if you don't."

"Really, Mr. Strong, I'm all right. And if I did take a vacation now, I wouldn't know what to do with my time."

"You would find plenty to do," Strong assured him. "How would you like six weeks' leave?"

"Not at all," Chase began to expostulate, when he caught a significant look in Strong's eyes. "Unless I had a chance for a flying trip abroad, to see what some of the men in my line are doing there."

"There would hardly be time to see much," Strong objected. "Besides, you shouldn't do any work for a spell. What about a jaunt around this country—'see America first?' There are dozens of good experimental stations you haven't seen. If the idea appeals to you, I think I can wangle your expenses."

Chase considered. "I can go anywhere I like?"

"Anywhere you are invited."

"I see. Then I'll accept, if I'm still as groggy tomorrow as I feel today, and if the offer is still good."

"In the meantime," Strong said, "don't turn down any chance that looks good. Now you had better go home and get some sleep. I'll take care of whatever turns up at your office."

No names had been mentioned, and not the slightest allusion to any authority higher than Strong's had been made. Nevertheless Chase knew, as clearly as if he had been told, the source of his orders. They had come down clear from the top. Thinking over the conversation with Strong as he walked home to go to bed, he realized that every word of it could have been reported before any court of law without incriminating a single human being, although the unexpressed meaning of everything that had been said was starkly clear and unambiguous. Strong's diplomatic approach was a masterpiece in the art of saying everything while saying nothing and keeping the mouth shut. Chase took the practical lesson to heart, and resolved to improve on it, if possible. He had an appointment that evening at eight with the Admiral.

The same men who had attended all the previous conferences were present at this, the final one. The proceedings were brief and to the point. All the cards were laid face up on the table, and there was no evasion of any kind. Spades were called spades, and Chase and his collaborators were made to understand clearly that it was simply to be a battle of their wits against Kott's and Serbin's. Whatever might be given out later—much later—for publication and official history, there was no avoidance of plain speaking in the instructions given or in the reasons for giving them.

The campaign had the beauty of simplicity, and it was based on sound principles of strategy and psychology. Kott being obviously the weaker of the two, would bear the brunt of the attack. With him eliminated, they could concentrate on Serbin. Arkol might be savagely brutal, Kott unscrupulous and fanatically obsessed, but Serbin had twice the brains of both together.

Kott's record had been exhaustively investigated by the proper agents. His claim to have been a student at the College of the City of New York was checked and verified. Further, having been born in New York City while his father was resident there as a naturalized American citizen, Kott was an American citizen. At the expense of considerable cabling, it was proved that Kott had never renounced his allegiance to the United States. All the privileges of citizenship were therefore still open to him, regardless of his political opinions, so long as he did not advocate the overthrow of the government by violence.

Kott had more sense than to do anything so futile, and in any event he was interested in a revolution far more fundamental than the overthrow of any form of government or economic system. So Mr. Kott was free to roam the United States at will and no one, least of all a secret service agent, would say him nay. He was the ideal medium for an involuntary exchange of ideas.

Kott's weakness was his inordinate conceit. A man with a sense of humor can brook even the rudest contradiction, while a conceited man goes straight up in the air if he is skillfully pricked in the proper spot.

Another defect of Kott's character—a defect, that is, for the job he had so blithely undertaken—was his irrepressible enthusiasm. A cool man like Serbin would never permit himself to be drawn into a heated debate, or allow himself the doubtful luxury of an angry retort. When Serbin got excited it was for the purpose of deluding his listeners into thinking that he really was excited. But when Kott exploded, he blew up all over the place, without decent reservations, mental or otherwise. It was the unhappy little man's misfortune to believe in himself and his cause to the pitch of fanaticism, and he could not help going all out in everything he tackled, from hating a bourgeois to crossing buffalos with yaks. His success with the yaks had been unbounded; his denunciations of harmless tradesmen had not caused one of them to lose a single customer.

Serbin and Kott had begged for an opportunity to enlist 'young skill, young talent' in their fifty year plan for the total elimination of drudgery from human life. True to his promise, Chase had laid their petition, verbatim, as closely as he could remember it, before

Admiral Simpson. The investigation of Kott's record and the long nightly conferences had followed immediately. The upshot of the conferences was to grant the petition.

Officially the favorable action of the committee was a gesture of friendship to a great power, which had courteously requested, through accredited agents, a reasonable favor. Unofficially, it was an unexpectedly good opportunity to find out exactly what was behind the courteous request. Chase and his associates acted on the unofficial side; Serbin and Kott on the official, although it is only fair to Serbin to record that he probably suspected the existence of the other side. However, he was forced to back up Kott in his recruiting of volunteers for the fifty year plan, so he expressed only the most cordial goodwill and gratitude to Admiral Simpson when told that he and Kott might proceed.

The final conference was nearly over. "Doctor Chase," the chairman directed, "please take a good look at these men and memorize their faces. You have been associated with them for several evenings now, so you should not have much difficulty in remembering them. One or two of them, but never more, will be in the audience whenever Mr. Kott speaks. To put it plainly, for the last time, these men will act as 'agents provocateurs'—of a refined type, no doubt, but still just that. They will consult you, as occasion arises, as to the kind of technical question best calculated to provoke Mr. Kott into a heated denial or a defensive discussion. The nearer their questions come to making him lose his temper, the more we shall learn. An exact record of all the discussion will be kept. We shall not trouble you with the record; it will be analyzed by other experts. Your work will consist solely in stimulating unguarded discussion by backing these men up and disputing their assertions when you think it advisable. Admiral Simpson, you may inform Mr. Serbin and Mr. Kott that our government—unofficially, of course—is only too happy to cooperate with them. You will transmit to them the arrangements we have made for their convenience. That is all, gentlemen. Good night."

Kott received the good news with effusive gratitude. Serbin expressed his thanks with restraint, but none the less effectively.

"We had no doubt, Admiral Simpson, that you would help us. All over the world the United States is loved for its cordiality and freehanded generosity to the savants of foreign countries. How different from some of the European countries. There we were received with open suspicion, and even the most distinguished scientists acted as if they thought we were going to steal their discoveries."

"Bah," Kott interjected with his usual vehemence. "As if they hid anything it would have paid us to steal." He favored the Admiral with a cunning look. "Do you know what they said about America when we told them we were planning a trip here?"

"No, but I can guess. What did they say, actually?"

"They said your research institutes and universities are a thieves' paradise."

"You don't say? And just what did they mean by that?"

"Over there," Kott explained expansively, "competition is so keen that nobody knows what anyone else is doing. Their jobs depend on it. The man who can get ahead of the man above him by anticipating his discoveries sometimes uses a passkey in his researches. You get my point? Ha—not bad. But in America everything except nuclear physics is wide open, and everyone is invited to help himself to what he fancies." He concluded his curious revelations with an outburst of engaging frankness and a backhanded compliment. "But we need not attempt to steal any of your work. We want only the opportunity to convince your young talent where its brightest future lies."

"And you have very generously accorded us the opportunity," Serbin added with dignity. "We shall not abuse your confidence."

"I am sure you will not," the Admiral agreed, and he meant it from the bottom of his heart.

All doors they cared to pass, except those barred by the military even to uncleared American personnel, would be open to them. To expedite matters, the Admiral had outlined a program for them to follow, with such modifications as conditions might dictate. A number of the leading universities, both state and privately endowed, had been approached with a view to securing lecture engagements for Kott, or opportunities for him to confer with their specialists in animal genetics. It was carefully pointed out that

Mr. Kott was an American citizen, now occupying a high position in the world of practical science abroad, and that he was a keen but impartial observer of international affairs and a distinguished amateur in world economics. In short Mr. Kott was the ideal man, scientific, impartial, with first hand information on existing conditions, to open a discussion on world affairs before any open forum of intelligent students.

The widespread interest of university students throughout the land in these questions was a well known fact, although some of the older conservatives, perhaps not unwisely, deplored the inevitable scattering of the students' attention on matters irrelevant to a thorough mastery of the Three R's or their university equivalent. Nevertheless, the carefully prepared statement went on, would it not be the better part of wisdom to meet the issue squarely and, by exposing the controverted questions to the merciless criticism of realistic young minds, render them innocuous? Finally, to allay any fears the trustees might have regarding possible civic indignation at the open discussion of questionable doctrines, Doctor Clive Chase, the well known head of the Division of Genetics in the United States Department of Agriculture, would accompany Messrs. Kott and Serbin on their tour of inspection of the genetic laboratories. Doctor Chase would be present at all lectures, discussions, and forums, on the platform, if desired. It was extremely fortunate that Doctor Chase's vacation happened to coincide with the visit of his distinguished friends from abroad.

When a draft of the original letter to university presidents and heads of departments of genetics was read to him, Serbin nodded gravely.

"It is indeed extremely fortunate," he said, "that Doctor Chase's vacation coincides with our visit."

"Oh," the Admiral replied carelessly, "if he had not been free, we could have arranged a leave. Kott must have someone who knows the scientific side of things to show him around. All the geneticists who amount to anything know who Chase is, even if some of them don't know him personally. With him along, you will really be shown things, and not be just shoved along from one busy man to the next."

Whether anything beyond the general letter was sent out, Chase was not informed. From the alacrity with which some invitations were issued, Chase rather suspected that polite personal representations had been made to some of the more influential institutions. With these as 'come-ons,' the less illustrious eagerly fell into line and waited their turn for a chance at the distinguished Mr. Kott.

Whoever concocted that letter knew his human nature as it is found in some universities, if not in all. The finishing touch that brought several doubters into line was the mention of the 'very reasonable' fee, which Mr. Kott would accept for his course of two lectures. As a matter of fact the fee was stiff enough. But any man who is willing to lecture on his own time for nothing is open to suspicion. The authorities concluded that this strongly recommended Mr. Kott must be the real thing and not a cheap quack.

The day before Chase was to set out with Serbin and Kott for their first engagement, he rang up Dorothy, and asked if he might call that evening. She said she would be at home, and glad to see him.

He found her alone, in the sitting room of her apartment. It was the first time he had seen her since the Admiral's luncheon. She was pale, and looked as if she had been crying, as indeed she had. Over a week had passed since Professor Brown's funeral, but she had not yet fully recovered from the shock of his sudden death.

Chase had decided it would be less harrowing to her if he were not to refer openly to Brown's death, but to express his sympathy silently. He began by asking after Gog. The big fellow was now mending rapidly, although still much too weak to sit up in bed. Dorothy was still nursing him.

"He would have wished it," she said, furtively groping for her handkerchief.

"I know, I'm awfully sorry. If there is anything I can do—or any of us—we will be only too glad to help."

"Thanks. But there is nothing. Gog will be up and about in two or three weeks. The experiment was a success."

"I suppose so. Does Arkol think it was?"

"He hasn't said anything about it. To spare my feelings, I suppose. But I shouldn't talk that way. He has been most decent. He cabled his government, and they authorized him to confer their highest decoration. Arkol gave his own. It was pinned on—"

Chase got up and turned over the magazines on the table. When she had got control of herself, he began talking naturally of his coming trip.

"The department has given me six weeks' vacation to show Serbin and Kott around the various genetical laboratories of the country. We're starting tomorrow morning. New York is our first stop, and we'll be up to our necks by eight tomorrow evening. They're giving Kott a banquet and a public reception before he lectures. He has been invited to talk on economic conditions, or something of the sort. If anything amusing turns up on our trip, would you like me to write?"

"I'd be glad."

"Then I'll see that something does turn up. You needn't bother to answer unless you really feel like it and want something to do. Well, I must be getting along."

"I'm sorry I'm such a wet blanket," she said. "But I can't help thinking about him. He meant as much to me as my own father, and I keep expecting to hear him every time I go near the hospital. He was so much himself, so cranky, so straight, so loveable. I can't believe he's dead. But I've got to believe it. Oh—"

He held out his hand. "Goodbye."

"Goodnight."

CHAPTER EIGHT
Arkol's Innocence

AS DOROTHY INTIMATED, ARKOL'S experiment had been a complete success. Brown's new antitoxin was better even than its discoverer had dared to hope. But one experiment proves nothing, and no one knew this better than Arkol, the chastened investigator of scores of optimistic failures. The antitoxin had saved Gog, but would it save his brothers? That question could only be decided at home, so Arkol began preparing vast quantities of the new antitoxin according to the detailed instructions of

Brown's notes. Greatly as he coveted the chance for an immediate check-up on his successful experiment, he lacked the nerve to approach Simpson with a view to enlisting American volunteers. The Admiral had been less cordial since Brown's death, though still polite enough, and Arkol sensed that he was not exactly liked. But his luck was still with him, and he gained his wish in spite of the Admiral's coolness.

Fortunately—from the scientific point of view—it was the open season for pneumonia. The black line on the chart in the public health bureau rose steadily as the prolonged spell of raw, depressing weather continued, and the outbreak showed signs of reaching the proportions of a minor epidemic. The hospitals filled rapidly, and the naval hospital got its share.

Through Simpson the result of Arkol's experiment was known to the medical officers, although the experiment had not yet been made public to the whole profession. The antitoxin was still in the doubtful experimental stage, and premature publicity could only do harm. But there could be no objection to trying the antitoxin as a last resort on cases that had been given up as hopeless. If these showed improvement, the use might be cautiously extended to less desperate cases.

The results of the first three trials—made simultaneously, as the men were sinking fast—were extremely gratifying. The improvement was almost immediate, and little short of miraculous.

Then suddenly, without the slightest warning, all three men began sinking rapidly at the end of ten hours. Within twelve hours after the inoculation, they were dead. This however proved nothing. After the fifteenth similar failure something seemed to have been proved, although no one cared to say exactly what, and further experimentation was abandoned. The hopeless cases died sooner, but they died naturally.

Putting two and two together, Gog's case and the recent total failures, Admiral Simpson decided to interrogate Arkol. That wily pathologist had not been told that Brown's new antitoxin was being tried out in the naval hospital, so he was rather at a disadvantage throughout the interview.

The Admiral began by informing Arkol point blank of the complete failure of the new antitoxin on American patients. If

Arkol was not shocked, he gave a very good imitation of consternation.

"But no! Impossible! I gave Gog enough pneumonia to kill a regiment."

"Why the excess?" the Admiral asked pointedly.

Arkol saw that he had blundered. According to the official version of what had taken place at one o'clock on that fatal morning, he had given Gog exactly what Brown would have suggested, but for Gog's heroic impatience to encounter the enemy.

"I wanted to be sure," Arkol confided in a burst of candor. "With only one volunteer I could take no chances."

"Nor could the volunteer, apparently. But don't you see, Arkol, that your very zeal may have defeated your purpose? If a tenth of a grain of strychnine is indicated for a certain disorder, would you do a thorough job and be done with it once for all by prescribing ten grains?"

"But it is different with antitoxins," Arkol expostulated.

"Just how do you know that?"

"Because I have proved it on hundreds of cases."

"You mean you think you have. I'm not a pathologist, but I will wager that a critical analysis of your hundreds of cases would prove that you have proved precisely nothing. Anyhow, it seems to me, Gog's case leaves you where you were a month ago."

"I beg to differ, Admiral Simpson."

"On what grounds?"

"The experimental evidence. I am satisfied."

"Well, I'm not. I wouldn't use the stuff on a dog. Nor would Brown, if he were alive. Unless," the Admiral qualified, discharging his carefully loaded broadside, "you were trying out the antitoxin on two things at once—a very dangerous stunt to try, I should imagine."

Arkol rocked with laughter. "Pardon me, Admiral Simpson," he apologized, subsiding, "but sometimes the scientific theories of a medical man are enchantingly naive. Dangerous? I should say fatal instead. Like meeting a cat and a tiger in the jungle, and aiming at the cat but forgetting the tiger." Again he shouted and rolled without civilized restraint, tickled by his own humor no less than by the Admiral's discomfiture.

Simpson was thoroughly nettled.

"When you recover sufficiently to take it in," he said with grim politeness, "I have some observations of my own to make on big game hunting."

"They will be of value, I am sure," Arkol mocked. "But remember, I have trailed tigers all my life, while you have been aiming at cats. You are a medical officer, a practicing and administrative physician. My humble lot has been cast on the battlefield of research."

"So the jungle is a battlefield now," the Admiral remarked drily. "However, let that pass. All I wanted to point out is simply this: you shot the cat."

Arkol looked puzzled. His self-satisfied smile changed to a pucker of bewilderment, like a baby's face when it is just about to cry.

"I fear I don't understand," he faltered.

"That's your fault, not mine. I didn't invent the cat and tiger metaphor. That was your contribution to this particular research. Mine was the simple observation that you shot the cat. Get it?"

Always the self-conscious actor making the most of any melodramatic possibilities in his far-flung battle against disease and death, the great pathologist sunk his bearded chin on his knotted fist and brooded in majestic, lonely thought like Rodin's well known graven image of the Thinker. It did not seem to have occurred to Arkol that no sane thinker off the stage, least of all a scientist, ever struck any such preposterous attitude while trying to think anywhere outside the privacy of his bathroom. Simpson let him brood undisturbed, wondering what queer egg all this prolonged sitting would hatch. The egg apparently was addled, for nothing came forth.

"I am still completely at a loss," the thinker finally confessed.

"Then I shall be forced to give you the benefit of the doubt, Mr. Arkol." The Admiral said it as if he grudged the admission. "To put it baldly, you did not take proper precautions when you inoculated Gog. Your instruments were not sterile."

Arkol leapt to his feet, his face black and working with rage.

"You—you—" he choked, "you, a paltry practicing physician, a political doctor, dare to insinuate that I do not know when instruments are sterile and when they are not. You—"

"Sit down. Don't make an ass of yourself. Now look here, Arkol. Our government is more than willing that its private citizens give you all the scientific help they can. But no one will put up with your playing fast and loose with our good nature. You got ahead of us with Gog. But you also got ahead of yourself. You inoculated him with something more than pneumonia, as was agreed."

"I did not!"

"No? Unfortunately I can prove that you did."

"You can not, because I know enough about my specialty never to have attempted anything so insane."

"I'll grant that—to give you the benefit of the doubt. Then the fact remains that you were grossly negligent. Your instruments were not clean."

"Prove it," Arkol challenged, with a contemptuous leer.

"Since you place so much faith in your science, I shall let you prove it yourself to your own scientific satisfaction. Come over to the pesthouse office for a moment."

Somewhat sobered by the Admiral's evident belief that he knew what he was talking about, Arkol sulkily followed in silence. Entering the office they found Miss Williams making out her daily report.

"Is Miss Grange about?" the Admiral asked.

"Yes, sir. She is with the patient. He is trying to walk a little."

"Will you please relieve her for a few moments and ask her to come here?"

"Certainly, sir."

When Dorothy entered, the Admiral closed the door and locked it.

"I am about to have a showdown on the irregularities in Gog's case," he said, "and I want a witness. One will be sufficient till I hear what Mr. Arkol has to say. Now, Miss Grange, who was responsible for the bacteriological preparations after Gog was inoculated?"

"Professor Brown made the first. I did all the rest."

"Have you examined the slide that Professor Brown made from the first preparation?"

"No."

"Why not?"

"He wished me to leave it alone."

"Did he ever tell you to leave other slides he had made alone?"

"It was a standing order. He wanted to be entirely responsible for the results of his own work."

"Do you know where the slide is now?"

"In that safe."

"Who has the combination?"

"I don't know. The safe has not been opened since Professor Brown's death."

Arkol had followed the questions with the closest attention. He now quickly interposed a question of his own.

"How do you know, Miss Grange, that the safe has not been opened since Professor Brown's death?"

Dorothy hesitated. "As a matter of fact, I could not swear that it has not been opened. But this room is locked except when Miss Williams, myself, or an orderly is in it."

"Ah," said Arkol with a leer of cunning satisfaction. "I am ready for your scientific proofs, Admiral Simpson."

"As soon as I can get someone to open the safe. I presume you will wish to see it opened in your presence."

Arkol favored the Admiral with a tricky smile.

"Not at all. It may be hours before you find a specialist who can open the safe without nitroglycerine. Will you telephone to my hotel when you are ready to proceed?"

"I suspect you are right," the Admiral admitted good-humoredly ignoring the sly sarcasm in Arkol's politeness. "But first I must insist that you and I seal the door to our mutual satisfaction."

"If you insist. But it is too late, I fear."

"What do you mean?"

"Your own proverb, Admiral Simpson. How does it go? Something about shutting a stable door—Oh, yes, I remember."

"Never mind," the Admiral snapped. "Miss Grange, will you telephone for tape and sealing wax?"

They sat down to wait for the supplies. Dorothy relieved the tension by starting a discussion on Gog's health. His powers of recuperation were amazing, and in the last three days he had made more progress than the ordinary convalescent makes in a month. The vast quantities of food he consumed were the wonder of the staff. Arkol contributed an interesting observation it this point. All of Gog's people, he said, were tremendous eaters. But Gog's appetite was phenomenal in another respect, which the staff could not appreciate as he, Gog's friend and constant companion for many months, could. Before his recent severe illness, Arkol declared, Gog had never shown any liking for meat. Indeed he had been practically a vegetarian—if one did not count milk. But now his appetite for meat was almost insatiable. The Admiral expressed great interest in this feature of the case. In his long medical experience he had known two or three cases of changes or perversions of appetite on recovery from severe illnesses, but he had never heard of a case exactly like Gog's. Perhaps Arkol had a reasonable hypothesis to account for it? Arkol modestly disclaimed any such expert medical knowledge as the Admiral possessed; he himself was merely a research pathologist. But if he might allow himself the license of a little speculation—not scientific, of course—he would hazard the suggestion that Gog's extraordinarily high fever had affected his ductless glands in some unusual way, and that the consequent imbalance of the hormones might account for the sudden change in his feeding habits.

The Admiral received Arkol's attempt at scientific speculation with eloquent silence. Dorothy, however, seemed to think there might be something in it. Or possibly she was just trying to be polite by keeping the ball rolling. She started something she regretted.

"Of course bacteriology is the only science I have had any real training in," she began, "but some authorities claim that the ductless glands do have a lot to do with one's character and personality. Anyhow, Gog's seems to be changing rapidly as he gets better."

"In what way, Miss Grange?" Arkol asked politely.

"Mainly his mind. I used to think he must be stupid. He isn't at all."

Arkol really let himself go this time. They thought he never would stop bellowing and roaring with harsh laughter.

"Gog intellectual?" he choked. "Oh my, oh my. This is too good. My dear Miss Grange, you can have no conception how stupid Gog is."

Dorothy flushed with anger. "He is *not* stupid. It is only because you have always treated him like an inferior being that he seems stupid—to you. If you had been really fair, if you had offered him the chance of an education, you would know."

Arkol sobered. "I beg your pardon, Miss Grange, I was not laughing at you. I was thinking of Gog. If you could converse with Gog in his own language—or in what little he knows of ours—you would soon discover that Gog is a miracle of dumb, brutal stupidity."

"That is just what he is *not*," she insisted. "He is picking up English at an astonishing rate."

"Gog learning English?" Arkol echoed incredulously. "My dear Miss Grange, you must be misinformed. Who told you?"

"Nobody. Ever since he nearly startled the life out of an orderly by asking for water, I have been teaching him. It was a word at a time at first. I would point to something, say its name, and he would repeat it after me till he got it right. Now it is whole sentences—often as many as ten words. By the time he leaves the hospital I will have him reading the editorials in the *Post*," she concluded, her face flushed and happy at the success of her pupil.

As Arkol seemed speechless for the moment, the Admiral carried on.

"There is just one thing I can't understand in all this," he remarked, looking pointedly at Arkol. "If Gog is as stupid as you claim, how did he understand enough to volunteer of his own free will for your experiment?"

"Oh, that. We had no difficulty in making him understand. It was very simple."

"So I imagine," the Admiral remarked. "Well here's the sealing wax."

After they had sealed the safe as the Admiral insisted, with Arkol's thumb print on one seal and his own on the other, Arkol bowed ceremoniously and left.

"Well?" said the Admiral.

"Just that," Dorothy nodded. "Shall I telephone about a man to open the safe? Then I should relieve Miss Williams. It is my spell."

"I'll see about the man. Where shall I find you if you are off duty when he comes?"

"At my apartment. If you telephone, I will come down. I suppose it will be all right to leave Gog with the orderlies if you want me while I'm on duty."

It was nearly ten hours before the police unearthed a competent expert. Half an hour later Arkol turned up, oily beaming, to be followed in a few minutes by Dorothy. Having made Arkol examine the seals and testify to their integrity—an unnecessary formality, Arkol insisted, as he was perfectly satisfied to take the Admiral's word—Simpson instructed the expert to proceed. Arkol stood nonchalantly by, humming a meaningless tune. He seemed rather bored, or feigned most convincingly that he was. The expert departed, and the Admiral silently prepared the microscope for Arkol.

"There is the scientific evidence," he said, slipping the slide into place. "Take all the time you want to study it."

Arkol took his time. His immobile face betrayed no emotion whatever. This time he might have posed for a study of a thinker. His mind and his senses were focused in an impersonal intensity of seeing and understanding. He was unaware of his body. Too absorbed to pose, he made the perfect pose unconsciously.

"Well?" the Admiral demanded when Arkol straightened up.

"I rest my case, I have nothing to add to what I have already said." There was a certain dignity about his manner, and the Admiral was frankly puzzled.

"You saw nothing more than pneumonia bacilli?"

"I saw a great deal more."

"And it means nothing to you?"

"It means more than I would have thought possible in a country that has extended the hand of friendship to a visiting scientist seeking only to advance science."

"May I ask what you mean? To me, that slide is conclusive evidence of gross negligence in your technique. It proves beyond the shadow of a doubt that you disregarded the most elementary precautions of sterilization when you went ahead with your unauthorized inoculation of your assistant. Is that plain enough?"

"Almost too plain, Admiral Simpson. I am disappointed. So this is the open-handed generosity of which you boast?"

"You expect us to let you attempt murder and hold our tongues?"

"Murder? What do you mean to insinuate now?"

"Let us forget what is on that slide for a moment. By your own admission you gave Gog enough to kill a regiment."

"Really, Admiral Simpson, I did not expect you to descend to this. The slide, I admit, has the elements of cleverness in its conception. But this other is unworthy of the stupidest police frame-up—I think that is what you call it—in your most corrupt court of law. I never made any such 'admission' as you say. If you insist that I did, it is your word against mine. And what unpurchased judge would credit your oath after what you have tried to do with this slide—before a witness, fortunately for me."

"Your idea of fortune differs from mine," the Admiral replied. "Miss Grange won't go to pieces under cross examination."

"She will never be cross examined." Arkol turned to Dorothy. "Am I right in remembering that you can not swear that the safe was not opened after Professor Brown's death—until Admiral Simpson ordered it opened?"

"You are perfectly right. I cannot swear to anything."

"Then, Admiral Simpson, that seems to settle it. You have no evidence against me. On the other hand, if I were ungenerous, I might take a very strong position against you. Those bacteria on the slide that are not pneumonia are utterly new to me. It follows that they must have been placed on the slide with malicious intent to destroy my character, and possibly to make a felon of me."

"The law can do nothing, I suppose," the Admiral admitted. "Doubtless you will take it as a high compliment to your ingenuity that you have made a watertight defense out of what I know, and you know, is a clear conviction of negligence, if not of something worse. Possibly if I were in your position I should do the same. But let me give you one piece of advice for your own good. Don't mention those new germs to anyone outside of this room. Their very newness, which you claim as a point in your defense, might easily be turned against you. They are new in America, too. Brown had never seen anything like them. It may follow that you brought them with you on your dirty instruments."

Arkol blazed up in a flaming passion. "Impossible! I will investigate. Unless some agent of yours placed them on the slide to incriminate me, they must have been in Brown's antitoxin—"

He got no further. Dorothy forgot herself and sprang at him.

"Don't you dare," she cried, as the Admiral grabbed her arm and pulled her back. "Don't you dare fling mud at Professor Brown's name! He was twice the scientist you will ever be, and he was the straightest man that ever lived."

Arkol apologized profusely and insincerely. There was a gleam of cold cruelty in his eyes. Having satisfied Dorothy—the fight had gone out of her with the sudden overwhelming memory of her benefactor—Arkol turned to Simpson.

"What the object of your government may be in trying to 'frame' me and persecute me, I do not presume to guess. Nevertheless, as an inoffensive man of science, I think it contemptible. And as an administrator of some experience I would advise your government to choose more competent agents for its espionage. I can overlook the humiliation and indignity you have heaped upon me as an individual. But I cannot ignore the insult you have offered my state in insulting me. Were it not that my duty compels me to remain here until my assistant is well enough to travel and my collaborators have finished their work, I would leave your shores immediately. As I must stay, I take the only sensible course by offering to forget this whole regrettable episode if you will do the same."

"That almost seems to go without saying," Simpson agreed with caustic emphasis. "I understand you perfectly, and I shall do as you propose."

Arkol bowed. "I knew you would be reasonable."

On the way out he took a parting shot at Dorothy.

"Oh, by the way, Miss Grange, we did not quite finish our discussion of Gog's intelligence. I believe you are entirely right. On my recent visits I have noticed a new light in his eyes as they follow you about."

"You had better leave, Arkol," the Admiral said curtly.

Dorothy's jaw set. "I will pay him back if it is the last thing I do."

"Better not, Dorothy. He isn't worth it."

"He killed Professor Brown."

CHAPTER NINE
Invited

THE SIX WEEKS' TOUR OF SERBIN AND KOTT was a triumphal progress of animated open forums, after dinner speeches, and impromptu addresses to discussion clubs. But as every triumph presupposes a battle of some sort or another, Kott's progress was not without its share of spirited skirmishes. Even where the world-famous animal geneticist and distinguished amateur of economics and world politics was most enthusiastically received, there were always one or two rude, pointed questions in the free discussion after the formal talk, not to mention a scattering fire of barely audible expletives mostly of one syllable, aimed at the lecturer's personal appearance, his too effusive manner and his wide-open enthusiasm for the new gospel. Young America was thinking, and was not afraid to do some of its plainer thinking out loud, especially when the inevitable policeman on duty was at the other end of the hall. The cop himself had a positive genius for being in the wrong place when any particularly prickly epidemic of heckling burst out.

Serbin's attitude through it all was one of tolerant good nature.

"Let them have their fun," he said. "Their hearts are sound. And they are thinking. Presently they will begin to think seriously."

Kott took the barbed stings less philosophically. At least twice a week he was stung to a sharp retort or a vigorous denial of accusations that might have been hinted—if one were unduly sensitive—but which certainly were not openly made.

It takes a young man or woman of eighteen to twenty-two really to get under a sensitive skin or a tough hide and make the poison of a plain question or a deadly accurate personal observation rankle. The splendid idealism of youth is a proverb; only those who have experienced its merciless but just realism know fully what it means, as the perspiring Kott learned to his acute discomfort. "Balony!" by a disrespectful sophomore in civil engineering can demolish an entire pyramid of philosophical or economical speculation just as the capstone is about to be set delicately in place. The man who cannot keep his temper and his sense of humor when the sausages begin to fly is lost. Kott would have been routed at the end of the first week but for Chase's cool good temper.

It did not take much to turn imminent disaster into uproarious victory. Once Chase saved the day by what was no better than a silent pun. Kott was lecturing on animal genetics before the agricultural college of Chase's alma mater. He took fifty minutes to extol the brilliant work of his own countrymen in animal breeding, leaving only five minutes for the rest of the world. This was all right, as most of the work he described was new and interesting. But his enthusiasm and conceit betrayed him into an incautious slur on all American work in the same field. Chase was on the platform, as usual.

A gangling youth in a soiled leather jacket rose in the middle of the audience.

"Are you going to take that sitting down, Doctor Chase?" he demanded in a raucous voice.

Chase promptly stood up. It was unnecessary for him to open his mouth, and Kott's hasty concluding remarks were lost in the uproar.

On the sober scientific side, Chase admitted that the visitors had little to fear from competition. They had done as much in ten years or less as the rest of the world in half a century. On the practical side they were crowding their nearest competitor. All this, Kott declared, was due to the unselfish devotion of the best minds working for the common good, and for that alone. Whether Serbin accepted this explanation without mental reservations, Chase could not decide. But he suspected the self-contained Serbin of cynicism on this as on everything else.

The complete competence of the visiting geneticists astonished the experts whom they met and 'consulted'—mostly as a matter of courtesy. Only eight or ten times on the entire trip did Serbin find anything of sufficient interest to merit a brief note in his pocket diary. Everywhere he went he seemed to know more of the experiments and what they meant than the experimenters themselves. He took them in at a glance and, without any offensive show of knowledge, casually dropped hints for revolutionary improvements.

"How do you do it all?" the director of one great agricultural station asked with flattering astonishment. "We thought we were pretty good ourselves. But all this is like A.B.C to you, apparently. What's your secret formula?"

The white-haired young-old man smiled wryly. "I do not want to be shot for incompetence."

"So they drive you by fear?" the director caught him up eagerly. "We wouldn't tolerate that in this country. It would be the quickest way of bringing on a revolution—which nobody wants."

"We had a revolution," Serbin reminded him. "No, fear is not the driving force. I am not afraid of being shot. But I do not want to be shot. My work gives me too much pleasure."

"Still, a man can't do his best work under pressure."

"It depends upon the pressure," Serbin remarked enigmatically.

"Just what is pressing you, Mr. Serbin?" the director quizzed.

"Call it my conscience, if you like. Personally, I ceased to believe in the human conscience when I was nineteen."

The director was shocked into silence. He was a good man, a thoroughly decent sort, and he detested cynicism, real or assumed.

"How old are you now?" he asked at length.

"Older than I may look," Serbin replied with a smile.

"You look sixty, although your features are still young. Take a more human attitude toward life and you'll grow younger. And healthier."

"Thank you for your advice." Serbin bowed stiffly. "I shall endeavor to follow it."

The recruiting of 'young talent' went forward slowly but surely at the conferences after the formal talks. A considerable number signed up at once when the salaries were mentioned. The more cautious held off until they had gathered what information they could on the probable cost of living. When they found that the salary barely balanced the cost of living in the style to which they were accustomed—as students, on next to nothing a month—they demanded more for their services, and they nearly always got what they asked. Only those who were not in the top five percent of their classes in engineering or the mechanical trades were told that they could take the original offer or leave it. A drastic medical examination was insisted upon before the contract was signed.

All this could not go on without public discussion. Editors all over the country were deluged with indignant letters protesting against 'this wholesale debauching of our youth, this draining of the best young blood of our land.' To which some of the young blood retorted with cool realism that, if there was to be another depression, it preferred a white man's job to walking the streets or clearing the weeds off country back roads that no one ever traveled anyway. If there was overproduction of brains, as well as of everything else, why not try exporting to the best market. Anyhow, exile would be better than thin soup and lousy flop houses if a slump came. Letters of this tone, when printed, only fanned the controversy. If the recruiting had not stopped when it did, it would have been smothered under a tidal wave of outraged public opinion, and the offending schools would have been summarily closed.

One coolheaded editor at last came forth with a practical suggestion. Why not send an American abroad to make a thorough investigation of working conditions before the 1200 young men who had signed up were given their passports? If the agents, Messrs. Serbin and Kott, would get the consent of their government to such a plan, and if the American investigator reported favorably, it might be the best possible thing for these young men at the most critical period of their lives to find steady, useful employment at their trades and professions. Neither industry nor the military had suitable jobs for them at the moment.

The proposal took, in spite of obvious objections that might have been (and were) raised by the more conservative elements.

The next thing was to find the proper man to make the investigation. Admiral Simpson stepped into the breach, in a two-column letter to the leading New York and Chicago papers, strongly suggesting Doctor Clive Chase as the ideal investigator. The laudatory account of his character, ability and personality, which Chase read in the public print, made him blush for shame.

The Admiral's letter appeared just before Kott's final lecture on the six week's tour, and Chase was greeted with an ovation when he appeared on the platform with the grinning lecturer. He was elected by popular acclaim, and he needed only a sufficient leave of absence from the Department of Agriculture.

Kott's farewell appearance on the American platform was staged at a large State University in the middle west. This great institution had been honored with the last lecture because the state was famous for its magnificent crops and herds, largely the result of half a century of scientific experimentation at the University.

To do full honor to the occasion, Kott had chosen to deliver the sizzling lecture, which had been pent up in him for six weeks. It was on the specialty in which he had first won international fame, and the topic was one that would draw a crowd anywhere—sex.

Hours before the auditorium doors were opened, the crowds milled and fought all over the campus. Only a tenth of those who battled under the infrequent arc lights gained admission. The rest however continued to press forward in the hope of overhearing something of interest. Only a torrential downpour finally sent them scurrying for shelter, and the police breathed freely once more.

A section of two hundred seats in the center aisle had been roped off for university students specializing in biology and medicine, and about fifty invited members of the medical profession. The holders of tickets to these were admitted early by way of the service door in the rear.

Young men and women were about equally distributed in this reserved section. They appeared to be a serious lot. Most of the young women had fat notebooks with them, and nearly every young man sported at least one fountain pen, although comparatively few had bothered to bring anything to write on. They were used to lectures, and few anticipated anything worth taking down from a public lecture. But before the proceedings ended they were scribbling desperately on the backs of envelopes and trying to borrow paper from their sisters, cousins, and sweethearts.

When the chairman shepherded Kott, Serbin, and Chase onto the stage, the packed audience rose in a mass and cheered. Not unnaturally, perhaps, Kott thought the ovation was for him. He walked to the center of the stage and acknowledged the cheers and applause with smirks and profound bows. The racket doubled, mingled with confused shouts. Kott bowed lower and grinned wider. Then some genius in the reserved section had an inspiration. A young man in a sweater bearing the large block numeral of the varsity football team popped up like a jumping jack and waved his arms like a yell leader. The students howled their college yell, ably seconded by leather-lunged alumni in the balcony.

In the slight lull caused by this diversion, the yell leader managed to pass the word for the next yell. He raised his arms horizontally for a moment like a scarecrow. Then he beat out the tempo with emphatic vehemence.

"We want Chase! We want Chase!" the students yelled. The crowd took it up and roared till the auditorium shook.

The chairman proved equal to the occasion. Taking the gaping Kott by the arm and leading him into the wings, he explained that the students were merely greeting Chase as an old football hero who had captained the team, which had robbed them of the American championship seven years previously. It was an able fabrication on the spur of the moment, but it was not quite able enough, as the embarrassed chairman learned two minutes later. For the moment Kott seemed mollified. The chairman hurried back on the platform. Abandoning Kott he dashed over to Chase.

"Get up and say something to quiet them."

"But I've got nothing to say."

"Say anything. Be a sport. Help me out of this mess. Get up!"

"Oh, all right." He stood up. There was an instant hush. "Well, here I am," he said. "What do you want?"

"You!" a voice in the gallery shouted.

"I can't get up there." For some reason or another the crowd found this funny. When the laughter subsided, the self-appointed spokesman in the gallery amplified his remark.

"Go and investigate," he shouted. "Bring back the truth. We will believe you."

The uproar left no doubt as to what the crowd wanted. Chase shuffled from one foot to the other, his hands behind his back, waiting for an opportunity to reply. When at last he could make himself heard he brought the house down again by a suggestion to the gallery spokesman.

"You get me an invitation."

Undismayed by the howls of delight, which greeted this retort, Serbin rose from his seat at the back of the platform and walked quietly to Chase's side. Chase had neither seen nor heard his approach, and he started violently when he found Serbin by his side. This seemed to please the crowd even more than the exchange with the gallery. Chase was now a firmly established popular idol; his picture would be on every front page in the country the following morning. The crowd quieted quickly in its eagerness to hear what the distinguished-looking man might have to say. He was signaling to the chairman.

"Mr. Chairman," Serbin began in a strong, clear voice, "may I say something?"

"Certainly, Mr. Serbin. Ladies and gentlemen, allow me to introduce Mr. Gregory Serbin, Director of the Fifty Year Plan in Genetics of our great sister republic."

The crowd applauded briefly. It was on edge to hear Serbin's message.

"Ladies and gentlemen! Allow me to congratulate you on the excellent wisdom and sound common sense of your popular nomination. Mr. Chase, if I may express my personal opinion, is the ideal investigator to study our Fifty Year Plan in Genetics and to report the result of his investigations to the people of America. As Director of the Fifty Year Plan I have the authority to invite whom I please to visit our experimental stations and see the plan in the present state of its development. It is my belief, based on impartial science, that the plan, when fully executed, will banish brute labor forever from the world and crown human toil with a new joy and a higher dignity. I am honored to extend now to Doctor Chase a cordial invitation to visit our experimental stations and to investigate our plan in any way that he deems necessary for the discovery of the truth. And now I will trespass no longer on the lecturer's time and your good nature." He bowed, and walked back to his seat.

There was almost a riot. At last the chairman got order. The gallery spokesman shouted his last question at Chase.

"Well, what about it?"

"If I can get leave, I'll do it."

Unnoticed in the following uproar, a short, bald headed man in the last row of the balcony left his seat and quietly slipped from the auditorium. The lecture, which was to make history, began.

CHAPTER TEN
Serbin's Attack

KOTT WAS IN A COLD RAGE. EVEN THE Chairman's flowery eulogy of the speaker of the evening could not cover up the humiliating fact that Chase had stolen Kott's show before the curtain rose. For once the impetuous little man was cool and collected, although he tingled all over as if he had been thoroughly spanked. His mind was already made up before he bobbed his acknowledgement to the chairman's compliments. He would get even with this ill-mannered audience in a way its youngest and its oldest would remember till their dying days. And, what was more, he would do it within the limits of his announced subject and within his rights as a scientific lecturer on his subject.

"Ladies and gentlemen," he began, with a satisfied smirk into the expectant faces of all ages and both sexes, "the subject of my lecture, as the chairman has told you, is sex. From the large and representative audience before me, I see that sex is as vital an issue in your great commonwealth as it is elsewhere. The main topic of my lecture will deal with certain experiments of the highest practical importance to the human race, which have been carried out in our laboratories under my direction and supervision. But to provide the proper canvass for those epoch making experiments, I must first outline with some boldness what I may call the classical aspects of sex. So I shall review the major theories of sex now current.

"To an audience such as this it is probably superfluous to recall that a true understanding of the normal can only be gained through a minute study of the abnormal. Need I remind you that the greatest advances in surgery are made through a thorough analysis of the morbid, and not through prolonged contemplation of the healthy? To understand the normal functioning of sex, we must first master its abnormalities, which I shall consider in some detail first.

"The chairman tells me that about fifty medical men have honored me by attending this lecture. It would be an impertinence on my part to review any of the pathology of sex with which they, as physicians, are familiar. I shall therefore choose illustrations from the unpublished case histories collected by our research workers among some of the more barbarous tribes of Central Asia. If time permits I will include one or two of the more unusual abnormalities, hitherto unreported, which our psychologists have observed among the higher apes."

These preliminaries out of the way, Kott figuratively rolled up his sleeves and plunged into the major operation, which he had outlined. Not more than two consecutive sentences of his 'classical review' could have been printed in any newspaper or periodical to which the mails are open. Hardened reporters laid down their pencils and gaped. Kott out-Freuded Freud and made Kraft-Ebbing sound like a pamphlet on etiquette for young ladies in a finishing school. True to his promise, he went into details on practices, which any medical man in the audience would have believed physically impossible till Kott explained every refinement, and convinced the most skeptical that the art of love as practiced by civilized races is in its infancy.

Possibly all but a fraction of a percent of the audience would have paid handsomely to escape from the hall, but none dared to get up and walk out for fear of what everyone else might think. They squirmed and suffered in hot discomfort, trying to convince themselves that science is just science and nothing more. One of the first things Kott had done, as a matter of sound tactics, was to cut off their retreat. This he did by blocking all exits with the usual argument of the psychoanalysts, that whoever is uneasy when the 'unmentionable' is freely discussed in public is secretly guilty of something much worse. He had them cornered, and he gave them everything new his fellow workers had collected, from the latest in the clinics of Vienna to the startling new researches in the jungles of Borneo.

Through all that torrid hour and a quarter, the students in the reserved section were the coolest and most self-contained. The faces of the majority were expressionless and unflushed. Not a note was taken during this long preliminary to what Kott had announced was to be the main topic of his discourse. A few of the students looked frankly bored, and now and then a weary sigh escaped audibly. One or two of the girls looked openly hostile, and began reading in the voluminous notebooks, cramming for their next examination. But such resentment as there was, was at having been trapped into wasting an hour and a quarter on anecdotes that did not particularly amuse them, when they had cut into a busy evening in the expectation of getting something of scientific value for their time.

Breathless and redder than any of his audience, Kott paused and wiped his face with his handkerchief.

"Are there any questions or comments on what I have said," he asked, restoring the handkerchief to his back pocket, "before I proceed to the new experiments?"

There was dead silence. Kott smirked happily. He had succeeded in shocking this bourgeois audience into insensibility with a few scientific facts that any girl of fifteen should take for granted. Of course he was not so thick as to believe that anyone actually would rise and ask a question. After what he had said it would be impossible to open one's mouth on the subject of sex without convicting oneself of all sorts of bizarre eccentricities. But it gave him a warm glow of superiority to stand there grinning into their helpless faces.

Receiving no requests for further information from the audience as a whole, Kott singled out the reserved section for social attention.

"Perhaps some of the medical gentlemen like to offer some remarks? If I have not been clear, I shall be glad to try to remedy the defects."

All he got from this was a battery of disgusted stares. None of the medical gentlemen could think of anything they would care to say in public.

Kott next tried the students.

"In my adopted country," he grinned, "the students are hungry for knowledge, and I have been led to believe that the same is true here. Indeed, I remember that it was so when I myself was a young student in one of your great colleges. Sometimes the eagerness of the students embarrasses the lecturers. They ask such penetrating questions. Come on now, boys and girls, see if you can ask the professor something he doesn't know."

One young lady in the students' section forgot her manners for a moment. She had brought a liberal supply of paper, and her fountain pen was filled just before she left her room. So far she had not taken down a single note, and she was mad clear through, for she should have been cramming for an examination in obstetrics.

"Rats," she said, quite audibly.

The reserved section got it. The self-elected yell leader jumped up, signaling for a cheer. There was a pause of three seconds while he passed the word. Then the staccato yell crashed out.

"Rats! Rats! Rats! Kott!"

The furious applause lasted but a few seconds. The crowd released all of its tense discomfort in a well timed, thundering echo of the students' effort.

The poor chairman was at his wits' end. He sympathized with the audience, and with Kott, but he could do nothing for either. The audience solved his problem for him. The tension relieved, they were in high good humor, and inclined to treat it all as a huge joke. They roared with laughter.

"Give him a break!" somebody shouted in the gallery.

This was sufficient. They clapped till their hands ached. Literally dragged to the front of the platform by the chairman, Kott was forced to bow his thanks. The jumping jack was on his feet again. The crowd hushed.

"All together, now," the yell leader commanded, and led them off in singing "For he's a jolly good fellow." That finished, he called for a skyrocket from the students for Kott. If that hallmark of student approbation or forgiveness could not mollify Kott, nothing on earth could. The yell leader subsided, and the chairman resumed his normal functions.

"Mr. Kott will now tell us of his interesting experiments, as he promised. I am sure I am expressing the sentiment of the audience when I assure him that we are all eager to hear what he has to tell us, in spite of the lateness of the hour."

"Mr. Chairman!" Serbin's voice boomed out. "May I have the privilege of a word?" The chairman assented, and Serbin continued.

"Ladies and gentlemen, Mr. Kott asks me to express his deep appreciation of the cordial reception you have given him. He is particularly appreciative of the warm response of the students, as he himself was once a student in one of your great institutions. But, owing to the lateness of the hour, Mr. Kott has asked me to give a brief summary of the researches he promised to describe to you. With your chairman's permission I will do so in a moment.

"First, let me beg all to be so kind as to remain till the end of my remarks. After finishing my report of Mr. Kott's researches, I should like to add some observations of my own, which I believe will be of the greatest interest to all of you. May I particularly ask the gentlemen of the press to remain? It is very important that an accurate report of what I shall have to say appear tomorrow morning in the newspapers of your great country."

Without further preliminaries, Serbin proceeded to give a coldly scientific summary of the results, but not of the detailed methods, used in animal breeding in the laboratories under Kott's direction. With just hints enough to whet the appetites of the students for more, he first described the control of sex, telling how it is possible to make a mother bear only sons or daughters as desired (not by her, but by those in control). The success in these experiments had been practically one hundred percent. He then reported in greater detail on controlled fertilization. By artificial fertilization one healthy male with desirable traits could impregnate a thousand females, and a considerable proportion of the progeny would inherit at least some of the desirable traits of their common father. Also, the period of gestation could be greatly reduced. There was much more, but these items appeared to be those of greatest interest to the audience. At the conclusion of his scientific report, Serbin asked if there were questions or comments. As it was late, he requested brevity.

A medical man in the reserved section was the first to rise.

"Have these experiments been tried on human beings also?"

"Yes."

A large, florid woman in the front row stood up.

"I call it disgusting," she said, and sat down.

"That, madame, I can understand," Serbin replied. "But nature is always disgusting when men defile it."

"Then why do you do it?" a man in the second row demanded.

"For the good of humanity."

A student rose next.

"Are you really as cynical as you try to make out, or is it just part of your pose?"

Serbin smiled. "An unanswerable question, my friend."

"Why?" another student asked.

"Because if I say I am, I am not; if I say I am not, I am."

The audience pondered this in silence for a moment. Then in rapid succession several students, of both sexes, rose and asked short, technical questions. Serbin answered them all, briefly and fully, even to explaining details of the methods used when these were asked for.

The reaction of the general audience through this part of the proceedings was curious. Those with scientific training listened intently, fascinated by these lightning stabs into the thick darkness hanging over the mystery of life. To them it was the opening of a new chapter in the history of the human race. The rest suffered acutely. All of Kott's pseudo scientific obscenities were as clean to them as newly fallen snow beside this, the real science. They felt that the inmost sanctity of life had been violated and defiled. Serbin realized this, and apologized.

"Fifty years from now," he said, "all that I have told you will be a world wide commonplace. Nations that do not accept controlled breeding will be unable to compete in the struggle for survival. But at present it seems strange and unnatural, and I appreciate your repugnance to the whole conception of a consciously controlled human destiny. Fifty years hence the strong of mind and body will look back on us as a pitiable society of weaklings and sentimentalists."

"That may be all very well," an elderly man, who looked like a retired minister, objected, "provided you can get human beings to agree what sort of future they want. Who is to decide what human traits we shall attempt to strengthen and perpetuate in your 'consciously controlled human destiny?' And, more important, who shall say who is unfit to propagate his species?"

"Those are difficult questions," Serbin admitted. "But unless we attempt to answer them to the best of our knowledge, we shall make no progress. Or, if you object to the word progress, we shall change too slowly by natural selection to avert disaster."

"What disaster?" the elderly man enquired.

"Extinction. Unless we change radically, we shall have committed scientific suicide before another century has passed."

The questioner muttered and sat down. Serbin let the matter of who was going to control the breeding of the future human race drop.

"I promised not to keep you longer than I could help," he continued, when no further questions were forthcoming. "I shall conclude briefly with some observations of my own, which I ask the gentlemen of the press particularly to note.

"During the past six weeks Mr. Kott and I have been received everywhere in your great country with generous hospitality and tolerance, except in one respect, which I shall mention presently. For the hospitality and tolerance we wish to thank the people of your country sincerely. For the rest we have only regret. We feel that the unfortunate feature of our tour is not a true reflection of the feeling of your people as a whole, but the expression of a groundless suspicion on the part of a few.

"Mr. Kott's lectures have invariably been followed, as you know, by questions from the audience and free discussion. As an impartial listener to the questions asked, I have noticed an unmistakable likeness, a general trend, running like a scarlet thread through certain of the questions asked at each and every conference or lecture. To put the matter beyond all doubt, I have kept a careful record of these peculiar questions. I am convinced that anyone who knows the elementary principles of testimony and evidence will agree that all of the questions were inspired by one person. When analyzed, these questions all ask, in more or less skillfully disguised form, for details of the execution and purpose of the fifty year plan in genetics, which no student or casual seeker after scientific information would be likely to ask. The complete logic behind the entire set of these questions rules out any possibility that they are the results of chance. The implications, I think, should be sufficiently clear to all of you. We have been deliberately spied upon.

"Needless to say, I have tried to identify the questioners at successive meetings. But as they often spoke from the gallery, I was unable to see some, and of the others, I was disappointed to find that they changed from meeting to meeting. I have remarkably good memory for voices. My efforts to fix two or more of the gallery questioners as the same inspired questioner failed until this evening. I am positive that the same gentleman spoke from the gallery of the Crown Theatre in Detroit when Mr. Kott lectured there five weeks ago. If he has not already left the hall, I shall be glad to shake hands with him after we adjourn.

"I wish merely to say that both Mr. Kott and I regret this lack of confidence on the part of a few who, no doubt, are irresponsible individuals acting without the knowledge of any authorized group of citizens. It is not necessary for anyone to spy on us. Our work is open to any properly accredited investigator you may care to delegate. We cannot, of course, throw open our laboratories to mere curiosity seekers or to those who lack the sufficient scientific background to understand what they see. In view of all this, it gives me great pleasure again to beg Doctor Chase to accept our invitation. I thank you for your courteous attention."

The crowd filed out in a daze. If Serbin were bluffing, he should be brought to book and clapped into jail. If not— The answer to that alternative did not seem so clear, and excited groups formed outside the auditorium to debate the possibilities.

As Chase followed the chairman off the stage, a messenger handed him a telegram. It was from Admiral Simpson.

"Congratulations," the message read. "Our mutual friend asks me to tell you that in his opinion Alexander could not have done it better."

Chase crushed the yellow paper into his overcoat pocket.

"Wait till the Secretary sees the morning papers," he thought to himself, "if he hasn't got the news already by private wire. Somebody seems to have blundered."

CHAPTER ELEVEN
Red Roses

TWO DAYS AFTER THE SHOWDOWN WITH Arkol, both the Admiral and Dorothy received contrite notes from the wily pathologist.   Arkol apologized abjectly for the scene he had precipitated, and almost got down on his knees to his 'benefactors' lest they think him an uncivilized barbarian with no finer feelings.

The notes were not identical. Dorothy's almost made her sick. When, half an hour after the note had been delivered by special messenger, five dozen gorgeous crimson hothouse roses on stems a yard long arrived, she felt quite faint, and for a moment had difficulty in breathing.

"The beast," she panted when she recovered her breath. Nevertheless, anticipating that the roses would shortly be followed by the penitent himself, she summoned the janitor's wife, and with her assistance got the flowers conspicuously displayed. Then she opened all the windows and sat down to cool off, inwardly and outwardly. When the expected ring came, she was ready. Opening the door she found the humble Arkol parked in the hall, a good yard from the door.

"Am I forgiven?" he mumbled in his beard.

"What do you suppose?" she countered, with a wave of her hand toward the crimson show behind her. "They're lovely."

Greatly relieved, and confident that the redheaded Dorothy would not fly at him and slap his face, Arkol took her gesture as an invitation to enter.

"I am humbly grateful," he said, stepping into the spicy bower, "that you are so generous. Need I say more?"

"No," she answered curtly.

For so large a man he felt remarkably small. Studying her averted, indifferent face with crafty eyes, Arkol decided that she was just another nice American girl, good to look at, thoroughly wholesome, and incapable of guile.

"There will be a more substantial token of our appreciation later," Arkol announced coyly.

"Oh?" said Dorothy.

"Roses wither," Arkol observed, letting a slight sigh escape him.

"Do they?" Dorothy asked.

Arkol began to have doubts about her wholesome simplicity. Hurrying over this awkward break, Arkol told her that he had telegraphed to Serbin the preceding day, and that Serbin had replied at once, agreeing that Miss Grange should be 'remembered' by their government in some fitting manner, which she herself would choose if free to ask for what she really wanted.

"Have you any suggestions?" Arkol concluded with oily humility.

Dorothy gave him a straight look.

"It is too late now," she said. "But I should think you would have telegraphed to Mr. Serbin at least a day earlier."

All belief in Dorothy's guilelessness vanished from Arkol's troubled mind. Her last remark sounded suspiciously like a declaration of war. He *had* telegraphed to Serbin, of course, immediately after his row with the Admiral, and Dorothy was not afraid to let him know what she still thought of him and his peace offering of roses. She had done it neatly, he admitted to himself, and in a much more civilized way than he himself would have considered necessary. When Arkol started a war he thought a formal declaration a piece of bourgeois superstition. Attack first, declare your intentions later, was his practical working rule. His black eyes became absolutely expressionless and his yellow face a bland mask of vacuous serenity like a Buddha's.

"We shall do our best to anticipate your wishes," he assured her.

"Thank you," she said. "But I am not sure myself exactly what I want. Before Professor Brown's death, I knew—or thought I knew—what I wanted in life. Now everything is different."

Arkol was instantly sympathetic.

"Professor Brown was very dear to you. I understand."

"I am afraid you don't," she said calmly.

"Oh, but I think I do," Arkol protested earnestly. "You had for him a far deeper attachment than any romantic fancy."

"Exactly."

"Now that you see I am not so obtuse as you imagined, won't you let me try to help you?"

"How?" she demanded.

"By helping you to find yourself again. You are a young woman, little more than a girl. It is not natural for one of your age, your vitality and your talent to be thinking always of the past. You must open your eyes and see the present. Then you will be able to foresee the future and plan for it."

"Must one always be planning?" Dorothy asked innocently.

Arkol affected to relish the dig. "Our weakness, I know," he confessed with a hearty laugh. "But we *must* make the future, unless we wish it to make us. Now, let me suggest a plan for you. You must develop a new interest."

"What, for instance?"

"Bacteriology, I should imagine, could never be the same to you again. Nor, I should think, would any of the cities in which you have lived. The associations would be too poignant."

Arkol paused, imagining that he was making a good impression. To give his sympathy a good chance to soak in, he was silent for a full five seconds. Dorothy grew slightly impatient. Her brusque words knocked the wind out of him and left him gasping.

"In short, you want me to become your assistant? Bacteriology and pathology are not so far apart. At least your specialized kind is not so different from what I have been trained in. There must be a lot about Professor Brown's work that you don't know, and that I do. Thank you, Mr. Arkol; I shall consider your offer very carefully."

"Intuition," he gaped. Then he saw the humor of it, and laughed quite heartily. "The older novelists were always talking about 'woman's intuition,' but I never believed much in it till now. You prove their case. How did you guess?"

"You have been having trouble following the instructions in Professor Brown's notes for the preparation of serums A, P, and S."

"How do you know that?" Arkol shot at her with sudden suspicion.

"It is my business to know. I am Professor Brown's scientific heir, or legatee, or whatever the lawyers would say."

"Did he dispose of his scientific materials to you by will?"

"It was not necessary. For years before his death Professor Brown had a premonition that he might die suddenly. His work sometimes was extremely dangerous, and he was not always as careful is he should have been. And he never asked any man to take a risk that he would not take himself. I know that he often tried out things on himself when he had no definite knowledge that they were not deadly."

"But his materials, his notes?" Arkol insisted.

"I was coming to that. Two years ago, when he considered my training finished, he made me promise to carry on his work if he should go suddenly. To make it possible, he used to give me all his unpublished notes for safekeeping as soon as he had finished a particular series of experiments."

"What did you do with them?" Arkol asked quietly. Only the trembling tip of his beard betrayed his eagerness.

"When any series was definitely abandoned—either because it was superseded by later work, or because if proved to be a false lead—I destroyed the notes concerning it."

"But the others? The experiments still in progress?"

"I kept the notes, of course."

"Where?" Arkol demanded sharply, unable to repress his feelings.

"Until a few hours ago they were in a safe deposit box at the First National Bank."

Arkol had difficulty in keeping his seat. "You have them here?"

"Yes. They are in the fireplace."

Arkol sprang up and strode to the grate. It was black and cold.

"There are only ashes here," he said, his voice hoarse with rage.

"Why not? I felt cold this morning, so I lit a fire. It has warmed up considerably, so I let the fire die down."

Arkol controlled himself, although his muscular fists clenched and unclenched, and the corded veins bulged on his forehead.

"Won't you sit down?" Dorothy begged. She feared he might become violent unless he were suddenly distracted.

Arkol walked to the nearest chair and sat down heavily, not trusting himself to reply until he had recovered his habitual diplomacy.

"It was a rash thing to do," he said finally, with an unmistakable threat in his tone. "I would not have taken such a risk lightly myself."

"I have taken no risk," Dorothy retorted coldly. "The notes will never be stolen now."

Arkol ignored her last remark. "Do you realize, Miss Grange, that you may have set the world back a century or more?"

"No. Have I? How?"

"By frustrating our fifty year plan. I have seen men shot for blunders that were shining triumphs of creative genius for our plan compared to this blunder of yours."

"But I am not interested in your plan, Mr. Arkol."

"Perhaps you are even hostile to it?" Arkol insinuated.

"I know next to nothing about it. Mr. Serbin and you have told me something, of course. But it has all been very vague. So why should I be hostile?"

"Why indeed?" he echoed with savage sarcasm. "Because you have no vision. The future of the race means nothing to you. So long as you have your bourgeois comforts, your—"

"Roses?" she suggested sweetly.

"Yes, roses!" he shouted. "While millions sweat in brute labor, breaking their backs pulling flax, pulling weeds, hacking the soil—"

"I know," she interrupted with a sigh. "I've heard it all before from Mr. Kott."

"Why must you be so callous?" he stormed.

"Why must you get so excited?" she retorted. "Shouting won't save humanity."

Arkol pulled himself together. "I beg your pardon. Let us consider what you are to do with your life. All that fine training Professor Brown gave you is too valuable a thing for society to be allowed to rust or go to seed. I am not going to preach again," he continued with a shrug. "I am looking at this from your point of view. You are the sort of girl who would be miserable keeping house for a man with nothing else to occupy your mind. Let me give you some advice. When you do marry, pick a man who can afford to give you a servant. Then go on with your work."

"I shall," said Dorothy.

"Why not as my assistant?" he took her up eagerly.

"I said I would consider it. And I shall."

"When may I expect a decision?"

"When Mr. Serbin and Mr. Kott return from their tour."

"And in the meantime?"

"I am busy with Gog."

"Ah," Arkol exclaimed. "I was going to talk about that too. I see a plan—"

"Another?" she quizzed.

"Yes, and a glorious one." Arkol's face lit up with genuine enthusiasm. "Gog's people shall be redeemed from stupidity. And their redemption," he added cryptically, "shall be the salvation of humanity."

"It sounds like a riddle to me," she said. "But possibly you know the answer. What then?"

"You shall see with your own eyes if you become my assistant. You were entirely right about Gog, and I apologize for doubting the accuracy of your observations the other day. I have tested him myself. He seems to have an extraordinary powerful mind, but it needs training. The high fever must have been the match to set the haystack afire. Gog is ablaze with intelligence, and your wonderful patience with him has worked miracles already."

"I tried to tell you it had," she said quietly. "But you wouldn't listen. Are you more patient with him now yourself?"

"I don't have to be patient," Arkol burst out. "He absorbs new things like a blotter soaking up water. That brings me to the main object of my call."

"Yes?"

"Miss Grange, there *must* have been something in Professor Brown's antitoxin that I knew nothing about."

"Are you sure?" she asked, looking him squarely in the eyes.

"You must believe me! By everything that I hold sacred, I swear that I was not responsible for what Admiral Simpson showed me on that slide. Will you believe me?"

"What difference will it make?"

"All the difference in the world. Suppose that a new bacillus was responsible for the fever. Did it kill the patient? No! It generated its own protection as the fever rose—how, I do not see."

"Nor do I," Dorothy agreed. "But I am only a bacteriologist. Go on."

"But look at the facts. Gog is alive. Therefore what I say is not absurd. Accept the experimental facts, and let explanations wait for the present. What is the second fact of vital, overwhelming importance? When Gog recovered, his dormant mind was fully awakened. One poison neutralized another."

"Aren't you theorizing again?"

"What if I am? The observed facts are all that matter. Miss Grange *that experiment has got to be repeated.*"

Dorothy was startled. "On Gog? I won't allow that. He has had his share."

"No, no. Not on Gog. On scores—hundreds—of his people, until we can duplicate the success in his case at will. Then we shall understand it, and our problem will be solved."

"But you may not rediscover how to prepare the antitoxin, especially if it contained something Professor Brown told you nothing about."

"Serums A, P, and S, for instance?" Arkol prompted with a penetrating look.

"But you are following Professor Brown's notes, aren't you?"

"Yes; but the notes seem to have gone cold." Arkol glanced at the grate. "You must have helped Professor Brown many times to prepare A, P, and S?"

"We worked together on them for nearly six months."

"Then we can do it! You remember, of course?"

"I am afraid I don't. The technique was very complicated, and I only followed the typed instructions."

"But you can't, you must not forget," Arkol insisted, tense with anxiety. "When you begin working, it will all come back to you."

"If I ever do take it up again, things may come back. But," she declared emphatically, "you do Professor Brown an injustice when you imagine him capable of letting what you saw on the slide get by him."

"It did not get by him, as you say," Arkol insisted. "He put it into the antitoxin himself, deliberately. And you know that he did, and you know exactly what that new thing is and where he got it."

Dorothy was silent. Receiving no encouragement, Arkol reiterated his innocence of all the Admiral's accusations.

"How can I convince you?" he wound up, almost pleading.

"I'm not good at riddles. But you and Professor Brown simply can't both be right."

"You don't believe me!"

"I did not say that. Has it struck you, Mr. Arkol, that you are very unscientific when you let your plans run away with you?"

"How so? I don't see—"

"It is as plain as day to an outsider like myself. Instead of looking at your problem soberly, as you would examine a puzzle in pathology, you forget all your scientific training when it comes to purely human values, and let your desires run away with your judgment. 'Wishful thinking,' I believe is what the psychologists call it."

Arkol regarded her in silence for some moments.

"We shall see," he said with a sigh. "I must not inflict myself on you longer; I can see that you are nervous and not quite yourself. You will give my offer your careful consideration, as you promised?"

"Yes."

When he was gone, Dorothy strolled over to the grate. Thoughtfully and daintily, so as not to spoil her satin shoe, she toed the crisp cinders away from a spot near the front of the fireplace, under the grate. Having uncovered the handle of the iron lid covering the ash receiver, she grasped the handle with her handkerchief and lifted the lid. The ash receiver was almost full. On top of the ashes lay a neat roll of white paper tied with red string. She lifted out the roll and untied the string.

There were about a dozen sheets of single spaced type. Settling down comfortably in her crimson bower, Dorothy flattened the papers and proceeded to give herself a silent examination. Evidently she passed it to her own satisfaction. S he reached for a match on the cigarette table. Then, with one final glance at the last sheet, to reassure herself that she was letter-perfect, she laid the papers under the grate and lit them. When they were black and crisp she reached for the poker and stirred till nothing but fragments that would have passed a sieve remained. As a final precaution she swept everything into the ash receiver.

Before Arkol's visit Dorothy had intended returning the papers to the bank that afternoon. She had taken them from the vault to refresh her memory before resuming work on serums A, P, S, as Brown would have wished her to do. Now she felt that the notes were best out of sight for good. Professor Brown had not expected to die when he did. How did she know that she herself might not follow him within a week?

The Admiral also had been burning things, but with no misgivings after the first was consumed. His weakness was expensive cigars, which he could not afford, Arkol's apology to the Admiral was accompanied by a box of a hundred cigars that ordinarily retail for a dollar apiece. At first the Admiral was inclined to call the janitor and tell him to stick the box, cellophane and all, into the incinerator. But a hundred were too many for his caution. Assuring himself that the revenue stamps had not been tampered with, he opened the box.

"Arkol can't have been such a melodramatic ass as to squirt any of his infernal germs into these," he said, lighting the first. "Well, anyway, here goes."

Feeling no ill effects from the first, he lit another. He must have been engaged on his fourth just when Dorothy was busy with her notes.

"Arkol is a harmless sort of idiot, after all," he mused. "But his taste in cigars is excellent."

CHAPTER TWELVE
Her Problem

THE MORNING AFTER KOTT'S LAST LECTURE, Dorothy was lying lazily in bed at half past seven, wondering whether she could square her conscience with another half hour's nap, when the bell rang. It was the office calling her.

"There's a telegram for you, Miss Grange. Shall I send it up?"

"Please, tell the boy to slip it under the door."

She hurriedly began to dress. "What's up, I wonder?" She heard the envelope slide over the floor, and darted out of the dressing room to pick it up. Tearing it open she glanced at the signature. "Clive Chase. Oh, what has happened to him?"

The brief message did not enlighten her. It said simply, "Please do not think me such a ninny as the papers make me out. Will be home the day after tomorrow. I can explain everything."

Dorothy's toilet was finished in record time. She did not take a paper herself, but usually bought one on the street or read the *Post* in the cafe. This morning she dashed out on the street and bought four. Then in the seclusion of a private booth in the cafe she read every word of the voluminous accounts of Kott's last lecture.

The story of Chase's election by popular acclaim to the post of investigator at large of the Fifty Year Plan brought a warm glow to her cheeks. She was as proud as Punch's dog Toby. Chase had kept her amused and diverted with his queer, stiff letters for six weeks. Now here he was a popular hero, with the papers printing his classic remarks in heavy type and his abashed face on the front page. Best of all, a late dispatch reported that Mr. Strong, United States Secretary of Agriculture, had willingly granted Chase the necessary leave of absence. Doctor Chase's work was of great importance for the welfare of the farmers, Mr. Strong was careful to point out, but this service to the youth of the whole land was of equal importance. As Doctor Chase was uniquely qualified, he should be spared for a short leave. Thus did Mr. Strong soothe the sensitive taxpayer, and forestall any charge of junketing from the House floor.

As for Serbin's accusations of espionage, Dorothy read them a dozen times, trying vainly to see what they really meant. She succeeded no better than the journalists. The press speculated on all manner of interesting possibilities, but arrived at no satisfactory conclusion.

Opinions varied between two extremes. The milder dismissed Serbin's accusations as the delusions of a hypersensitive man who had experienced so much underhand spying in his own country that he saw spies wherever he went. The United States, according to this opinion, was not interested in spying on its neighbors, least of all when they came to pay us a friendly visit. Mr. Serbin was advised to forget it, and go back to his scientific work.

At the other extreme were the mysterious hints that all this was part of a diabolical plot to involve the United States in an Asiatic war. The logic by which this gloomy conclusion was reached was far from clear, but the alleged plot stuck out like a wart on a beauty queen's neck. Mr. Serbin was advised to deport himself before an outraged and longsuffering people demanded of the proper authorities that they perform that necessary office for him.

Dorothy knew quite a lot of the constant gossip and whispering that goes on in government circles. The Admiral had often shared some of the choicer bits—that never get into the papers—with her, and she rather sympathized with the moderates. These halfway journalists neither dismissed Serbin as a harmless scientific crank, nor howled for his deportation. They merely suggested that Mr. Serbin or his agents had been decoding instructions to the United States secret service men, and had not properly understood what they decoded. This theory was inspired no doubt by the investigation, then going on in the Senate, of the similar trick being played by American amateurs on the short-wave code messages of foreign powers. The moderates somewhat cynically advised our great competitor to employ code experts who really understood their business, and who would not read all sorts of fantastic nonsense into straightforward code messages from the Department of Justice for the apprehension of thugs.

It was clear that a first-rate controversy was already well started. Unless the visiting scientists could manage to slip away before the matter led to questions in the Senate, they might as well give up all hope of ever seeing their own laboratories again. Dorothy hoped it would not come to this. The thought of Arkol being within easy pestering distance for months, possibly years, was more than she could face calmly. She finished her coffee, and hurried out to make an early morning call on the Admiral. She found him pacing the floor, chewing savagely on the last of Arkol's expensive cigars. That he had forgotten to light the cigar was an indication of his state of mind.

"Someone has made a complete fool of himself," he burst out.

"You think the story may be an invention?"

"No, I knew it before it went on the printing presses. Chase telegraphed."

"It must have cost him something," Dorothy remarked.

"Not a cent. He had it charged, collect."

"Oh," said Dorothy. "So there really is something in it?"

"A lot," the Admiral groaned "And now it has all come out."

"What has come out?" Dorothy asked quietly.

"I am not at liberty to tell you."

"Perhaps I can guess."

"If you do," the Admiral warned her sharply, "I cannot admit that you have."

"I shall not ask you to. We can help one another without saying one word of why we are working for the same end. You remember what I said about Arkol when he insulted me about Gog?"

"You said you would get even with him, if it was the last thing you ever did."

"Yes; and I mean it now even more than I meant it then. There is a lot I haven't told you of what has been going on the last six weeks. In fact I have told you nothing of any real importance."

"Surely you did not distrust me?"

"Of course not."

"Then why haven't you discussed things freely with me, as you did after Professor Brown's death? I would have been glad to help you at any time and in any way I could."

"I know that. I have kept things to myself for two reasons. I did not wish to embarrass you—that's the first. The second is that it is *my* duty, if it is anyone's to find out who murdered Professor Brown. I cannot expect you to drop everything and get yourself into hot water by being openly suspicious. So I have worked alone, and I shall continue to work alone. All I ask is that you will not try to hinder me because I happen to have guessed what is behind Serbin's speech last night. I give you my word that I will not interfere with any other investigation in any way, and that I will never tell anyone but you of my own. But I must tell you, as you are my witness to what happened when Arkol looked at that slide."

"I see. And what is your guess?"

"Serbin was telling the truth. So were you, when you said that everything has come out. Serbin and Kott were spied upon, and the spies got careless. Serbin has very cleverly turned the tables on the spies by appealing to our American sense of fair play, and he has invited Doctor Chase to go and investigate, whether Arkol has been spied upon these last six weeks, I don't know. Nor have I the slightest idea why anyone should want to spy on Serbin and Kott. It is none of my business. What Arkol does, and what he intends doing, is very much my business."

"What does he plan to do?"

"That I can't tell you."

"Why not?"

"For the same reason you cannot tell me whether my guess is right, or why anyone should want to spy on those two."

"You are wrong there, Dorothy. Surely you have not given your word to anyone not to talk?"

"I did not mean it that way. If I were to tell you Arkol's plan—that is, if I am right in what I guess it to be—I should only weaken my own chances."

"Suppose we are both trying to find out what Arkol is planning? What then?"

"We can still work best independently."

"Rather a poor compliment to me," the Admiral observed ruefully.

"Not at all," she flashed. "Don't think me self-righteous or sentimental, but have you ever thought of the line 'Thrice armed is he who knows his quarrel just?' I know my quarrel is just. What about yours? Is it your own, or are you merely fighting in the dark for someone else who has ordered you to fight? What crime has Serbin committed? Or Kott? Unless you know, your fight will be only half-hearted. I intend to go all out in mine."

"I pity Arkol when you catch him," the Admiral remarked, looking at her as he had never looked before. "You mean what you say. But do you honestly believe that Arkol is the most dangerous of the three?"

"That has nothing to do with my problem. I know nothing, and I care less, about Serbin and Kott. Or," she modified her assertion, "I should rank Serbin as the brainiest, Kott as the stupidest, and Arkol not much above Kott in brains. But in cruelty I would put Arkol equal to Serbin."

"It has not struck me that Serbin is particularly cruel. Aren't you misjudging him?"

"Perhaps. But I believe Serbin is as cruel in a refined way as Arkol is in his brutal way. Arkol is all passion and emotion. Serbin is cool and calculating, and he feels nothing now, whatever he may have felt once."

"So you have been studying our friends? Well, so have I. And I'll say frankly, I can't make them out. They are all for humanity, and they will save the human race even if they have to cut its throat in the process. A queer religion, but millions believe in it."

The telephone bell cut short the Admiral's reflections. He had been expecting the call, and looked nervous.

"I'll go," Dorothy said. "I have an appointment with Arkol at ten."

She left the Admiral to his telephoning and hurried to keep her appointment with Arkol at the bacteriological laboratories.

Gog had been discharged from the hospital nearly three weeks previously, and was now sharing Arkol's suite at the hotel. During the day, Gog helped Arkol in the mechanical details of preparing serums, taking his exercise by walking after dark, when he would be less likely to attract a crowd wherever he went.

Step by step with his rapid progress in purely intellectual activities, Gog had developed an extraordinary sensitiveness in his fingers. His manipulations of delicate apparatus were as skillful as a Chinese jeweler's. Arkol found him invaluable as a collaborator and taught him much 'for the good of his own people.' Gog seemed to care nothing for anyone's good, so long as he had a good time playing with the apparatus. Or, if he did indulge in ethical speculations, he never shared the fruits of all his silent thinking with his preceptor and benefactor Arkol.

Dorothy found the pair already deep in their work. Arkol, she was forced to admit, was a most marvelous technician, whatever else he might be. He knew his trade from the inside out and from the outside in, and he did automatically what less gifted men toil at laboriously with sweat and frowns. Arkol's very skill condemned him in her eyes. Such a man simply could not have blundered in the elementary matter of making a clean inoculation. Whatever had caused Gog's phenomenal fever was neither an accident nor a mistake. Arkol did not make mistakes. Therefore, in Dorothy's merciless logic, Arkol was guilty of murder, for the strange infection that killed Brown had come from the new bacteria on that first slide.

Gog looked up as she entered. His eyes worshipped her.

His huge hands dropped to his side, and he sat like a statue of expectancy watching for her slightest movement. The intelligence, which his fever had unchained, lightened only his eyes; his flat-nosed, hairy face, with the heavy projecting jaw was as pathetically repulsive as when Dorothy first saw him and was shocked. Now she was used to him, and she had taught him to speak English and to read it with perfect ease. His ambling gait as he followed her about, day by day, listening with all his body and soul to her crisp instructions, no longer gave her a sensation of eerie strangeness. She was used to that too, although the crowds in the streets were not, and everywhere that Gog ventured by daylight he was a spectacle to the curious and a jest to the heartless. The crowds snickered and made remarks, which he could understand perfectly as his command of English increased. Dorothy never even smiled, and her personal remarks were confined to strictly impersonal corrections of his errors in pronunciation. The result was what might have been expected, Gog would have sold his soul for her.

It never occurred to Dorothy that Gog could fall in love with her. Had she stopped to reason, it would have seemed the most natural thing in the world, indeed inevitable. She had helped to save his life in a long and distressing illness; she was the first human being who had ever spoken a decent word to him, or who had treated him like a human being; she had discovered his awakened mind, and she had taught him how to use it for his own inexhaustible pleasure. But she had considered none of this as anything more than an interesting professional problem. His helplessness in the fire of Arkol's constant, sneering abuse had aroused her anger rather than her sympathy. To put Arkol in his proper place she would show him that Gog was not the unteachable brute he supposed. As her efforts met with ever greater success, she conceived a sort of humorous affection for him, as one might for a great, shaggy, awkward dog. But to love him as a woman loves a man? That was grotesquely, inhumanly impossible.

Arkol was in the back of the room when Dorothy entered. His curious, calculating eyes watched Gog closely as the hulking fellow followed every move Dorothy made.

"Good morning, Miss Grange," Arkol said pleasantly. "Punctual as usual, I see. You would make an ideal assistant."

"Punctuality is no rare virtue in a trained nurse," she retorted. "Good morning, Gog; I didn't see you when I came in."

Gog gave a husky cough and bent over his work without acknowledging her greeting. Arkol had been watching both of them closely. He beckoned her into his office and shut the door. For some moments he deliberated how to attack his subject.

"You are fond of Gog, Miss Grange?"

"Of course. But surely you didn't make this appointment to ask me that?"

"No, no. I hardly know how to put it. But before I come to the other, I must say something. Personal."

"Don't mind me," she laughed. "A nurse hears all sorts of things. And," she added with a quizzical look at the perturbed Arkol, "she forgets most of what she hears—if she has any sense."

Arkol labored to express himself, and Dorothy actually blushed. What she was expecting to hear, she has never confessed even to herself. What she did hear left her white and speechless.

"Gog is in love with you."

When she recovered her breath, she took a quick step toward Arkol.

"You—you—" she stammered, not knowing what to say.

"Please, Miss Grange," he begged. "I am not trying to humiliate or insult you. What I say is the truth. Gog is madly, violently in love with you."

His manner, for once free of any hint of guile, convinced her that he was speaking what he believed to be the truth.

"It isn't so! You must be mistaken. Why I— What makes you think so?"

"My dear young lady, if it is obvious to me, it should be doubly obvious to you. A woman knows by instinct when a man is in love with her."

"But I have never thought of Gog as a man," she began to defend herself, stopping short when she noticed the expression on Arkol's face.

"How so?" he asked slowly, fixing her eyes with his own.

"I didn't mean to insult Gog," she apologized, "and I am ashamed for what I said. But don't you see how it would be? He is so foreign, so different from the men I have known. There is something about him——"

"Yes?" he encouraged, when she hesitated.

"Well, to be brutal, I feel sometimes as you said you felt about Gog before his illness. He is barbaric." A sudden inspiration for turning the tables on Arkol flashed across her mind. "Would you be willing to marry a woman of Gog's people?"

Arkol exploded with laughter, rocking helplessly till his swarthy face purpled. At first Dorothy was inclined to join him, till she thought of the hulking, faithful fellow in the adjoining room. Then she began to lose her temper.

"Stop it!" she cried. "You make me feel like dirt."

Arkol sobered, and his face grew crafty.

"Pardon. I was not laughing at Gog."

"Then what were you laughing at?"

Arkol repressed a titter.

"Women's logic. Always the particular, never the general."

"You haven't answered me," Dorothy retorted coldly.

"Then let me be both fair and polite. No, Miss Grange, I would not marry a woman of Gog's tribe so long as I retained my vision and my logic."

"What has logic to do with it?" Dorothy demanded suspiciously. "People don't fall in love because of logic."

"No," Arkol admitted, "but it is conceivable that a lack of logic might prevent them falling in love."

"Oh, your riddles make me tired. Why can't you say what you mean without trying to be subtle?"

"I am saying exactly what I mean," Arkol insisted, "and there is no other way of saying it. Some day I may ask you to remember this conversation. Then you will agree with me." His eyes narrowed. "What you are too blind to see may be the turning point in your life. I have tried to warn you, as one human being might feel obligated to warn a blind fellowman who is about to plunge over a precipice. If you will not stop playing with Gog's feelings, he may begin playing with yours in a way that will not be pleasant."

"I have never played with his feelings."

"That is a woman's excuse. Unless you are made of wood you must know instinctively what your studied indifference would do to a man of Gog's temperament. Any woman would know. You have not tried to discourage him because you have been too much of a woman to forego even the conquest of a savage who could not read or write six weeks ago."

Dorothy was silent. Arkol's indictment of her was at least logical. Had she subconsciously played lady bountiful to Gog in order to make a paltry conquest? She honestly believed she hadn't.

"You are mistaken. Gog has never been anything to me but an unusual and interesting problem. I have never given his emotions a thought."

"I shall believe you." He bowed stiffly. "But let me warn you now Miss Grange, for the last time, that unless you do give very serious thought to Gog's emotions you will wish you had when it is too late. You must discourage him in a way he will understand. Make him hate you."

"Perhaps you can tell me how to do it? If my indifference only makes him worse, what would open rebuffs do?"

"How should I know?" He shrugged his shoulders. "If a woman does not know how to get rid of a man, what man can tell her?"

"Oh, don't be so superior. Suggest something, and I'll do it. I like Gog, and I can't let him go on this way—if he really does believe he is in love with me. What am I to do?"

"That is your problem. If I knew the answer I would be a better psychologist than anyone in America. You must solve your problem yourself, in your own way. Well, let us go on to the next thing. Possibly it is more important."

"I hope so," she murmured.

Disregarding her attempt at lightheartedness, Arkol drew a sheaf of letters from his pocket.

"These are from Serbin. They concern that first slice, which Professor Brown made. Serbin agrees with me that it is of the highest importance for our program. Our government would be willing to pay handsomely for it, if you care to part with it."

"What would I do with the money?"

"Surely a healthy young woman with the best of her life ahead of her need not ask such a question?" Seeing from Dorothy's expression that he had blundered, Arkol instantly made his offer more tempting. "You might wish to endow chairs in bacteriology at the leading American universities in memory of Professor Brown." Sensing that this bait was no more attractive than the first, Arkol concealed the hook entirely. "If you do not care to part with the last thing Professor Brown did, you need not. A micro-photograph of the bacteria on the slide would serve our proposals well as the original slide itself."

"I see. Then in that case I see no objection. But I want no money for it. And I will not accept anything else."

Arkol bowed solemnly. "I understand perfectly, Miss Grange. When may we take the photograph? If it would not inconvenience you, Mr. Serbin would like to do it as soon as he returns. We are anxious to leave America as soon as possible. You have seen the morning papers, I presume?"

Dorothy nodded. "Of course you will be anxious to get home as quickly as possible now that your work is done here. Suppose we say eight o'clock in the evening, the day after tomorrow? I have a luncheon engagement that day, and the rest of my time until the evening will be taken up with things I must do."

"That will suit us perfectly. Thank you Miss Grange." Arkol eyed her speculatively. "There is just one thing before you go. If Gog annoys you in any way, I can stop him. You need only let me know."

"But why should he?"

"Gog might do anything in his present state of mind. To put you on your guard, let me tell you something I discovered by accident the other night. I had been out late, and I decided to walk home—the drinks had been a little heavy. My way took me past your apartment at two o'clock in the morning. Half a square before reaching it, I saw a large man ahead of me suddenly emerge from the shadow of the trees opposite your apartment. You know how Gog walks—more of a shuffle than a walk."

"Well?" she asked, although she guessed what was coming.

"I am positive the man had been watching your window, possibly for hours, from across the street. Of course it was Gog."

"But wouldn't a policeman have seen him and made him move on?"

"Not necessarily. Gog is very strong and quite agile at rough sports. I imagine he passed several pleasant hours in one of those trees. Of course he would not be so foolish as to drop on the policeman's head."

Dorothy suddenly felt faint.

"I'll get another apartment," she said.

"That will not be sufficient. For your own good, Miss Grange, do what I have advised."

"I would if I knew how. But I don't. Goodbye, and thanks."

CHAPTER THIRTEEN
Her Knight

WHEN DO YOU LEAVE?" DOROTHY ASKED. "Next Saturday," Chase replied. "Serbin is anxious to get away before these silly questions in the Senate get any sillier."

"I don't blame him. The whole affair is utterly ridiculous."

Chase regarded her speculati vely. Without betraying confidences, how much dared he tell her? At her request he had taken her to lunch at a quiet little place famous for its steaks and black beer. The flashy palace with its big name orchestra, which Chase had proposed, was too expensive, Dorothy declared, for a struggling young geneticist, and she liked the food at the other place better anyway. Their talk at first had been rather constrained, as Chase felt that she must think him an awful sap for having stepped into the limelight as he had. Gradually, as Chase allowed himself to be coaxed into a bald account of what had actually happened at the historic lecture, he loosened up and became natural. His coming trip as investigator at large fascinated her.

"I wish I had your chance," she sighed, when Chase finally made up his mind to keep his mouth shut and share none of his speculations on the motives of Serbin, even with his charmingly provocative companion.

"It won't be so hot," he said. "A lot of hard work and dinners with cabbage soup."

"Just think of the places you will see. I'm so fed up with civilization. Always the same thing, never anything startling or exciting."

Chase slowly went a brick red. Now or never was the time to do it.

"Like to come along?" he blurted out.

"How? I haven't been invited like you."

"As my wife, we could get married on Saturday morning before the boat sails. Or, if the license is held up, the Captain could marry us when we get beyond the twelve mile zone."

Dorothy carefully extinguished her cigarette before replying.

"I can see you have been making plans, too. That suggestion about the Captain was no sudden inspiration."

"You are not turning me down, then?"

"No, and yes. Not now. I have been planning too, and there is something I must do before I can settle down and become a sedate married woman. By the way, our friend Arkol gave me some free advice the other day. I wonder what you would think of it?"

Chase instantly grew jealous and suspicious.

"What right has he to give you advice? Has he been proposing to you?"

Dorothy laughed. "Not exactly. But I think he would with a little encouragement."

"If you do, I'll—"

"What?" she asked mischievously. "Perhaps you had better kiss me now. Then we will both feel better."

Chase rose to the situation. Dorothy was entirely satisfied.

"Now I can tell you what Arkol said with a clear conscience," she resumed when she had recovered her breath. "He advised me not to marry a man who could not afford to give me a maid. Will you go that far?"

"Two, if you like," Chase promised enthusiastically. He would have promised her the moon in his intoxication.

"One will be enough," she said. "If you are hard up, or get another cut in salary, I can get along on none. I was only preparing you for the major shock."

"Let's have it. I'm prepared."

"Will you let me go on with my scientific work when we are married?"

"You are not the girl I take you for unless you do. That was one of the reasons I asked you to marry me. I hate stuffed pigeons."

"You're really a very satisfactory young man. So it is all settled."

"Then you agree to my plan about the Captain?"

"The Captain? No. That would be a little precipitate. I must see my own plan through first. Really, I am in deadly earnest. You have been so reasonable about everything else, I know you will take my word for this."

He gave her a long, thoughtful look.

"The proper thing for me to do now, I suppose, is to play the ardent lover and overcome your maidenly hesitation. Well, I shan't. I'm not a conceited ass, in spite of what those sappy papers say."

"We shall get along together famously. I can't stand having everything explained to me with diagrams. You have really said nothing, and neither have I. But we understand one another perfectly." She paused reflectively, and lit a cigarette. "Do you know, I have a feeling I may be on the boat when you steam out of the harbor?"

"Why don't you do it? We would have a grand time."

"There is the awkward matter of finances, for one thing."

"That is not what is worrying you," he said shrewdly.

"No, it isn't. My lack of nerve has held me back so far. The prospect of having those three on my hands in their own native country was a little too much for me. But with you somewhere in the neighborhood, my nerves wouldn't be so jumpy if anything should go off unexpectedly with a loud bang. I think I shall fish for that invitation Arkol is dying to give me."

"So he has hinted to you, too? Serbin remarked the other day that Arkol thinks his government owes you something for all your trouble with the serums."

"Did he suggest a trip abroad?"

"He said you had told him you were crazy to travel and see the world."

"Then he let you put the two together?" Dorothy suddenly threw back her head and laughed till the tears came. "I wonder if Serbin thinks he is playing cupid? The way those poor men plot and scheme to get what they want is rather pathetic. Why don't they come right out and tell us what they are willing to pay? Then I wouldn't be nearly so suspicious, and it would cost them far less in the end."

"They are not made that way. Just think of all the fun they would rob themselves of if they couldn't believe the whole world is against them. Life wouldn't be worth living unless they were gloomy and suspicious of everyone and everything."

"Including Senators who asked pointed questions? Well, I think I shall accept that invitation when it comes."

"*If* it comes," Chase corrected. "They may have discovered some new mare's nest before Saturday."

"Oh, it will come. I shall see that it does."

"When?" Chase demanded curiously. "You seem pretty sure of yourself."

"Why shouldn't I be? Arkol and I have been as thick as thieves all the time you were away. I shall get that invitation tonight."

"Tonight?" Chase echoed in dismay. "Surely you—?"

"Don't be alarmed. Trite boudoir scenes bore me. And I rather suspect they bore Arkol too, or he would have tried to stage one long ago. He did send me some very gorgeous red roses, though. He won't try it again."

"He had better not, if he knows what's good for him."

"You needn't worry. He won't. Arkol really has a lot of good common sense. If you like," she added to reassure him, "I shall put off getting the invitation till tomorrow morning."

Chase was offended. "I hope you don't think I'm that sort of a chump. You do it any way you like, and send me the bill."

"I knew you weren't silly. Still, just to show myself that I can, I will get the invitation tomorrow morning instead of tonight, as I had half planned." She opened her purse and extracted a neat wooden box, about three inches long, an inch wide and half an inch thick. The lid was sealed with red wax. "Will you keep this for me?"

Wondering, he took it, and turned it over speculatively. As Dorothy showed no desire to tell him what it was, he had sense enough not to ask. "What shall I do with it?"

"Keep it on you, always, where it will be safe. Not in a pocket. I don't want it stolen."

"I can manage," he promised. "And of course I won't go broadcasting that you gave me anything."

Dorothy nodded. "Thanks. If I were the heroine in a play I would ask you to defend that box with your life. Not being a heroine, I shall simply ask you to hang onto it, and if you are ever asked to give it up, throw it into the sea, or drop it on the floor and smash it with your heel. The thing in the box is quite fragile. If you do have to step on it, do a thorough job."

"They won't get it away from me while I have my health," Chase promised.

"No, no," she exclaimed, "that is just what I don't want you to do. Smash it if there is the least danger of it being taken. You never know how a fight is going to turn out when it starts."

Chase promised to obey orders, and Dorothy got up to go. "There will be guests at the hospital laboratory tonight, and I must be getting along to prepare for them."

"Big bugs?"

"Not so big, although they think they are enormous."

"That's usually the way," Chase remarked. "Some of the biggest guns in my line never even ask to be shown about officially. They just ask one of the caretakers where the greenhouses are, and conduct their own tour."

Dorothy thanked him with her eyes for his tactful lack of curiosity. "If I don't see you in the meantime, look for me on deck number one on Saturday morning."

Dorothy's preparations for her guests were brief. Before going to lunch with Chase she had attended to the most important. Professor Brown's will had been probated about a week previously, and Dorothy found herself in possession of all notes and materials relating to Brown's unfinished work. To enable her to continue his work, Brown had left her a modest sum, sufficient to tide her over a year or two, until she could find a suitable engagement. She had deposited the most valuable notes and slides in a drawer of the safety deposit vault of her bank. These included the series of preparations from Gog's case. That morning she had transferred the necessary material for the evening's work to the bacteriological laboratory on the second floor of the pesthouse, where she had agreed to meet Serbin and Arkol at eight o'clock. All that remained to be done was to get out the microscope and arrange the proper lights for microphotography. She had borrowed other apparatus from the Department of Public Health.

Her preparations ended, Dorothy sat down to wait for her guests. She had had no dinner after her feast with Chase, but she was too excited to heed the promptings of hunger. The clock showed fifteen minutes to eight. It was almost dark, and the dense foliage of the maple tree shadowing the second story windows cut out the last daylight from the upper sky. Although the room was flooded with light, Dorothy peered about as the minutes crept by, vaguely apprehensive. She had an irrational feeling that someone was in the room watching her, but she could discover no possible nook in which a spy might have concealed himself. Wishing the men would come, she got up and opened the door into the hall. Someone was moving about in the wards on the first floor. She knew the wards were empty, and for a moment she was tempted to bolt. Then ashamed of her unreasonable nervousness she walked to the head of the stairs and called down.

"Who is there?"

"Only me, Miss Grange. You asked me to be on hand to unlock the outer door at five minutes to eight. You said you would let yourself in."

"Oh yes. Thank you, Mr. Johnson."

Feeling decidedly foolish, she walked lightly back to the laboratory and fussed with the apparatus till she heard footsteps ascending the stairs. There was a rap at the door.

"May we come in?" Arkol's voice called.

"Of course. Everything is ready."

"Good evening, Miss Grange," Serbin bowed. "Quite a long time since I saw you last. You look more charming than ever." As if appreciative of Dorothy's new charm, Serbin took full advantage of his foreign privileges and kissed her hand.

"You make me feel like a grand duchess," she laughed.

"I trust not, Miss Grange," Serbin replied with a peculiar smile. "Some of the grandest of our duchesses came to very shocking ends."

"There you go again," she retorted. "America hasn't changed you a bit. Shall we take the photograph? Perhaps I had better do it, as I understand this trick camera. It can be quite temperamental when it pleases."

Before replying, both Arkol and Serbin inspected the apparatus. They shook their heads.

"This is beyond me," Arkol confessed. "It must be a thousand years old."

"Not quite. The regular outfit has been loaned for a few days to the Department of Public Health. They sent me this antique this morning when I asked for a handout."

"Have you ever used it before?" Serbin asked.

"Often, in a pinch. There really is nothing to it when you master its disposition and practice for a month or two. I have it thoroughly tamed now. Shall I go ahead?"

They nodded, and Dorothy adjusted the slide. Arkol and Serbin exchanged glances, and Serbin moved toward the door, ostensibly to inspect some horrible looking specimens in jars of alcohol in a glass cabinet by the door. Dorothy said nothing, although she wondered just what Serbin was up to.

"Shall I lock the door?" Serbin asked. "Someone may blunder in and upset us at the critical point."

"I suppose you had better," Dorothy replied, without looking up from her work.

She was aware that Arkol was watching her face. Pretending to have difficulty with a stubborn screw that had once been as shiny as a new gold piece, but was now stiff with green rust, she asked Arkol to start it for her. While his attention was thus distracted, she managed to see what Serbin was doing. He was apparently absorbed in the glassed horrors, and was trying to open the cabinet door, the better to inspect them. His movements were unnaturally awkward, and Dorothy suspected that he wished her to observe his blundering clumsiness. She did. She observed also that his elbow was sawing up and down dangerously near the electric light switch. With difficulty she repressed a smile of contempt for the plotting pair who could invent no neater way of stealing the coveted slide than by 'accidentally' turning out the lights and substituting a duplicate on the platform of the microscope at the critical moment. She went on with her work, confident of her ability to outwit them, even in the dark.

The expected and the unexpected happened within two seconds of one another. Dorothy was just about to press the bulb for the shutter when the light went out. An apologetic exclamation from Serbin may have been intended as a signal to Arkol to work fast. Dorothy had barely time to avoid Arkol's groping hand in her effort to move the apparatus beyond his reach, when a crash of shattered glass made her jump clear of the table instinctively.

A huge form bounded furiously about the darkened room, overturning tables and chairs, wrenching cabinets from the walls and ripping them to pieces, and darting like a tarantula after the three terrified human beings in the room.

Arkol and Serbin were shouting to one another in their own language; they seemed to have forgotten Dorothy. A hand gripped her shoulder. She felt herself lifted like a doll, while another hand passed lightly over her face. She was set down in a corner, unharmed.

Then began a systematic destruction of everything the enraged creature could get its hands on, as it groped in the dark for the two men. Once Arkol squealed in terror as his coat was ripped from his back, but he escaped. Serbin, keeping his head, fared better, till the missiles began to fly.

The destruction of furniture and apparatus had been deliberately panned. Failing to catch his enemies in the first rush, and being outwitted by them in the dark, the attacker began a bombardment. Nothing fell in Dorothy's corner. How the siege would have ended if it had gone to the limit, neither Arkol nor Serbin cared to speculate after it was all over. Both had been hit, but neither received more than painful bruises and cuts.

Johnson, still on duty downstairs, had started up on the run when he heard the first crash. By the time he had battered down the door and turned on the lights, the attacker had vanished.

"The tree," Arkol panted pointing to the window.

But the tree was uninhabited. The attacker had vanished.

"I should like a drink of whiskey," Serbin observed, ruefully binding up a cut on his left wrist. "And if anyone has one, Miss Grange would doubtless like it even better."

Johnson hurried downstairs for his pocket flask, which he had left in his coat with his lunch.

"What was it?" Dorothy gasped, although she knew only too well.

"Your Knight coming to your rescue, Miss Grange," Arkol informed her with a mock bow. "When the lights went out he imagined we were about to attack you.

"Yes," Serbin agreed. "I fear Gog is still uncivilized, in spite of all Miss Grange has done for him."

"But why on earth—?" Dorothy began, when Arkol silenced her.

"I warned you to be careful," he said. "Now look at that." He pointed to the wreckage of the apparatus. The solid brass platform of the microscope had been twisted out of shape, and the stout steel rods of the photographic apparatus were tied into knots.

"But I don't understand how he could have done it with his hands," Dorothy protested.

"Gog is strong," Serbin remarked. "If he had caught one of us in his rage he would have pulled his victim apart as you pull a shrimp. On the whole, I am glad I was not caught. Ah, here is Mr. Johnson with a glass and something better."

Dorothy declined the drink. Arkol and Serbin gulped theirs greedily, and Johnson had two himself.

"The next thing is to call the police, I guess," he said, moving toward the door.

"No," said Dorothy decisively. "If we do that there will be an investigation, and these men will miss their steamer on Saturday."

"Then what am I to do, Miss Grange?" Johnson asked in perplexity. "Somebody will be investigating me unless I turn in a report."

"Wait," said Dorothy. "I've got it. Telephone to Admiral Simpson, and ask him to come here at once. He will be responsible and do any reporting necessary."

Johnson left them, but half-satisfied with this solution. "Well," said Serbin, "we are alive. What magnificent strength! But our experiment? Done for, I fear." He picked up the twisted platform of the microscope. "The slide has been ground to powder."

"You don't seem particularly put out by it," Dorothy remarked with a shrewd glance in Arkol's direction, Serbin's cool retort gave her a shock.

"Are you, Miss Grange?"

She recovered instantly. "You suspect that I put Gog up to this?"

"Never mind Gog," Arkol cut in. "He will be properly taken care of."

"Not while I know what I am doing," Dorothy retorted.

"Oh, not here," Arkol remarked lightly. "At home. We sail shortly, you know."

"You will never sail," Dorothy said slowly, "unless you promise to let Gog alone."

"Really?" Serbin inquired sarcastically.

"Really, I mean just what I say. You are not going to take any revenge on poor Gog. He foolishly thought he was protecting me, and I'll not have him suffer for his mistake. So if you sail on Saturday, you must give me your word that all this will be forgotten the moment you step on deck."

"May I ask how you propose to prevent us from sailing?" Serbin demanded with obvious sarcasm.

"Sorry, but I can't tell you, because I don't know myself. But Admiral Simpson will doubtless drop a hint of this to the proper authorities. The investigation may drag on for years."

Serbin bowed. "We give you our word that Gog shall come to no harm on account of this knight-errantry."

"That is sufficient," Dorothy said, ignoring the slur.

"Miss Grange!" Arkol expostulated with mock sincerity, "you must not believe what a couple of scoundrels like Serbin and myself promise."

"Perhaps I don't. Nevertheless I trust you to do as you promise. Better still, you will send Gog back to his own people, where he will be far enough away not to tempt you."

"How do you know all this?" Serbin inquired mockingly.

"Doctor Chase can arrange it easily enough. Until he is satisfied that Gog is beyond reach of your spite, he can hold up the report of his investigations."

Serbin laughed heartily. "We had no intention of persecuting Gog. All we were trying to do was to test you, Miss Grange. You are a very earnest young woman."

"Admirably suited to be a scientist's collaborator," Arkol added enthusiastically. "After this little mishap we shall need you more than ever. In fact you are now indispensable to us. You promised to give me your answer, you remember, when Mr. Serbin returned. Have you made up your mind?"

"Yes—but I hear Admiral Simpson coming. That's his step. I'll tell you in the morning."

"Excellent," said Serbin. "Possibly something that I may have to say will influence your decision in our favor."

The Admiral took one look at the wreckage and glanced at Dorothy. It was unnecessary for her to speak.

"This had better be kept quiet," the Admiral said. "We can't afford any delays now that Chase has his leave. What happened?"

Arkol told him, carefully omitting any reference to the probable reason for Gog's outburst.

"But what made him do it?" the Admiral asked in bewilderment.

"Heaven only knows," Serbin replied with smug fervor. "The motives of primitives are beyond the understanding of civilized human beings."

"Will he be fit to travel? What if he should go mad some night at sea?"

"I think Gog will be tame enough," Arkol assured him, stealing a sly glance at Dorothy. "We shall take along a sedative."

CHAPTER FOURTEEN
Gog's Request

DOROTHY HAD FINISHED BREAKFAST AND HAD just returned to her apartment when the telephone rang.

"I knew it," she cried, giving three skips to the telephone.

Mr. Serbin and Mr. Arkol had called, and would be honored if she would overlook the unusual hour and receive them.

"Come right up," she said, and hung up. "Now to look as if I weren't expecting a medal," she said composing her face before the mirror. "After all they may fool me and hand me a beautifully engraved note of thanks. Oh well—"

The doorbell rang. She took her time about answering. With misgivings she noted that her callers were in formal morning attire, as if making a call on the President. Was it to be the engraved note after all? Ignoring her invitation to sit down, they remained stiffly standing.

"Miss Grange," Serbin began, "I have the honor to present you with a slight token of appreciation from our government for your invaluable services to our scientific commission."

He drew a bulky envelope, heavily sealed, from his inner pocket and tendered it to Dorothy with all the stateliness of an ambassador conferring a decoration for his sovereign.

"Oh, thank you. But I have done nothing. May I open it now?"

"Please do."

Dorothy broke the seals with becoming deliberation and extracted a half dozen papers from the envelope. The first was a beautifully illuminated, short, but adequate expression of official thanks, on parchment. The next two were passports. All they lacked was her signature. Provision had been made to record this before the proper witnesses. Dorothy remembered having given the Admiral a good snapshot of herself. Here it was, reduced to the proper scale, on the passports. For one unworthy moment she wondered whether Arkol had borrowed the snapshot from the Admiral, or whether he had just picked it up on his way out after a pleasant evening of cigars and cards. She forgot to ask the Admiral the next time she saw him. The fourth item in the envelope was a steamer ticket. The fifth was a free pass over the railway and steamboat lines of Serbin's great country, and the sixth was a letter of credit for a sum, which took her breath away.

"Good heavens," she gasped, "what am I to do with it all?"

"Travel," Serbin replied. "Have you forgotten what you told me the day we met?"

"Oh, but this is too generous of you. Your government should not squander money and travel on me, when it needs all it has for the fifty year plan."

"Our government will have made the best investment it ever made," Arkol declared solemnly, "if it convinces you that we are your friends and well-wishers."

"I have known that all along," Dorothy said simply. Then, just as a gentle reminder that her loyalty was not for sale, and as a sufficiently clear declaration of her intentions, she amplified her remark, "Ever since Professor Brown's death, I have felt that my professional career must be bound up with Mr. Arkol's."

Arkol beamed. "Then you accept my offer? You will become my assistant?"

"Yes. When do my duties begin?"

"There is no hurry, Miss Grange. After the somewhat trying experiences of the past six weeks, we all need a little relaxation. Personally, I shall not resume my work till I return to my own laboratory."

"That suits me. I shall be ready to go to work the day you start. There is just one condition, however. To do decent work, I must have a reasonable amount of freedom—as to hours, and so on. If you will tell me what you want done, I shall do it. But I must be free to work in my own way, without constant supervision. Set a time limit, if you like, on any job, and I will get it done, or else tell you at the beginning that I shall need more time. Is that satisfactory?"

"Perfectly, Miss Grange. Your duties will not be heavy."

After they had left, Dorothy seated herself at the writing desk and I studied her gifts minutely. At last she was satisfied.

"If there is a catch in any of this," she mused, "it is well hidden. As I can't see it, it will be my own fault if I get properly hooked.

But I shan't—by Arkol. That's that. Now to lay in supplies." She called up Chase, and asked him if he could spare the hours before lunch.

"You may as well get broken in early," she said, "and endure a woman's shopping. No, no; I'm paying all the bills this time. Later, perhaps, I shall be calling on you for that. Come and help me pick out what I'm likely to need for a long trip. Yes, I'm going too."

Chase's incoherent reply was lost. Dorothy hung up and flew around to get ready.

The morning passed in a whirl. Dorothy insisted on treating Chase to lunch at the swank restaurant to which he had intended taking her.

"I may never hear another 'good' orchestra," she explained, when Chase objected. "Not that I want to, but it will be something to remember America by."

"Aren't you planning to come back?" he asked seriously.

She teased him for his sober mood. "What a question when I haven't even started."

"But seriously, Dorothy, you don't plan to spend the rest of your life as Arkol's assistant?"

"Of course not. But the choice may not be mine."

He eyed her curiously for a moment. She was trying to tell him something she did not care to put into words, and he thought he understood, but he wished to be certain.

"Not expecting to be shot, or anything of that sort, are you?" he jested.

She gave him a straight look. "No. Are you?"

"Not unless I go stalking big game," he laughed, "and some nervous fellow hunter mistakes me for a tiger or something bigger in the jungle."

The Admiral had told Dorothy of Arkol's metaphor of the cats and tigers in describing his fight against disease, and she wondered whether he had also told Chase. If so, why? Was Chase going abroad as more than the official investigator at large of the fifty year plan? She chilled at the thought. Why did he not confide in her? But of course he could not talk, if his word were pledged, even to the girl he was to marry. Intuition came to her aid. Chase was offering her a code—cats and tigers. She decided to put her intuition to the test of experiment.

"What if the nervous sportsman were to mistake you for a cat?"

"Oh," Chase replied lightly, "then he would hold his fire. Nothing short of a tiger can throw a scare into your real big game hunter."

She reached quickly across the table and touched his hand lightly.

"Promise me you won't go tiger hunting just for sport."

"It's a go, if you promise not to stroke any cats the wrong way just for the fun of it. They say white cats are the most vicious."

"Then let's drink to our return on the same ship." She beckoned to the waiter. "Do you suppose you could bring us some champagne? This is rather a special occasion."

When the waiter brought the bottle in its tub of ice they pledged one another in silence.

"You will be nice to Gog on the trip, won't you?" she begged, putting down her glass.

"Of course. Poor devil."

As both had much to do, they parted, promising to meet at the dock on Saturday, half an hour before the boat sailed. What with final preparations and leave-takings, the time slipped by before ether realized that Saturday had really come.

Prompt as always, Dorothy appeared exactly thirty minutes before boat time. The Admiral had come to see her off. They found Chase waiting.

"Our friends have already gone aboard," he announced. "Traveling seems rather a bore to those three."

"What a waste for them to be going," Dorothy sighed happily. "Just think of it, the day I have longed for all my life has come at last. Aren't you excited?"

"Horribly," he confessed. "From what has happened already, I anticipate the worst."

The Admiral was instantly alert. "What's happened?"

"Nothing much yet. But all the flunkeys treat me as if I were the mayor. I hope they don't expect a mayor's tips out of me."

The Admiral said he would not go aboard, as the time was growing short. He shook hands with Chase.

"Take care of yourself. Good luck. May I kiss Dorothy?"

"We'll both be offended if you don't."

If Chase was treated like the mayor, Dorothy was welcomed as if she were a princess returning to her native land. The Captain himself bobbed up from somewhere to welcome her. Somewhat puzzled by all this flattery, Dorothy allowed herself to be personally conducted up the gangplank by the Captain. When she saw her quarters, she gasped. The luxury suite deluxe was to be hers, and the drawing room was a bower of crimson roses.

"Arkol again," she exclaimed.

"I beg your pardon?" the Captain apologized.

"I beg yours. You say I am to be in this, this—"

"Suite, Miss Grange. Yes; we call it the royal suite."

"But why on earth—?"

"Very special orders from across the water," the Captain explained mysteriously.

"Good Lord," said Dorothy, sitting down suddenly. "They don't mind expense, do they?"

"Money seems no object," the Captain agreed, as he bowed himself out.

"No wonder the Captain showed me in," she mused when she was alone. "What do they expect to get out of me?" Her face set. "Well, *one* thing they won't get, just because they want it so desperately. Do they think I am a child?" She rang the bell. A trim maid glided in from somewhere. "Will you please find out where Mr. Clive Chase is, and ask him to come here?"

"Yes, madam."

Chase, as a matter of fact, was just outside the door, but it was some minutes before he was located. When he finally was ushered in, his jaw dropped.

"You're clean out of my class," he laughed. "Mine's like a dugout compared to this. And I thought mine was the last word in masculine luxury. No wonder they kow-towed. Whew!"

"Rather an attractive jungle, though, isn't it?" she quizzed.

"Too attractive by half—for a jungle. Still, not half bad. I hope you won't high-hat me if you run across me in the steerage. Just nod and pass on; I'll understand." His manner changed. "Servants satisfactory?"

"Only one has appeared as yet. A very nice looking maid."

"You will change for dinner, of course?"

"One has to live up to it all, I suppose," she sighed. Then she read in his expression an unexpressed warning.

"They gave you a lady's maid to go with all this?"

She saw what he was driving at. "They must have. What on earth shall I do with her? I've never been maided in my life. Do you suppose she will pull on my stockings for me? Or what?"

"If it is going to bother you," he said slowly, "why not simply say you are not used to such service, and prefer to take care of yourself? I fired my valet the first thing. Then I came here on the run to see how you were making out."

"Oh, the maid won't bother me. I shall let her take the lead, and do what she seems to expect. It will be rather fun."

"Sure?" he asked.

"Dead sure." She gave him one of her looks that said everything she dared not say aloud for fear of being overheard. "You were quite right, though, in getting rid of the valet. I could not stand a man who couldn't put on his own shirt."

They were interrupted by the noiseless entry of the maid.

"When would you like dinner served, madam?"

"Do I dine here?"

"If you wish, madam. The dining room is on your left."

"Eight o'clock, then. Will you see that Mr. Arkol, Mr. Kott, and Mr. Serbin are asked? Oh—I'll write a note." Dorothy had just spied the writing table buried in crimson roses. While the maid stood respectfully by, Dorothy dashed off three cordial invitations to dinner. "I needn't send you one," she remarked to Chase. "Consider yourself invited." She handed the notes to the maid. "Tell the steward there will be five for dinner."

"Yes, madam. Shall I send in your maid?"

"Please."

Chase beat a hasty retreat. "Don't let her make a monkey of you," he implored, loud enough for the parlor maid, or whatever her official title was, to hear. "We're only simple folk who have never been on a boat before."

The beautifully served dinner was a complete success. Even Kott was in festive mood, and some of his reminiscences as a humorously persecuted infant prodigy at the C.C.N.Y. were really amusing. Serbin seemed to have left his irony and his sarcasm ashore, and the heavy Arkol loosened up under the humanizing glow of good wine and became quite jovial. Chase alone did not take anything stronger than water to drink, excusing himself on the ground that it always made him sleepy, and he did not want to miss any of Kott's stories. Dorothy sipped at hers to keep her guests company, but contrived to take only a tablespoonful or two. Her abstinence passed unobserved by her guests. They were having too good a time to bother about her.

"Is Gog comfortable?" she asked during a lull in the conversation.

"Entirely," Arkol assured her. "On the trip to America, he traveled steerage. Now, thanks to all you have done for him, he is promoted to the second cabin. He could have gone first, if he had wished."

"But he preferred to be inconspicuous?" Dorothy suggested.

Arkol frankly told her the truth. They had decided against promoting Gog to the first class to save Dorothy embarrassment. As a second class passenger, Gog would not have the entry, without invitation, to some quarters of the ship. If Dorothy cared to see him, she could invite him to call.

"Let's ask him in now," she cried. "It would be rather fun to hear what he thinks of all this."

No one dissented, and a messenger was commissioned to unearth Gog and bring him to the party, which had now reached the drinks only stage. Arkol seemed to have thrown off all his scientific inhibitions. He was putting away an astonishing quantity of good liquor. The only effect it seemed to have on him was to make him more human. Dorothy, sober as an icicle, began to wonder whether she had been misjudging him. She had heard that a man's true nature floats to the surface if sufficient alcohol to float anything is supplied, and as a medical student and trained nurse she had frequently verified the saying. If this was indeed the real Arkol, then he was not such a bad sort after all. She noticed that Chase also was looking puzzled.

Gog shuffled in, an enormous book in one hand. Without any preliminaries he blundered his way to Dorothy's side, and placed the book in front of her.

"Teach me," he begged, tapping the book with the back of his huge hand.

The men stared at him curiously, Dorothy turned the book up to see the title.

"Sorry, Gog, but I can't. You see, this is in Italian, and I don't know enough Italian to teach it to anyone."

Gog looked miserable. He loomed above her, ungainly, crestfallen, and strangely inhuman. With a profound sigh, he picked up the book and shuffled awkwardly toward the door.

Arkol stopped him. "Let me see it, Gog."

Gog handed him the book, and Arkol glanced through it, keeping up a running fire of questions in his own language, which Gog answered in monosyllables. Arkol handed back the book.

"Italian is not what he wants," he said to Dorothy. "Your specialty has taken his fancy. Is that right, Gog?"

Gog appealed to her again. "Teach me," he implored, holding out his ungainly arms.

"Bacteriology?" she questioned. "Why do you want to learn that?"

Arkol explained for him. "He says he wants to understand what he is doing when he helps me with the serums. Some of the diagrams in this book caught his eye. See." Arkol reached for the book and exhibited several drawings of slides with various bacteria.

"Where did you get the book?" Chase asked Gog.

Gog fixed Chase with his appealing eyes, and glanced down on Arkol. He did not reply.

"Ask him to tell you," Dorothy suggested to Arkol. "He seems embarrassed."

Arkol questioned him in his own language. Gog, it appeared, had bought the book at a secondhand store.

"If he is to help you," Serbin observed, "it will be an advantage if he understands the reasons behind the dull routine."

"Undoubtedly," Kott agreed. "Sound psychology. Eh, Miss Grange? You should know; you are a successful teacher."

"It would give him something to do," she said. "All right, Gog, I'll give you two hours a day. Come tomorrow morning at nine. I shall layout the lessons in the mornings, and you can come again at five in the afternoons to let me check what you have done. If you do as well at bacteriology as you have at everything else, you will be giving me lessons before we land."

Gog was overcome. His eyes filled with tears, and he shuffled from the room without a word. They sat silent for some moments after he had gone.

"Do you think it wise?" Arkol asked.

"It would have been inhuman to refuse."

"Perhaps I can be of assistance," Chase spoke up. "Suppose I take lessons too?"

"That will solve it," Serbin exclaimed. "Why did I not think of volunteering myself?" He favored Dorothy with a gallant bow. "With Miss Grange to help me over the rough places, I believe I could learn bacteriology myself. Gog," he continued with evident sincerity, "has naturally a far more powerful mind than I have. His brain, I am willing to wager, weighs more than mine. All it needed to flame up into genius was a salutary fever and the understanding sympathy of our charming hostess."

Dorothy bowed mockingly. Nevertheless she flushed with pleasure. Kott suddenly burst out laughing.

"What if Gog should take it into his wise young head to bully us as we used to bully him? You will not try to start him off on a counter revolution will you, Miss Grange?"

"Not if I can help it. Gog seems to me to have the stuff in him for making a very useful member of society. Doctor Chase and I will do our best to bring him up in the way he should go."

The party broke up shortly after Gog's exit. Dorothy signaled to Serbin to stay a moment as the others filed out.

"Really," she said, "your government shouldn't have done this. I am not used to any such luxury as this."

"You mustn't scold us," he replied good-humoredly. "Believe me, Miss Grange, our government knows exactly what it is doing. Your good will is worth infinitely more to us than a thousand times all this. If you are pleased, we are amply repaid."

She gave him a doubtful look. "Tell Mr. Arkol and Mr. Kott that I appreciate what you have done. And you might pass that on to whoever is paying the bills. In return I promise to work my head off for Mr. Arkol."

"We knew we could rely on you," Serbin replied, somewhat enigmatically. "May I express the thanks of all of us for this evening? You are an ideal hostess."

When she was alone, Dorothy sat down at the writing desk to think out what it all might mean. That there might be an adder concealed somewhere in the roses, she was modest enough to consider as one of the possibilities, for she simply could not believe that her probable services to Arkol as his assistant could be worth any such staggering sum as was being squandered on her. "What *do* they want?" she asked herself a dozen times. She found no plausible answer. The maid looked in twice, but said nothing, diplomatically hinting by her manner that it was long past bedtime. Dorothy continued to brood. Finally, just as the mad appeared for the third time, she accepted a partial solution of her problem. They obviously wanted something they had not yet dared to hint for, and they were hoping to smother her natural wariness under a cloying syrup of extravagant luxury before venturing to put their question.

"Well," she sighed, getting up from the table and stretching sleepily, "a tenth of a percent of the purchase price would have been just as confusing. What waste!"

"I beg your pardon, madam?" the maid inquired deferentially.

"Just my way of saying it is long past my usual bedtime. Is the bath ready?"

"Everything is ready, madam," the maid replied, deftly beginning to peel her embarrassed mistress.

CHAPTER FIFTEEN
Confidences

SERBIN'S ESTIMATE OF GOG'S BRAIN POWER erred on the side of modesty. After the fourth session, Chase gave up trying to follow his competitor, and sat humbly by, following with astonishment the swift, unerring precision with which Gog grasped old facts and reached out after new. Arkol and Serbin dropped in frequently, Kott only occasionally. Kott's air was one of 'I told you so,' although he seemed to have been as contemptuous as the others before Gog's awakening. To see him strut, one might have thought him, and not Dorothy, responsible for Gog's humanizing.

Dorothy's brief explanations were often interrupted by questions from Serbin or Arkol to Gog, always in their own language. Dorothy grew curious.

"Giving him an examination?" she quizzed after one prolonged exchange of questions and answers.

Serbin apologized. "We are very rude, Miss Grange, but Gog still thinks more naturally in our language. Yes, we were examining him."

"What for?" Chase demanded. He had been half asleep, but something in Serbin's tone put him on the alert.

"Investigating already, Doctor Chase?" Serbin retorted with a touch of his old sarcasm. "We dock tomorrow morning at eleven."

"Thanks for reminding me; my mistake."

Dorothy took a hand. She also was curious to know what the constant cross-examination of Gog meant. "Hadn't you better let Doctor Chase share your confidences?" she suggested pointedly.

"Why so?" Serbin asked coolly.

"Doctor Chase was invited by your government to investigate the fifty year plan, was he not?"

"Without a doubt."

"Then why don't you satisfy him—and me too, for that matter—on a perfectly reasonable question? We are not children."

"Far from it," Arkol spoke up with startling abruptness. "Mr. Serbin has just told you work does not begin till tomorrow at eleven. So why persist in prying into what does not concern you?"

"Look here," Dorothy flashed, standing up and facing Arkol, "I've had enough of this. Now, before we land, is a good time for a showdown. Leave Doctor Chase out of this. He can ask his own questions if he wishes, later. For over a week you two have treated me with a studied rudeness that no woman with an ounce of spirit would stand. You have carried on long conversations in my presence in a language I don't know a word of. Is that your idea of common courtesy? If so, it isn't mine."

Serbin sneered openly. Arkol pretended to be bored.

"So that's your answer?" Dorothy was thoroughly angry. She caught her breath and took a grip on herself. "Then listen to mine," she continued calmly.

"You are not going to resign before you begin work?" Arkol asked in mock alarm.

"I keep my word. Now, if you will not answer a reasonable question, I shall forget my breeding too, and ask a third party what you have been saying."

"Whom will you ask?" Serbin inquired lazily.

"Gog."

Through all the altercation Gog had sat like a stone, apparently indifferent to what was going on. Serbin accepted Dorothy's challenge.

"Ask him," he said contemptuously.

"Gog," she said, "will you please tell me what sort of questions Mr. Serbin and Mr. Arkol have asked you before me?"

"No," Gog answered in his deep, husky voice.

While Dorothy stood aghast and speechless, Gog gathered up his belongings and shuffled from the room. Arkol guffawed. Serbin turned to Chase.

"Have you any questions you would like to ask?"

"For the life of me," Chase retorted, "I can't think of a single one that is necessary."

"By which you mean?" Serbin prompted.

"Just what I said. Gog said it all. His answer will make very interesting reading in my report."

"What if your report is never written?" Arkol insinuated with sinister irony.

"Then, I suppose, Gog's immortal words—pardon me, word—will be lost to the hundreds of our 'young talent' whom you have enlisted."

"You misunderstood me," Arkol hastened to explain. "I had no intention of conveying a threat in my question. That sort of thing does not happen on sober, scientific investigations."

"No?" Dorothy interrupted. "What did you mean?"

"Simply that Doctor Chase's proposed investigation may now be unnecessary—thanks largely to you."

"So all this luxury has been squandered for nothing. What a joke!"

"Now that you have had your 'showdown', as you call it," Serbin remarked, "perhaps you will keep your temper and listen to me. Mr. Arkol and I have intended from the first to satisfy your very natural curiosity and tell you what we have been saying to Gog. Your excitable suspicion rather irritated us, after our poor efforts to win your confidence and show you that we are your friends and well-wishers."

"Yes?" said Dorothy. "Please go on. I am duly grateful for all you have done."

"Gog's extraordinary mental development under your expert teaching," Serbin continued without a trace of emotion or sarcasm, "has suggested a revision of one great campaign in our fifty year war on brute labor. Within a week, we hope, you will understand this as clearly as we do. But let me anticipate this much: If it is possible to bring the average man of Gog's people up to only one tenth of Gog's level of intelligence, we shall be able to reduce the fifty years required for our present plan in genetics to ten, or possibly only five. Our questions to Gog have all concerned this possibility. Knowing his own people far better than any outsider possibly can, his opinions on the educability of his race are invaluable."

"And what does Gog think?" Chase inquired unexpectedly.

"Gog is optimistic," Arkol replied. "In fact he told Kott only yesterday that we have not even begun to scratch the intellectual resources of his people."

"Better not scratch too hard," Chase advised.

"You don't believe in intelligence?" Serbin asked with a sarcastic inflection.

"For the masters it may be all right," Chase retorted. "But for those condemned to run the machines and do the rest of your dirty work, I should think it would be all wrong. For one thing they might throw a monkey wrench into the machinery."

"Ah," said Arkol craftily, "that is just what we must control. Gog's people in their uncivilized state are as stupid as Gog was when you first saw him. Our problem is to rouse their intelligence, but not to waken it completely. We must keep them just stupid enough to be first class mechanics in love with their machines. They must idolize their tools and revel in drudgery as their greatest pleasure."

"What a hellish idea," Chase remarked. "To breed a race of poor devils predestined to brutal slavery, with no desire for anything better, seems to me the last word in cynical contempt for the human race. Serbin must have thought of it."

Serbin modestly disclaimed fathering the idea. "The inspiration came to Mr. Kott one night as he lay awake, unable to sleep after an excellent but too heavy dinner. I have often thought," he mused, "that the stomach must be the seat of the soul. All the really brilliant ideas for the betterment of the human race have emanated from men who have had either too much or too little to eat. However, that is beside the point. Kott was inspired, and our original plan is now tentatively modified to take advantage of Kott's inspiration."

"And may I ask what your original plan was?" Dorothy inquired.

"So far as it concerns Gog's people," Serbin replied, "it was simple enough. One man of his tribe can do the work of ten ordinary men—unskilled work, that is. They can be taught to run tractors and the like, but it would be a little dangerous to make them drivers of railway locomotives. Our problem, as we explained to Professor Brown, was to make them resistant to the pulmonary diseases that ravage them. The death rate is appallingly high in the labor camps."

"Then why do they stay?" Chase asked pointedly. "I should think they would take the first train home."

"There are so few trains running to their part of the world," Arkol explained with a sly smile, "that your suggestion is impractical, Doctor Chase."

"For another thing," Serbin added, "Gog's people are so entirely devoted to the fifty year plan that only one in ten thousand is ever tempted to revert to a state of nature. You can have no idea how the slogan 'all for one and one for all' can transform the rugged individualism of an entire people into the highest type of social idealism."

"Shall I put that in my report?" Chase asked drily.

"By all means," Serbin agreed cordially. "No American will believe in the transformation."

"So no American will believe the rest of my report? I shouldn't be surprised if you were right. This investigation promises to stand all my own preconceived notions on their heads. Now, will you answer me a straight question?"

"What is it?" Arkol demanded cautiously.

"Simply this. Since we left the United States, all three of you have steadily cooled off in your enthusiasm for my investigation. Sometimes I feel you would give a good deal if I were to take the next boat back without leaving the dock."

"Doctor Chase!" Serbin expostulated in a shocked voice. "You pay our poor attempt at hospitality an even poorer compliment."

"As a matter of sober fact," Chase retorted, "I am reserving all of my compliments, poor or other, for my report. What I want to know is this. Are you as keen for a favorable report from me as you were when we sailed?"

"Not quite," Serbin admitted indifferently.

Arkol backed him up. "Any sort of a report will be a luxury for our historical archives if the revised plan suggested by our collaborator Gog should turn out as successfully as we hope and expect it will."

"Then you will have no use for all that 'young talent' in engineering and the mechanical trades you signed up?"

"I would not go so far as to say that," Arkol replied judiciously. "We shall still be able to use a few geniuses—say two. And if we may offer you some kindly advice, you will not try to export more, in spite of your glutted stock. You will need all the talent you have if the revised plan succeeds. And," he concluded emphatically, "it is going to succeed. Then the United States of America will recede within ten years—possibly within six—to the ignominious position of a vassal province in the great empire of world industry and trade."

"Really? You alarm me."

"You do not alarm us," Arkol retorted. "At least not to the point of laying a blueprint of our plan before you for inclusion in your report. You cannot taunt us into showing off before an unscrupulous competitor."

"It might be better for you if you did show off a bit."

"How so?" Serbin demanded.

"That question from you," Chase replied, "is a bit of a shock. Arkol might have asked it, but not you. Don't you see? But of course you do. With only my suspicions to work on, I am likely to invent a sensible parody of your revised plan that will set all of our own technicians working like the devil to go it one better. Why? Because my take-off will be at least sensible—I have no romantic imagination. But suppose I do learn the actual plan, revised or unrevised. To give you a watertight international patent on it, all I have to do is to publish the details in full."

Arkol eyed him suspiciously. "Are you trying to be sarcastic?"

"Not at all, I am telling you what I believe to be a plain fact. Has Kott told you exactly what happened at his last lecture?"

"We have a stenographic report," Serbin cut in. "Very illuminating."

"Almost an index to the American character?" Chase suggested.

"We are filing it in our archives as such," Serbin agreed with a wry smile.

"Then has it not occurred to you," Chase continued, "that there are some things for which Americans will not stand?"

"Even at the cost of receding to the status of a vassal state?"

"At any cost. You can't train a clean beast to live on filth."

"You put it rather strongly," Serbin replied. "But I agree with your position. Where I differ," he went on with unassumed cynicism, "is in the classification of beasts. I have never seen a clean one. Putting that aside, however, allow me to compliment you on your perspicacity. You have evidently grasped the essential features of our plan."

"Oh no," Chase protested.

"But I think you have," Serbin persisted quietly.

"All I know," Chase replied, "is what you and Kott kept dinning into me on that lecture tour."

"Concealment seemed unnecessary," Serbin remarked indifferently, lapsing into abstracted silence.

"Tell me," Arkol begged, "do you think America would oppose us if it learned of our plan?"

Chase intercepted Dorothy's danger signal. "No," he replied. "Why should it?"

"You have just told us yourself," Serbin spoke up. "There are some things for which no American will stand. Once they hear that we are determined to press our campaign on all fronts they will be roused to furious indignation. We shall be implored to desist—in the name of humanity. But our offensive will continue. Prayers in the name of humanity will gradually change to imprecations. There will be war—and what war! Our respective populations will be reduced to a tenth of their normal numbers. But through it all we shall continue to press our major offensive on all fronts. Victory there will be the final and lasting defeat for all of our enemies—including those who imagine their humanity superior to our own. You will be glad to forget your ideals of humanity and accept the generous peace we shall offer you. Then the human race shall go forward together to one goal, instead of squandering its efforts on a hundred opposing futilities."

"What if we prefer futilities to a robot lockstep?" Dorothy asked.

"Then you will have the comfort of them in your graves," Serbin replied. "Extinction or progress. Take your choice."

Chase was left alone with Dorothy a few minutes later.

"Want to turn back?" she asked.

"Too late," he laughed. "Have you guessed what their grand plan is all about?"

She shook her head. "Here comes the cat," she whispered. The parlor maid glided in to ask when Dorothy would like dinner.

"The usual hour," she said carelessly. Then to Chase, "It's stuffy in here. Suppose we take a turn round the deck?"

"I've still got it," he confided to her as they leaned on the rail watching the swift waves flash by.

"Remember what I told you," she whispered. "Step on it if you must. Sure you don't want to turn round tomorrow and go back?"

"What about you?" he countered.

"Don't you see? I'm the bait."

"You mean," he asked slowly, "they have never meant to let me make a report?"

"Perhaps not that. At first they may have intended taking you on a carefully supervised tour to see just what they wanted you to see. Now they seem to have something sharper up their sleeves."

"A, knife, for instance?" he suggested.

"Possibly."

"But will they have the nerve? What would our government do?"

"What could it do? They could laugh in its face."

"I must say you are in a cheerful mood this evening," he muttered.

"Say practical instead. We must keep our wits about us. I don't expect either of us to be shot in the public square with reporters present, or anything of that kind."

"Then what do you expect in your practical way?"

"Nothing much. One of us might die naturally but suddenly. Professor Brown did."

"You're imagining things. They did not kill Professor Brown."

"Not intentionally, perhaps. Arkol is scientific, remember. A lucky accident has often led to a valuable practical discovery. They will know how to make the accident happen now when it is least expected."

He tried to laugh her out of her morbid suspicions, but she persisted.

"You remember what Serbin said a while ago about war? Well, does that suggest anything to you? The nation with a deadly new bacterium and two weeks' start could do pretty much as it pleased."

"But what would they want to do it for—now?"

"Ask some diplomat," she replied. "But I suspect they won't want us running round telling everything we know."

"We know nothing," he said with conviction.

"They seem to think you have made some pretty good guesses. Have you?"

"How should I know?"

"Good boy," she said with approval, patting his arm. "You won't talk, even to your red-headed sweetie. Just for that I'll promise to take the same boat as you do."

"That's talking. So we are coming out, after all?"

"In some boat or another. For all I know it may be Charon's. If so, we sail together."

That evening Dorothy dined alone, excusing herself from attending the party given by Kott to the others on the ground that she had a headache. The men lingered till past midnight over the drinks and cigars. The talk was peaceful enough, but the minds of all seemed preoccupied. Nonetheless they sat on, possibly in hopes that one side or the other would drop a card. Neither did, and with cordial wishes for a good night all round, the party broke up.

Chase strolled to the upper deck, and leaned over the rail where he had stood with Dorothy. Their conversation that afternoon came back to him, and he half expected her to slip out and join him. "I wonder which boat we shall take back?" he thought. "What real difference does it make, so long as it is the same one?"

A hand was gently laid from behind on his shoulder, and he turned with a glad exclamation, expecting to see Dorothy's face in the moonlight. Instead he was staring up into Gog's somber visage. It was heavy and black with brooding. His approach had been noiseless, for Gog disliked his awkward boxes, and frequently strolled about barefoot after the passengers were asleep.

"Beautiful night," Chase volunteered. Gog's hand still rested on his shoulder. The huge fellow's grasp now tightened suggestively.

Gog did not respond. What was troubling him and keeping sleep from him came out without warning.

"You love her?" Gog whispered huskily.

"Yes. Do you?"

"Yes," Gog acknowledged. "Does she love you?"

"Yes. Does she love you?"

"No," came the despairing whisper. "She pities me."

Chase felt the iron grip on his shoulder tighten like a vise. Saying nothing, he stealthily unbottoned his shirt. The pressure on his shoulder grew almost unendurable; he felt that the bones must snap unless Gog let him go instantly.

"The sea is deep," Gog observed dispassionately.

"Very," Chase agreed. His shirt was unbottoned, and he was prepared to swim for his life if he must. The intolerable pressure on his shoulder suddenly relaxed.

"Never mind, old fellow," he said, facing Gog. "You will forget when you go back to your own people."

"Never," Gog sighed. "She is my life."

"And mine."

"Do *you* pity me?" Gog asked after a long silence.

"No. Why do you ask?"

"Everybody pities me. All but those three. They used to laugh at me. Now they need me."

"What for?" Chase asked.

The only answer Gog permitted himself was a profound sigh. Chase learned nothing.

"Do you mind if I ask another question? Don't answer unless you like. Why did you ask Dorothy to teach you bacteriology?"

"It is hers."

"I'm afraid I don't quite understand."

"I thought if I made myself her equal in intelligence she might not pity me."

"I see. But Dorothy does not pity you the way you think she does. She is only sorry for you because of all the unfair things those three did to you."

"I know that is not true!" Gog burst out. Then he seemed suddenly to go mad. Throwing back his great head he let out a sharp, barking roar. His enormous chest expanded to its limit, and he beat upon it with his knotted fists till the hollow expanse thundered like a war drum. Chase's efforts to stop him before the crew came on the run were futile. Gog continued to bark and roar, beating his chest as if he neither knew nor cared that he was making a spectacle of himself.

Kott had heard the first roar. He beat the second officer to the upper deck by a yard. Arkol and Serbin, in their pajamas, followed within five seconds.

Kott shouted at Gog in his own language, but the maddened giant was oblivious of everything but what was present in his own mind.

"Look out!" Serbin shouted. "He will begin smashing things in a moment."

They fell back just as Gog, with startling abruptness, stopped roaring. True to Serbin's prediction, Gog started smashing things.

The rail was ripped from its bolts and twisted into a knot before Gog hurled it with maniacal fury into the sea. With one bound he leapt from the deck upon a lifeboat. The canvas covering was shredded in a matter of seconds. Then Gog began systematically ripping the boat to pieces with his bare hands. At a sharp command from the second officer, curiosity seekers were barred from the deck, and only a few members of the crew, with Chase and his companions, witnessed Gog's madness.

Revolver in hand, the Captain appeared.

"I shall have to shoot him in the foot or the leg if he tries to bolt," he warned Serbin. "Twenty men couldn't hold him."

"It will be over in a moment," Serbin prophesied, as the wrecking of the lifeboat proceeded. "He is nearly exhausted."

Gog suddenly wilted. He seemed to collapse as if every bone in his body had turned to jelly.

"Quick," Kott shouted, darting forward.

Arkol and Serbin rushed after him. Between them they dragged Gog's limp body to the deck.

"Get a bucket of water," Kott ordered. When a sailor brought the bucket of salt water, Kott dashed it in Gog's face. "Give him room to breathe. He will be all right in a minute."

Groaning as if he were in great pain, Gog twisted himself into a sitting posture, knuckling himself up with the backs of his hands. The ring watching him was silent. Some wondered where they had seen movements like Gog's before, but they failed to complete the memory. Serbin walked up to the squatting figure.

"Are you better now?"

Gog groaned. Serbin turned to the Captain. "There is no danger now. He will be quiet. I will see him to his quarters." The Captain dismissed his men, but stood by himself.

"Does he have these spells often?" the Captain asked curiously.

"Quite often. His mother was subject to them,"

"Poor devil," said the Captain. "Probably epileptic."

Kott disagreed. "I think not. J ust savage."

Arkol drew Chase aside. "I wouldn't say anything about this to Miss Grange, if I were you."

"Why not? She should know if Gog is likely to be in the same laboratory with her."

"It would only make her nervous. I give you my word we shall take every precaution."

"What sort of precaution?"

"Guards with high powered army rifles."

"These outbursts are the usual thing, then?"

"We think it best to take precautions," Arkol replied evasively. "While he was in America we kept him under sedatives when he began to show signs of an approaching attack. You will not tell Miss Grange?"

"Perhaps you are right. There is no point in upsetting her. You are sure she will be in no danger?"

"I give you my word. Miss Grange and I will be working in the same building. To protect myself—if you insist on looking at it that way—I must protect her at the same time."

Chase said no more, and was about to go, when Gog stood up. For a few seconds he tottered drunkenly. Then he saw Kott. The effect was instantaneous and peculiar. Gog snapped into a different being. Standing rigid and erect, he released a torrent of words at the puny little man before him. Although Chase failed to understand the meaning of a single word, he followed the drift of Gog's denunciation. Kott was the helpless recipient of as thorough a cursing as one man ever got from another. Finishing with Kott, Gog turned on Serbin and cursed him at even greater length. His climax however was reserved for Arkol. This contained several sentences in English, from which Chase gathered that Gog cursed Arkol for having exhibited such a vile thing as the hairy, misshapen body and hideous face, which were his, to Dorothy. Gog did not threaten Arkol; he merely tried to waken his shame. Arkol turned his face aside to conceal the broad smile, which he was afraid Gog might misinterpret in the moonlight.

Chase turned and walked away. His business was to use his eyes and hold his tongue. He had seen enough to keep him talking for a year when the time should come for talking. What he had just witnessed made him resolve to go all out in his fight, as Dorothy had said she meant to do in hers.

CHAPTER SIXTEEN
At Work

A FAIR PART OF DOROTHY'S DREAM WAS NOW a reality of the past. She had traveled farther than she would have dreamed it possible for her ever to travel less than three months before. She had seen the best of the Mediterranean, the Aegean Isles, and Constantinople. There had been unforgettable excursions in Greece and Italy, marred only by the effusive travelogue of the encyclopedic Mr. Kott, but even his inexhaustible store of ancient history and archaeology could not quite smother the perfect beauty of the islands. Serbin never explained anything; Arkol confined his remarks to tips on what to eat and what to leave for the waiter. Chase was the ideal traveling companion; he never raved. And now all this was only a gorgeous memory, as Dorothy stood in her white uniform in the steel and glass central office of a vast, box-like structure of steel, concrete, and glass without a friendly stick of wood anywhere in its severely scientific and sanitary construction. Work had begun, and it had begun in deadly earnest.

Arkol angrily flung down the report he had been scanning. The report was typed on pale red paper, to indicate danger and urgency. The numerous reports on white, gray, or green paper were still untouched.

"We've got to stop it," he exclaimed, glancing up at Dorothy.

"Stop what?"

"This infernal plague. It has broken out worse than ever in the concentration camps. Over three hundred dead yesterday in camp 27, eighty in camp 30, and so on all through the fourth and fifth districts." He pointed to a wavy black line on the red paper, beginning in the lower left hand corner and rising steadily to the right. "The history of the last ten days. We should have got here sooner."

"I am waiting for instructions," she reminded him.

"Yes, yes. Of course. There is no use treating those already infected. The mortality is one hundred percent, and they will all be dead within twenty four hours. We must inoculate the healthy."

"Is the serum prepared?"

"Only what I made in America. Get busy at once and lay out everything for giving us a continuous supply." He pushed a button. "You will have all the technical assistance you need. I expect you to take charge and be responsible for the finished product. The assistants will obey your orders."

A soldier in dingy olive gray answered Arkol's summons.

The man had his army rifle, with fixed saw-tooth bayonet, slung across his shoulders. Arkol fired a rapid stream of curt orders at the man, who listened intently, turned upon his heel, without saluting, and hurried from the office.

"Excuse me for not using English," Arkol apologized. "Our guards know only our language. I have sent for a woman interpreter. You can give your orders through her. If there is any insubordination, you need only point out the guilty party to one of the guards. You will find them efficient and trustworthy."

Dorothy made no comment. Since Arkol had set foot on his own soil, he was a different man from the easy-going host and agreeable companion of the steamer. His movements were quicker, his voice sharper, and his whole manner indicated the ruthless commander who exacts instant, unquestioning obedience.

The armed guards, tough-looking scoundrels, two at every door and six to ten in each of the laboratories, had made Dorothy wonder, but she had asked no questions. From her cursory inspection of the laboratories as she followed Arkol to his office, Dorothy guessed that the vast building of glass and steel was indeed one of the world's finest bacteriological laboratories, if not the very finest. But why the brutal guards with fixed bayonets and full cartridge belts? As Chase had told her nothing of Gog's outburst she was completely at a loss. Possibly, she reflected, this was just a vivid detail in Arkol's theatrical dramatization of his heroic war against disease. But she was too perturbed to smile at his expense.

The guard returned, preceded by a chunky young woman with close-cropped black hair, tortoise-shell glasses, bare red arms and a grim visage on which bigotry and fanaticism had left their harsh lines. Her uniform was like Dorothy's except that it was a dirty blue instead of white.

"Your interpreter," Arkol said.

Dorothy offered her hand. The interpreter crushed it in hers. "I did not get your name?" Dorothy inquired politely, trying not to wince.

"Lena," the strong young woman replied in a gruff voice, not without a certain harsh music.

"Mine's Dorothy. You understand English—or rather American—well?"

"You bet," Lena boomed.

"Show Miss Grange to Laboratory A," Arkol ordered. "Until relieved, you are under her orders."

Without a word Lena marched from the office, evidently expecting Dorothy to follow. But Dorothy hesitated. She had just heard a husky cough outside the door, and she thought she recognized its peculiar quality.

"You said I am to have assistants?" she asked, inventing the pretext to linger.

Arkol swelled with pride. "The best in the world, Miss Grange. And if you need any supplies, tell Lena what you need."

"Thank you, I shall." She turned to follow the impatient Lena, and almost bumped into Gog. The awkward fellow blocked the exit. Behind him were two of the villainous soldiers. This murderous looking pair had unslung their rifles and were carrying them in the most suggestively businesslike position. Dorothy retreated toward Arkol's desk. Gog gave her a heartrending look and stepped before Arkol. The great pathologist's face clouded. For a moment he seemed to be on the point of ordering Dorothy to follow Lena. Then the old crafty look oiled his heavy features and he motioned to her to stay.

"You remember," he said, fixing her with his black eyes, "how Professor Brown doubted that Gog had volunteered of his own free will for our little experiment back in America?"

"Did he?" Dorothy asked with well-feigned surprise. "He never told me."

Arkol favored her with a malignant smile.

"Professor Brown seems to have been a more reticent man than our mutual friend Admiral Simpson. You remember our little session with him? When he asked me to look through a microscope?"

Dorothy nodded, and Arkol continued. "Professor Brown was quite outspoken in his doubts to me. As a guest in America, I could not very well contradict him." Arkol seemed to be enjoying himself. To give his next revelation its full force he paused and stroked his beard with all the dignity of a Tartar potentate. "If Professor Brown were present now—as he cannot be, alas—he would be the first to admit that he had misjudged me. Gog!"

At the sharp command Gog started violently. His eyes had been gloating on Dorothy's hair. But Arkol was not reprimanding him for his public adoration.

"I shall need twenty-five volunteers in Laboratory B in two hours from now. See that they are there. Answer in English."

"Yes," Gog answered in a husky whisper.

"You see," Arkol exclaimed, turning triumphantly to Dorothy, "this splendid soldier in the war upon disease has no hesitation in promising to find twenty-five more as brave as himself, and to do it within two hours. I would issue the call myself," he added, "were I not so busy and," he concluded with a harsh laugh, "if I understood the language of Gog's people as well as he does. Gog was invaluable to us as a recruiting sergeant before we went to America. I am pleased to see that his sip of foreign culture—and your splendid efforts in behalf of his intelligence, Miss Grange— have not sapped his superb sense of duty. Now hurry, both of you. There is not a minute to lose. The enemy—"

Whatever Arkol was about to divulge about the enemy was drowned in Gog's roar. Dorothy had never heard anything like it before from a human being. Arkol's face went a pasty yellow. The guards could not hear his command above the roar, but they acted instantly and efficiently. Gog's outburst ended as suddenly as it had begun. The blood oozed through two neat slits in the back of his smock, just below the shoulder blades, as he faced about, beating his chest with his fists, and silently preceded the guards from the office.

Dorothy swallowed hard before trusting herself to speak. When she felt sure of herself, she spoke quite calmly.

"Is that the way you keep a promise?"

"To what particular promise do you refer, Miss Grange?"

"You promised me that Gog would be sent back to his own country as soon as you got back home."

"My dear Miss Grange," Arkol expostulated, "I have never broken my word in my life."

"Then why is Gog still here?"

"Is he?" Arkol asked with heavy sarcasm, pretending to peer about the office for the vanished Gog. "I don't see him."

"I think you understand what I mean," Dorothy answered quietly.

"Really, Miss Grange, you have the advantage of me."

"Have I? Then let me repeat that you gave me your word—and Mr. Serbin gave his—to send Gog back to his own country without any delay the moment you returned here."

Arkol apologized profusely. "How stupid of me. I see now what you mean, and I understand your mistake perfectly. It is quite a natural one for anyone in your position to make. But I have sent Gog back to his own country. With an armed escort, it is true; but still I have sent him, as you saw for yourself. Perhaps it is the armed guard that is troubling you? That may be interpreted as a mark of honor, if you like, such as we would accord any visiting king or president. In short, Miss Grange, Gog's country is *here*—or not more than half a mile away."

"But this place is highly civilized."

"Why not? Have you no barbarians in your own highly civilized country?" Arkol sneered. "I seem to recall meeting several. I give you my word as a scientist that I have told you the exact truth and nothing more."

"You gave me your word before, and I understand it no better now than I seem to have done then."

"It will all be plain enough in a day or two," Arkol purred. "Now, to work. You know what you have to do."

"I will do my best," Dorothy replied slowly, "but don't expect me to do the impossible."

"Such as remembering how Professor Brown taught you to put together those extremely complicated serums A, P, and S, for instance?" Arkol suggested with a sinister smile.

"As an illustration, yes. That might be impossible for me. Until I try, I don't know."

"I fear you underestimate your own capacities," Arkol insinuated, menacing her with a look, which made his meaning obvious. "The impossible has often been accomplished—under my personal supervision and direction—in this laboratory. I might almost say in this office."

"I have told you I would try to do my best," she said, walking from the office.

"Do," he flung after her. "Lena will be glad to help you. She is expert at knowing when some disloyal worker is malingering or contemplating sabotage."

Chase also was learning much of at least the outside of the fifty year plan. Serbin, as director of the whole plan, and Kott as chief of the division of animal genetics had taken Chase in hand, and were now showing him everything they wanted him to see. Most of the seeing was done from the back seat of a seven passenger car, which sped over the fine white highways at anything from fifty to seventy-five miles an hour under the expert driving of a burly chauffeur in a soldier's uniform.

Like most who have had no first-hand information of their neighbors, Chase was astonished at the purely physical aspects of the delightful country in which he found himself. Olive groves, palms, subtropical vegetation and deep, fertile valleys bathed in an atmosphere as balmy as Southern California's or the Riviera's, contradicted the grim tradition of a harsh, forbidding country with long winters, which he had always accepted as the only rational picture. His preconceived notions of the climate and scenery were as absurd as the similar confusion between Labrador and Northern Mexico, merely because both happened to be situated in the continent of North America. His astonishment reached a climax when Serbin pointed out a dense green jungle luxuriating rankly in an old river bottom.

"Bamboo," Serbin remarked laconically.

"Bamboo? Here?" Chase echoed.

"Why not? We are in the southernmost peninsula of my country."

"But why all the bamboo?" Chase persisted.

"Excellent fodder," Kott informed him with a misinforming grimace.

"For what? Elephants?" Chase asked. He remembered Serbin's cryptic remark about improving bamboo through breeding. At the time Chase had thought Serbin's comments part of his habitual sarcasm. Now here was the bamboo, hundreds of acres of it, and Chase hoped to discover why his severely practical companions should think it worth cultivating. The river bottom, he judged, must be some of the richest agricultural land in the peninsula. Serbin seemed to think Chase's inquisitiveness worth his personal attention.

"As a plant geneticist, Doctor Chase, you should see the unlimited possibilities of bamboo. Under proper conditions it can be stimulated to produce new shoots every four weeks. Have you ever tried fresh young bamboo sprouts?"

"Can't say that I have."

"The Chinese," Serbin continued, "have long considered them a great delicacy." His characteristic irony cropped out in spite of this purely impersonal subject. "On my flight through China—when I was young and still believed in the old order—I had many opportunities for testing the opinion of the Chinese epicures. In fact," he continued reminiscently, "at one time I subsisted entirely on a diet of bamboo sprouts for a period of twenty-five days. The shoots were as succulent as the epicures claim. I found them excellent, but insufficiently nourishing."

"Rather watery, I should imagine," Chase remarked.

"All water," Serbin agreed, "except for the undigestible cellulose and a deep tincture of chlorophyll to make the shoots appetizing to the uncritical eye. But it occurred to me when I was on the point of starvation that if bamboo could be successfully crossed with sugar cane, the boon to humanity would be inestimable."

"You really believe people could live on the stuff?" Chase demanded incredulously.

"Not those who have been lapped in bourgeois luxury," Kott cut in excitedly. "But who cares whether they live or die?"

"Then who could live on your glorified sweet asparagus?"

"Honest workers," Kott replied fiercely. "And at a minimum cost to the state. The green stuff and the cellulose would provide bulk, the sugar unlimited muscular energy, and we could round out the diet with liberal allowances of bananas. Where bamboo flourishes bananas do well. We are developing a new species adapted to cool climates."

"Where grows the lush bamboo, there blooms the rich banana, too." Chase observed facetiously, hoping to enrage Kott into further revelations. He was learning more than he had hoped for when they set out. "It sounds like the beginning of a Cuban love song, or a slogan for the Borneo Chamber of Commerce."

Kott's explosion almost wrecked the car. His enraged shout startled the driver just as they were taking a hairpin turn at something over forty. Chase had overdone it with his Cuban love song. Kott was so enraged that he spluttered an unintelligible froth of half a dozen European languages in addition to his native Yiddish. Only the word 'bourgeois,' used as an oath or an epithet of contempt with alarming frequency, gave a hint of the general flavor of Kott's effervescing denunciation.

"Thanks," said Chase drily, when Kott finally ran himself out of steam. "I get you."

A welcome diversion was afforded by the shrill screaming of a siren behind them. Glancing back, Chase saw a huge scarlet truck rearing after them at seventy miles an hour. Their own driver hastily drew up off the road and waited for the screaming monster to pass. As it flashed by, Chase had a curious vision. The truck was nothing more or less than a huge cage of two inch steel bars mounted rigidly on an American metropolitan hose truck. Four men in uniform, one the driver, occupied the front seat, inside the steel cage were three figures, two of them in uniform. On top of the cage, at each of the four corners, machine guns were mounted, and sitting behind each were two men in the now familiar olive gray uniform.

"Wasn't that Gog in the cage?" Chase asked Serbin as their own car swung back on the road.

"Possibly," Serbin admitted.

"Where's he going?" Chase demanded.

Serbin stiffened. "Is that a proper question, Doctor Chase?"

"Perhaps not. I ask it merely because the Senate Committee back home will want to know the answer when they see the question in my report."

Serbin favored him with a cold, malicious smile.

"In that case you shall answer it with your own eyes." He gave the driver a sharp order and the car shot after the scarlet truck.

CHAPTER SEVENTEEN
Investigating

THE CHUNKY LENA GRUFFLY REPRIMANDED Dorothy for not having followed her more promptly.

"I was talking to Mr. Arkol," Dorothy answered shortly.

"You are not supposed to talk to him. Mr. Arkol will talk to you."

"Really?" Dorothy queried in the most exasperatingly honeyed tone she could command at the moment.

"Yuss," Lena retorted. "You are under orders now."

"Pardon me," Dorothy replied still more sweetly, "but I thought you were under orders. Mine, too. Mr. Arkol ordered you to obey me."

"That applies only to the interpreting," Lena retorted with an angry gesture. "I am your supervisor, assigned to this detail by the bacteriological workers' committee."

"Dear me," said Dorothy. "Where did you study bacteriology?"

"I ain't," Lena snapped.

"You what?" Dorothy queried in polite bewilderment.

"I ain't studied no bacteriology," Lena explained gruffly.

"Oh, I see. So you are to supervise my work. How intensely interesting you must find your duties."

"Cut out the comedy," Lena snapped. Her bigoted face set like an axe. "I don't know nothing about bacteriology, but I can damn well tell when a worker is slacking. Get me, lady?" The 'lady' was spat out with venomous emphasis.

"I get you, Lena," Dorothy replied with deadly calm. "By the way, where did you get your extraordinary command of English?"

With quite unnecessary obscenity, Lena told Dorothy that she had picked up the choicer fluencies of her vocabulary in that historic American institution known to all New Yorkers as the Tombs, where the passionate Lena had been incarcerated before deportation for speaking her mind too freely in Central Park.

"They framed me," Lena explained.

"And as turn about is fair play," Dorothy suggested, "you are now going to frame me? Is that it Lena?"

They were alone in a long dismal passageway leading to the laboratory where Dorothy was to work. Lena planted herself before Dorothy, her fists doubled on her hips, and her hard, shrewish face thrust temptingly forward. All she needed was the red cap to complete the pose for a bloodthirsty fishwife of the French Revolution. She made the perfect foil for Dorothy's daintiness and cool poise. Dorothy was the thoroughbred of one social order, Lena the equally finished product of another in its crude beginnings.

"Take it any way you like, you damned bourgeoisie. I am to report on you."

"How do you expect me to take it? Do you think I will submit to having my instructions to my assistants garbled by you? If you know nothing of bacteriology, how are you going to translate what I say?"

"Who gives a damn what you say?" Lena sneered, thrusting her face into Dorothy's.

"Then why am I here?"

"Ask Arkol."

"I shall," Dorothy retorted. "Now."

"The sooner the better," Lena agreed with a hideous laugh.

Dorothy marched back to the office, alone. Lena was still laughing herself silly in the passageway.

Arkol looked up frowning. He had just digested another of the reports on pale red paper.

"Well?" He glared at her angrily.

"Give me a competent interpreter if you expect me to do any work with my assistants."

"Lena is competent. Go back to your work."

"I haven't begun yet," Dorothy retorted. "And I have no intention of starting until you give me an interpreter who knows at least the sound of technical terms in bacteriology in our two languages."

"You will obey orders," Arkol snapped. His face was purple with suppressed rage. "Go to the laboratory."

Dorothy sat down. "When you give me a competent interpreter."

Arkol jumped up and stood over her. "Do you want me to ring for a guard? You saw them handling Gog."

"But I'm a woman."

"What has that to do with it?" he sneered. "Here you are a worker. Like Gog."

"I might resign, you know."

"You might," he agreed with sinister meaning. "But you will not. Now, go to work."

"I refuse, until I have had an opportunity to talk with Doctor Chase in private."

Arkol was about to burst into a passion when he had a brilliant inspiration, and he checked himself. His face became bland and crafty.

"I beg your pardon, Miss Grange," he apologized. He picked up the red paper he had been studying. "This plague is getting on my nerves. You will overlook my hastiness as the natural reaction of an overwrought man?"

"Of course," Dorothy said, eyeing him keenly.

"Then let us meet one another half way. Compromise."

"How?" Dorothy asked warily.

"You go to the laboratory and work as fast as you can till Doctor Chase returns, and I'll send him to you the moment he comes."

"He is coming here? Today?"

"It was not on his schedule. But I can easily telephone and make arrangements for him to drop in on his way home."

"Couldn't I telephone?"

"Impossible, I fear. None of the operators understand English."

"Oh. Then I shall have to trouble you to do it for me. What about Lena?"

"Won't you please put up with her for today? Tomorrow, I promise you, I will let you have full and exclusive use of a trained bacteriologist who speaks English. In fact," he added with a peculiar look, "it has been my intention from be first to do so the moment I could find the time to make the necessary arrangements myself. Your very natural impatience with Lena determines me to find the time today."

Something in his manner alarmed her, but she could see no other course but to accept his terms until she had seen Chase. Then a suspicion that chilled her to the heart caused her to hesitate. What if Arkol's promise to telephone about Chase was of the same stuff as his other promise to send Gog home?

"You are sure Doctor Chase can be reached in time by telephone?"

"Oh, positive."

"Then I'll get on the best I can with Lena for today."

"That's sensible," he purred. "I knew you would be reasonable."

Dorothy found Lena waiting where she had left her.

"So he sent you back?"

"Not exactly. We compromised."

"On what?" Lena demanded suspiciously.

"You. Mr. Arkol is to give me a trained bacteriologist who speaks English for my interpreter."

"When?" Lena asked curiously. Her harsh mouth seemed to have deliquesced into a loose-lipped smile of lascivious anticipation.

"Tomorrow," Dorothy replied curtly, trying not to look at Lena's revolting smile.

"So soon?" And for no apparent reason Lena howled and yelped like a laughing hyena.

"Stop it!" Dorothy cried. "This isn't the Tombs."

The next hour and a half passed quickly enough for Dorothy, as she supervised the setting up of the necessary apparatus in the splendidly equipped laboratory.

While Dorothy was thus engaged, Chase was making startling progress with his investigation of the fifty-year plan in genetics.

Another day of sightseeing, he felt, would enable him to write a sufficiently detailed report. Indeed, if he could have seen Dorothy then and there, he would have tried to persuade her to take the next boat back with him. He knew enough now, he believed, to satisfy the most inquisitive and the most talented of the 1200 or more 'young talent' whom Serbin and Kott had recruited for service under the plan.

For about ten miles Serbin's car followed the screaming scarlet truck down a broad paved highway, straight as an arrow, which traversed a flat valley between heavily forested mountains on both sides.

"A military road?" Chase asked.

"Just that," Serbin confirmed with his sarcastic smile.

"And those enclosures like old-fashioned stockades back against the mountains?" Chase pursued. "What are they? Barracks?"

"Camps," Kott answered curtly.

"Civil or military?" Chase demanded.

"You shall see for yourself," Serbin replied. He gave the driver an order, and the car swerved down a side road leading to one of the forbidding looking stockades. "There will be plenty of time to overtake Gog before he begins work."

Half a mile from the main road the car slowed down. Two pale red flags, one on either side of the road, indicated danger. The driver shouted. Presently he was answered by two shouts, from opposite sides of the road. The shouts were followed by two uniformed guards. The car came to a dead halt. Serbin stood up to show himself, and the guards signaled the car to proceed.

"Only the commander in chief may pass without a written order," Serbin explained. "I am the commander in chief. By the way, Doctor Chase, you are not averse on your investigations to risking your life, I take it?"

"If I must, I must. Neither you nor Mr. Kott seem particularly disturbed. So why should I worry?"

"Your employers might be provoked if you were to die suddenly," Serbin replied. "If either Kott or I fade from the picture, better men will step into our places. The resources of our country are inexhaustible."

"But what particular danger is there?" Chase persisted, as the car again came to a stop, this time before a removable barricade stretched across the road. A dozen or so soldiers, with fixed bayonets, stood behind the barricade. Again the car was allowed to pass when Serbin stood up.

"Plague," he answered briefly as he sat down. "We have not yet discovered any means of controlling these distressing outbursts among the workers. The disease is transmitted in much the same way as the most disastrous types of influenza. That is to say," he concluded with a sarcastic smile, "nobody knows how. It just steals through the air like a noxious gas. Shall we go on?"

"Yes," Chase answered. "The resources of America also are practically unlimited."

"You have the courage of ignorance," Serbin sneered. "What you do not understand you face fearlessly, whereas a squad of ignorant and brutalized executioners would find you as meek as the bravest counter-revolutionist."

"Well, why not?"

"No reason at all," Serbin admitted, "I was merely commenting on the peculiar psychology of the aristocrat and the bourgeois. A sudden death, provided it is 'natural' and unforeseen, is without terror, as any practical revolutionist will tell you. Yet its effect is precisely the same as that of the more humane execution."

The car had come to a stop again. Kott spoke up.

"We shall not go any farther," he said. "But if you wish to investigate the camp, the guards will let you pass."

Chase said nothing for the moment. He was busy photographing every detail of the scene on his memory. The stockade was thirty feet high, and it was not wood, but steel and concrete. Electricity from high-tension wires crackled and sputtered along the top of the wall, for the full two miles or more of it, which were visible from where they sat. About two hundred yards from the wall a cordon of machine gunners, one machine gun with its crew every twenty yards, stretched in an unbroken line as far as Chase could see. The gunners wore gas masks, and their guns were trained on the stockade.

"A necessary precaution," Serbin explained. "Desperate patients sometimes succeed in evading the dangers of high voltage."

"And when they do," Chase remarked, "I suppose they are shot?"

"In midair, as they leap. It is necessary."

"How do the medical officers get in and out?"

"They don't," Kott replied with a grimace. "As they could do nothing for the patients, why sacrifice their skill when the state can use it to good advantage?"

Chase took this without comment. Serbin sighed restlessly.

"Shall we go on?"

"I suppose we might as well," Chase agreed. "There's not much to be seen here. How long has this camp been under siege?"

"Since yesterday. The first case was discovered shortly after the workers left the mess hall for their morning labor."

"So you isolated the entire camp? Rather drastic treatment, I should think, for a single case. Wouldn't it be more economical to isolate the single case, and put the others under observation?"

Serbin grew quite animated. "At first we followed precisely that plan. We were forced to abandon it because it proved uniformly unsuccessful. Experience is the only reliable teacher in a novel experiment. We found it invariably more economical to let nature take its course. After the first twenty-four hours only the most resistant are alive. By the end of seventy hours only the very cream of a population of twelve or fourteen hundred has survived. From this naturally resistant nucleus we proceed to the next experiment."

"Yes," Kott added effusively, "the nucleus are our trusted shock troops in the major campaign. Of course," he added modestly, "we are still in the experimental stage."

"How many of these shock troops are in the field now?" Chase asked.

"Too few, unfortunately," Kott admitted reluctantly.

"How few?" Chase persisted.

"Well, to be exact," Kott confessed, "as a scientist I should not care to claim more than one."

"And that one, I suppose, is our friend Gog?"

"Exactly," Serbin said. "That is why Mr. Kott has such a high esteem for him. Gog, you see, was the sole survivor from a particularly disastrous outbreak, which wiped out a camp of over five thousand in less than a week. As chief of the division of animal genetics, Mr. Kott is naturally anxious that Gog be induced to perpetuate his splendid resistance. Unfortunately, Gog has hitherto evinced an unnatural repugnance to the very idea of marriage."

"Hitherto?" Chase asked sharply. "He has changed?"

"Gog's contact with civilization in America gave him a new and a more human set of values," Serbin elucidated. "We have observed a remarkable and very gratifying change in his attitude of late. I think Mr. Kott may be encouraged to hope for the best."

Chase wondered what Dorothy was doing, and wished he were within easy reach of the bacteriological laboratories. He kept his head and dropped the subject of Gog's remarkable conversion to the finer aspects of civilization. His mind was occupied with the problem of inventing a plausible excuse for visiting the bacteriological laboratories where Arkol had his office.

"Have I seen everything of the concentration camps necessary for my report?" he asked.

"You wished to see where Gog was going," Serbin reminded him. He gave the driver a sharp order, and the car shot down the highway at eighty miles an hour.

At that speed Chase had little opportunity for observation. He caught fleeting glimpses of groups of machine gunners guarding side roads branching off to other stockades, and the pale red danger flags were constantly in evidence. At length the car slowed to enable the driver to make a square turn, and the car leapt forward on the last lap of its pursuit.

The scarlet truck with Gog and his guards had already been swallowed up in the vast stockade—which Serbin euphemistically designated as a workers' concentration camp. This particular camp had thus far escaped the ravages of the present outburst of the plague although Kott confided to Chase that it had "suffered heroically" in two former "assaults of the merciless enemy."

The steel gates of the camp had not been closed after the entrance of the scarlet "emergency truck"—which would want to get away as quickly as possible once it got its load. But exit was not left to the discretion of the concentration workers; a full battery of machine guns parked just outside the gates presented an unanswerable argument against trying to run away from the job.

"What a remarkable establishment," Chase observed as the car was allowed to pass in.

"Typical of all the camps, Doctor Chase," Kott replied with smug satisfaction. "Sanitary to the last degree. And efficient. We are proud of our camps."

"I see no reason why you shouldn't be. Where is our friend Gog?"

The question needed no answer. The scarlet truck appeared in the distance, leaping toward them as if the world were on fire, and it was the last hope of controlling the conflagration.

"Quite dramatic," Chase observed. "Would you mind having the truck stopped?"

"Not at all," Serbin replied courteously. He shouted to a soldier and the man ran forward waving a red flag at the oncoming truck. There was a screeching and smoking of brakes, and the truck came to a halt.

Excusing himself, Chase left Kott and Serbin in the car and walked over to the truck.

"Investigating, Doctor Chase?" Serbin called after him.

"Not yet. I just want to pass the time of day with Gog."

"You will find him on the roof of the truck," Kott shouted, "with the guards and machine gunners."

"Thanks," Chase called back. "Mr. Serbin, will you give me the necessary orders for me to get onto the roof? I can't stand down here and shout."

The orders were given without hesitation, and Chase climbed up. Gog was still guarded by two ruffians with fixed bayonets. When he saw Chase his face became hideously distorted, and he tried to bury his head in his arms. A guard made him sit up.

"It's all right, Gog," Chase began. "I just want to ask you a few questions. First, who are all these men—evidently of your own race—in the cage? There must be well over twenty of them."

"Twenty-five," Gog corrected in a husky whisper.

"Twenty-five, then. Where are they going?"

"To the bacteriological laboratory."

"What for?"

"To be inoculated."

"Just as you were, back in America?"

"Yes."

"And they have volunteered, just as you did?"

Gog looked up, his face contorted with anguish.

"They know nothing," he said.

"Then why are they being taken?"

"Because I persuaded them to go."

"And who persuaded you to persuade them?"

Gog was silent. Chase pursued the inquiry.

"These men?" he asked, indicating the guards.

Gog shook his head. "They are tools."

"I see. You bear them no ill will because they are only doing their duty in carrying out orders. Whose tools are they?"

"Arkol's."

"Thanks, Gog. I think I had better ride back to the laboratory with you and your truckload of volunteers. Oh, Serbin," he called, "please tell the driver of this truck that he has an extra passenger. I have just remembered something that Mr. Arkol must know at once."

Chase could not see the expression on Serbin's face, but the necessary order was given, and the scarlet truck continued its rocket rush to the laboratories. The roar of the motor and the shrieking of the siren made further questioning of Gog on the way impossible, and Chase was reduced to studying Gog's face for possible clues to the truth and justice—if any—of the strange proceedings.

Gog's expression was like that of a dog that has been beaten by its master and would commit suicide if it knew how. The grotesque ugliness of the hopeless, defeated face but emphasized the lines of despair. Chase would gladly have shot any civilized human being in sight, but the guards had a monopoly on the weapons of civilized warfare, and Chase had nothing on him comparable. The necessity of being civil to Arkol in the approaching interview increased his discomfort almost beyond endurance. "Keep your mouth shut," he reiterated to himself. "Getting excited and raving like a fool will only make things worse. God, but I wish Dorothy were out of this. Why in hell didn't they send Alexander, if they think he is so damned good? But then I would never have met Dorothy. Cheer up, the worst can't be more than a mile off."

Arkol met the truck at the entrance to the laboratory yard. There was a rapid exchange of words between him and the driver. Chase, of course, was invisible from the ground. Evidently the driver reported his presence last, for the look of astonishment on Arkol's face, which Chase caught as he stood up, obliterating the great pathologist's self-conscious crispness, was genuine. For once, Chase imagined, he had caught the fearless leader in the war against disease off his guard. But it was only for a fraction of a second. Arkol recovered his wits and his false face instantly and simultaneously.

"Ah," he exclaimed, his oily countenance beaming with gratification. "I just missed you by telephone at the camp. Serbin tried to overtake you, but our emergency truck can outspeed any car on the road."

"You telephoned?"

"Miss Grange wished to get into touch with you, and I promised to locate you—which I did, after a little frantic telephoning to the various camps. I told Miss Grange I would send you in as soon as you came."

"Thanks," said Chase, climbing down. "Where is she?"

"In her laboratory, working." He shouted to a guard. "That man will show you where she is."

Chase hesitated. Should he follow the guard, or should he stay by Gog? If Dorothy were in any immediate danger, Arkol would not be sending him to her unless—and the possibility sent a chill up his back—this were a cunning trap to take them both at once.

Gog resolved Chase's doubt. As the big fellow climbed down, he contrived to nudge Chase in the back with his elbow. The direction of the urge was unmistakable. Chase followed the guard.

CHAPTER EIGHTEEN
Exit Lena

CHASE FOUND DOROTHY FEVERISHLY BUSY. Under the jealous, watchful eyes of Lena, she appeared to be completely absorbed in her supervision of about twenty expert assistants.

"Hullo, Dorothy," he called. "Everything going along all right?"

His voice startled her and she jumped round to face him.

"Oh—" she began, and stopped abruptly, eyeing the glumly observant Lena distrustfully. "Let's go into the passageway a moment. I need a breath of fresh air."

Chase glanced at Lena and raised his brows. Dorothy nodded.

But Lena would tolerate no loafing on the job. "Miss Grange is working," she declared gruffly.

"She'll be back in a moment, as soon as she's had a breath of air."

"She stays here," Lena announced, planting herself squarely between them.

"Please, Lena," Dorothy piped up. "I must go out for a minute."

Lena, graduate of the Tombs, was not unduly delicate before gentlemen.

"You went to the lavatory less than five minutes ago. What's the matter with you?"

Dorothy stifled the witty retort on the tip of her tongue, and faced the pest with firm civility.

"I wish to speak to Doctor Chase in private for a few moments. Mr. Arkol said I might. Does that satisfy you?"

"No," said Lena, shortly and angrily. "What you two say I'm going to hear."

"That's all right," Chase assured her, giving Dorothy a warning glance. "We have no objection to talking before you, I understand the situation perfectly. You are only doing your duty."

Lena flared up. "What the hell do you know about my duty?"

"Now that you ask me," Chase retorted good-naturedly, "I suppose I don't know much. What *is* your duty, by the way?"

"To see that Miss Grange does what she is told."

"A sort of overseer? Well, I won't take any of her time." He turned to Dorothy. "Really there was nothing of any importance I just wanted to tell you about my trip around the country. Great place—all sorts of unexpected plants. A regular botanist's paradise," he enthused, "and you should see what they've been doing with new species of bamboo." He included Lena in his complimentary remarks. "Your plant geneticists have beaten us out of sight. Why, that bamboo was the real thing—"

"Did you go through it?" Lena demanded suspiciously.

Chase laughed. "Go through it? I should say not. Why, I wouldn't even go into it without a machine gun or something of the sort. I'll bet that jungle of yours is swarming with tigers."

Dorothy instantly followed up his hint.

"You are always imagining things," she smiled. "I'll bet you saw a cat sneaking into the jungle, and magnified it into a tiger."

"You are dead wrong," he protested. "That bamboo is a natural jungle for the real cats—the big fellows with stripes and whiskers a foot long. I'm going to keep out of it. Unless I have a machine gun with me."

"Where will you get it?" Lena demanded with a malicious smile.

"Possibly I shan't. Perhaps—"

His speculations were cut short by a staccato voice that is never forgotten once it has been heard. Dorothy's startled eyes stared into his, and they stood white and speechless till the voice had stopped speaking. Lena's slack-lipped mouth straightened into a hard, cruel line, and her eyes brightened.

"That's one now," she said.

"It was in this building," Dorothy remarked.

"Yuss," said Lena.

"A machine gun in a bacteriological laboratory?" Chase queried. "Queer sort of gadget to fool with here, I should think. What do they do with it?"

"Shoot counter-revolutionists," Lena informed him.

"You don't say? That sounds as if it might be worth investigating. Want to come and see the fun, Dorothy?"

"Sure," said Dorothy. "Let's all go. The assistants can get along for five minutes more without me. Coming Lena?"

Lena planted her fists on her hips. "You stay here," she ordered curtly. "He can go if he wants. That's none of my business."

"Miss Grange is none of your business, either," Chase retorted. "Come on, Dorothy."

Lena burst into a harsh laugh. "You think they're going to shoot *you?*" she sneered, pointing a grimy finger at Dorothy. "So you want to run away?" She doubled up with mirth. "They wouldn't shoot you if you killed Arkol. You're too precious." Lena sobered. "They've only been shooting the ones that wouldn't volunteer for inoculation."

"Some of those that Gog brought back?" Chase asked sharply.

Lena shrugged her shoulders. "I guess so," she said indifferently. "Why make a fuss about it? We have plenty more."

Chase ignored her. "I think we had better go and have a talk with Arkol," he said, taking Dorothy's arm. "Come on."

Lena lifted up her voice in unclean vituperation and harsh command.

"Oh, go to hell," Chase flung back over his shoulder. "We haven't time to fool with you."

"You shouldn't swear at a woman," Dorothy reproved him.

"She isn't a woman," Chase replied curtly. "No more than that precious trio that brought us here are men. What have we got into anyhow? If I have to stay here a week I'll be like the rest of them. Don't listen to that virago."

Lena was following as fast as she could, cursing Dorothy with every foul oath she remembered from the slums and prisons of New York. Her frustrated rage expired in one last yelp of hatred just as Chase and Dorothy hurried past the guard outside Arkol's office.

"You wait," she screeched. "You'll get what's coming to you, you bourgeois—"

Arkol was in the midst of an excited colloquy with Serbin and Kott.

"What's all this?" he shouted. "Interrupting a conference when you should be at work? Insubordination—"

Chase calmly drew up two chairs and motioned Dorothy to sit down. Then he sat himself, and deliberately crossed his legs.

"When you get through shouting," he said to Arkol, "we can talk business. Mr. Serbin, can't you control him?"

Serbin was equal to the occasion. At an unmistakably sharp command, Arkol seated himself at the desk, swelling and blowing with rage. Chase gathered that Arkol had been having words with the director of the fifty-year plan in genetics. Kott also seemed to be not quite at ease.

"Now," Chase resumed in the dead calm that followed, "I want some information for my report." He turned to Kott. "Where were you, Mr. Kott, when Mr. Arkol telephoned a little while ago?"

"Telephoned?" Kott repeated in bewilderment.

"That's all I wanted to know," Chase cut him off. "Mr. Serbin, where were you?"

Before Serbin could reply Arkol shot a volley of words at him in his own language.

"You need not answer, Mr. Serbin," Chase smiled. "Mr. Arkol has just told us all where you were. Unfortunately for his story, I saw his face before he saw mine when I was up on top of that red truck. Mr. Arkol did not telephone, as he promised Miss Grange that he would. Now, Mr. Arkol, for my first real question. Why did you break your promise to Miss Grange?"

Arkol maintained a sullen silence. Serbin took the burden of explaining off his harassed colleague's conscience.

"Let me explain," he said with quiet dignity. "Mr. Arkol's message reached Mr. Kott and me at the next camp on our way home as we followed you."

"Thanks," said Chase. "Everything is explained. That truck I was riding was too fast for your car to catch. How simple things are when they are explained by someone who knows the facts. I withdraw my first question, with apologies."

Serbin accepted the apology gracefully. "You wished to ask something else?"

"Several things. Where is Gog?"

"Shall I answer?" Serbin inquired politely.

"If you please. I suppose Mr. Arkol is willing to let you do the talking."

"Gog is with the volunteers."

"Which of them?"

"I fear I miss your meaning," Serbin hesitated with a puzzled look.

"I mean is he with the dead or with the living?"

Serbin's face expressed polite astonishment.

"But none have died yet, Doctor Chase. They were inoculated only a few minutes ago. Need I say that we are most hopeful of the outcome? Mr. Arkol used the serum he prepared in America, following Professor Brown's instructions."

"What about those that refused to volunteer?"

Kott took it upon himself to supply the desired information. "Our workers are loyal, Doctor Chase," he explained expansively, showing his full battery of teeth. "They are only too eager to volunteer for service under the fifty year plan. It is their duty, and they welcome it as a high privilege."

"Yes," Arkol added in emphatic confirmation. "No worker yet has hung back when volunteers were called for. Nor has one changed his mind at the last moment and begged to be sent back to his fellow workers in the camps."

"Then," said Chase deliberately, "that woman—what's her name, Lena?—is given to flights of the imagination?"

The question evidently puzzled them. Instead of attempting to answer, they eyed him keenly. Arkol solved their problem by shouting for Lena. She was just outside the door. When she entered, Arkol began a rapid-fire examination in his own language. So far as Chase could make out, Lena denied everything. Arkol appeared to be thoroughly disgusted with her. In answer to an enraged shout two guards entered, grabbed Lena by the arms, and dragged her, kicking and screaming, from the office. But Lena had the last word, and it was in English.

"They're all lying," she managed to yell, before one of the guards succeeded in smothering her outcry.

Chase ignored Lena's testimony, and Arkol, too, seemed willing to forget it. Serbin however thought it worthy of a brief footnote.

"Lena has just confessed her outrageous attempt to terrify Miss Grange." He turned to Dorothy. "I trust you will forgive her," he said. "Indeed I am sure you will, for Lena's unkind effort was really the highest compliment one woman can pay to another. She was jealous of your charm, Miss Grange, and sought to prove your courage inferior to her own."

Dorothy received this dignified speech with a slight inclination of her head. "That's all right," she said. "I bear her no grudge."

Chase was just about to resume his examination when four rifle shots, practically simultaneous, cracked out. When the echoes died away, Dorothy spoke up.

"I trust that poor Lena kept her courage to the end."

Arkol expressed surprise that Dorothy should allow her ungrounded suspicions to misinterpret the daily rifle practice of the guards at the back gate. Chase continued.

"As Lena won't care to talk now, I shall ask you to send for Gog. There are one or two things I wish to ask him."

"Certainly," Serbin agreed.

A guard was summoned and dispatched to fetch Gog. Conversation died. Arkol fussed with his pale red papers, scowling and muttering in his black beard. Kott squirmed like a monkey on his hard, uncomfortable chair, and Serbin stared indifferently at the ceiling, as if the proceedings bored him beyond expression. Presently Gog shuffled into the room. He was alone, but two guards stood suggestively in the doorway. As he passed Dorothy, he looked down on her hair, and his head dropped in utter shame.

"Gog," said Chase, "did any of those volunteers you brought in today refuse to be inoculated?"

"No."

"Did you hear a machine gun a short time ago?"

"Yes."

"Were any of the volunteers shot?"

"No."

"Thanks, Gog. That is all I wanted to know."

As Gog shuffled out, Chase turned to Serbin. "You don't mind me trying to check up on things in my own way?"

"Not at all, Doctor Chase. Without a full and unprejudiced investigation your report would be of but little value."

Dorothy seemed to be listening. Arkol noticed her attitude.

"I give you my word, Miss Grange, you will not hear another shot. So pray do not be nervous."

Dorothy made no reply, contenting herself with a significant glance at the telephone, which stood conveniently near Arkol's elbow. He had the grace to redden uncomfortably.

"Is your present investigation concluded, Doctor Chase?" Serbin inquired politely.

"These questions, yes. In fact I think I have enough now to prepare a report."

"But you have seen nothing of the laboratory work in animal breeding," Kott protested.

"It isn't necessary for my report."

Arkol grinned. "On the contrary, Doctor Chase, your report will be like an egg without salt unless you do see Mr. Kott's extremely interesting experiments."

Chase eyed him coolly. "Are you sure I haven't seen enough of them as is?"

They received this in stony silence for some seconds, until Serbin took it upon himself to answer.

"I take it, Doctor Chase, that you consider further investigation of one phase of our plan superfluous?"

"More or less," Chase admitted.

"In fact," Serbin pursued, "you need never have left America to complete this part of your report?"

"Hardly that strong. Theories must be checked up, you know."

"And how have you checked yours, if I may ask?"

"By using my eyes. Gog brought back a truckload of evidence today that would prove a dozen theories, and I have only one. I consider my theory sufficiently well established to be included in my report. So I shall ask you to make the necessary arrangements for me and Miss Grange to leave for home tomorrow."

"Miss Grange stays till her contract with me expires," Arkol exploded.

"Miss Grange is engaged to be married to me," Chase retorted, "and she leaves when I do."

"Must you leave so soon?" Serbin insinuated. "Why not enjoy a vacation? Our country is beautiful."

"No doubt. But there are about twelve hundred young fellows at home waiting for my report. To say nothing of Congress and about a hundred and twenty million ordinary citizens—all the adults. Sorry, but I really must hurry back."

"Must you?" Arkol asked with obvious sarcasm. "Are you sure you must?"

What else he was going to say was silenced by a sharp order from Serbin.

"If you must go, you must," Serbin sighed, "although we shall be sorry to lose you so soon. Miss Grange, however must fulfill her contract with Mr. Arkol."

"I have no contract," Dorothy remarked quietly.

"In writing, no," Serbin admitted. "We thought such formalities unnecessary with you. Am I right in remembering that you promised to work as Mr. Arkol's assistant?"

"Yes. I promised."

"And you have no regard for your word?"

"Conditions have altered."

"What conditions?" Serbin demanded.

"Well, for one thing, you have just had my interpreter shot. I can do nothing without an interpreter."

Serbin sighed impatiently. "To avoid a profitless discussion, I will not contradict you. Assume if you like that Lena has been executed. We shall give you another interpreter, as I understand Mr. Arkol has already promised, and one far more efficient than Lena."

"Who?" Dorothy asked.

"One to whom you, Miss Grange, can have no possible objection," Serbin smiled. "A trained bacteriologist."

"I suppose you mean Gog?"

"We have meant to make him your assistant and bodyguard all along, and were keeping him as a surprise for you."

Chase took a hand. "I appreciate your thoughtfulness for Miss Grange's comfort. So don't think me ungrateful when I decline for her. We really must get away tomorrow."

Serbin appeared to be resigned. "As director of the fifty year plan I am virtually dictator of this province. It is in my power to cancel your passports and forbid you to leave until I wish. To take such a course would be as repugnant to me as it would be disagreeable to you, and I have no intention of arbitrarily exercising my authority. Instead, I shall appeal to your youthful generosity to help, not me, but all my people, to their freedom. Then, if your consciences will permit you to leave before Miss Grange's work is done, I shall say no more. You shall be free to go, when and where you will. What I am about to tell you, I have never confided to another human being. Pardon the personal nature of my revelations. They are not made in any spirit of self-esteem, or because I believe them to have any intrinsic interest, but merely to provide the necessary background for my activity in the fifty year plan."

While Serbin was thus disposing of the preliminaries to his version of his interest in the fifty year plan in genetics, the two Americans were not alone in the close attention with which they followed Serbin's introduction and tried to evaluate its sincerity. Arkol's eyes expressed wary distrust; Kott's, resentment and hostility.

One at least of Serbin's statements was the ungarbled truth; he had never thought it worth his while to take his collaborators into his confidence. Kott particularly had resented Serbin's aloofness, which, in spite of Kott's aggressive championship of the proletariat, gave the fussy little man a constant feeling of inferiority, as if Serbin, the aristocrat by birth, breeding, and education, proved by his very existence that there may be something indestructible in aristocracy after all. As a world authority on animal breeding, Kott admitted without any argument that breeding does play some part in animal economy. But as a flamingly loyal proletarian, the consciously inferior Kott was forced to exclude the human race from his scientific findings, and to prove—to his own satisfaction—that all aristocracy, except only that of the proletariat, was necessarily the perpetuation of the unfit who, by some unfair means, had somehow or another succeeded in outwitting and browbeating the fit. In short, the scientific Kott was as unscientific as the rest of us when his science collided with his emotions or his prejudices, and he became a very hot and gaseous body indeed when he collided mentally with the incarnation of all his dislikes, namely Serbin.

Arkol, on the other hand, was essentially a Mongolian potentate who loved the proletariat in direct proportion to the amount of power, honor, and personal glory he could squeeze out of their pliant masses. His secret dislike of the always cool and judicial Serbin sprang from his own deficiencies. It galled him to have to admit to himself that Serbin had a better mind than he had, and was in every way more valuable than himself to the success of the fifty year plan. Arkol would have stopped short of nothing to make himself dictator of the grandiose plan, and all that held him back from open rebellion was the certainty that Serbin could make a complete and final fool of him the moment an insurrection started. Kott could gladly have cut Serbin's superior throat in his impetuous way, but he never got a chance. Arkol refrained from attempting to shoot his superior officer because he knew that Serbin's aim was better than his own. Both Arkol and Kott now waited expectantly to hear what sort of man their chief would try to make himself out to be, for neither believed for a moment that Serbin would be foolish enough to draw a true picture of himself. They looked for an excess of self-depreciation. In this they were grievously disappointed. Serbin was too clever for them even on this detail.

CHAPTER NINETEEN
"Passports, Please!"

"I NEED NOT BORE YOU WITH A LENGTHY account of my experiences in the revolution, which abolished the last of my social class and put another in our place," Serbin began. "You doubtless all have heard scores of similar histories. My discomforts were no greater than those of my friends. A revolution without mob violence, inhuman cruelty and bloodshed is impossible."

"Why can't you have a peaceful revolution by lawful means?" Dorothy demanded.

"Can you recall such a revolution from your knowledge of history?" Serbin countered blandly.

"No," she admitted, doubtfully. "But still I don't see why human beings can't avoid cruelty and bloodshed."

"Precisely because they are human beings," Serbin replied coldly. "And that brings me to the first impact of our revolution on the fifty year plan. Had I not witnessed the revolution with my own eyes, I would never have proposed the fifty year plan to our great dictators who guide the proletariat in their search for political and economic freedom. Like you, Miss Grange, I did not see before the revolution why it should not be possible for human beings to achieve their common purpose—if there is one—rationally and peaceably. It took many months of the terror to awaken me from my dream.

"I could not find it in my heart to blame the people for their excesses. For centuries they had endured injustice, cruelty, and nameless indignities from those who held the power. I looked for this phase to pass soon. It did not pass. Violence begot violence, and only when there was no living object of hate to be destroyed did destruction cease.

"During my abundant leisure in prison I made an exhaustive study of the history of the human psychology of revolutions. For the essential books and documents I appealed to the generosity of the governor of the prison. As the necessary material was available in the great university library within a quarter of a mile of the prison, and as it cost the governor nothing, my request was granted. I obtained what I needed at a nominal cost to myself. In fact the governor thought he had much the better of the bargain, as I revealed to him the place where the women of our family had hidden the accumulated jewels of three centuries before they were taken to prison. The jewels of course were contraband and useless to my family. I shall always be grateful to the governor. He was executed for speculating in the property of the dispossessed aristocracy shortly after I became mayor of the city on my return from Holland. But I am running ahead of my story.

"My exhaustive study indicated that something more radical than a natural, human revolution must take place in human nature before human revolutions are robbed of their inhuman terrors.

"But my studies were not conclusive. Daily I witnessed acts of heroism on the part of my companions in prison, men and women, which caused me to doubt. Might not these splendid human beings become the leaders of a more rational society?"

"No!" Kott interrupted fiercely. "Damned, cold-blooded aristocrats all of them."

"You forget," Serbin reminded him with stinging sarcasm, "that I also was a damned cold-blooded aristocrat until my conversion."

"What converted you?" Kott demanded suspiciously.

Serbin smiled. "A woman," he answered, with a whimsical bow in Dorothy's direction. "She was utterly charming. Her vivid coloring was not unlike yours, Miss Grange. She was seventeen and I nineteen when we became engaged. When the revolution swept our class into limbo, we found ourselves in the same prison. Not in the same dungeon of course; that would have been too heavenly. The women's quarters were separated from the men's by an unscalable wall, heavily guarded. Although I never saw my fiancée while I was in prison, I contrived to get an occasional word to her, and to receive in return her adorable protestations of devotion. The guards, I soon discovered, were not incorruptible. The costliest was almost infinitely cheap compared to the governor, although he was an even more ardent revolutionist."

"You are slurring the revolution," Kott warned with a menacing frown.

"Not at all," Serbin retorted. "My remarks concerned only the revolutionists, not the revolution. There is a distinction."

"I fail to see it," Arkol exploded. He seemed to think Serbin was sneering at him in particular instead of at unreliable revolutionists in general, and he resented the imputation of graft.

"The point may be rather a fine one," Serbin admitted. "Possibly only those who have profited by the distinction are capable of appreciating it. That, I imagine, accounts for your personal difficulty. However, to return to my experiences.

"Many of my class had foreseen a possible revolution, although they had not anticipated that it would break precisely when it did and cut them off from the escape, which they had planned. To prepare for their anticipated flight, they had taken very considerable sums in gold and their most valuable jewels out of the country on preliminary trips, when egress and entry were comparatively easy to those who had the ear of the corrupt military authorities. The great wealth thus taken out of the country was deposited in rented vaults in certain of the banks in Holland. As Holland remained neutral throughout the war, it was considered by my farsighted friends that their wealth would be safe when the expected revolution broke. Unfortunately the revolution took an unexpected turn, and my friends all found themselves in prison before they could escape. Pardon me for giving all these details, but they are necessary for what is to follow."

"Did you export any of your own wealth?" Kott asked suspiciously.

"About half," Serbin replied. "No more could be converted into gold. Although I bribed the highest officials liberally, they declared that they were powerless in face of the strong opposition of certain of the nobility, conspicuous for their unselfish patriotism, who asserted that the export of gold and treasure at such a time was equivalent to high treason.

"I continue with the experiences of my friends in prison. I have often been asked why they did not swallow the capsules of poison, which most educated Europeans carry for use as a last resort in case of a hopeless railway accident, or fire from which no escape is possible. The prison authorities had, of course, confiscated all this 'life insurance'—as it is called."

Chase interrupted. "Do you carry insurance, Mr. Serbin?"

"Always," Serbin replied with a smile. "To return to my friends.

"Their execution was delayed to the last moment at least five times, because the revolutionary authorities were convinced that my friends had not yet disclosed the hiding place of the major part of their wealth. The police of course had access to the records of all banks and exchanges, and the secret agents of the old government ably aided the spies of the new in uncovering questionable transactions. The frequent threats of execution were a somewhat inefficient attempt to make the weaker members of the aristocracy talk."

"Who finally did talk?" Chase asked pointedly.

"I was coming to that, Doctor Chase. The threats of execution did not terrify me, for my fiancée and I were condemned together, and we cared for nothing so long as we were permitted to die on the same day. Our devotion to one another was so marked that it could not long escape the intelligent observation of the governor of the prison. His suspicions became certainties when one of the guards whom I had bribed to carry messages to my fiancée insisted that I was able to give him more than I had. On refusal to gratify his greed, he at once confessed his personal corruption to the governor, restored practically all that he had received from me to the treasury of the people, expressed himself desirous of serving only the cause of the revolution in future, and was generously pardoned by the governor, who immediately promoted him.

"Shortly after the guard had given this incontrovertible proof of his loyalty, the governor sent for me. The interview was short and satisfactory to both of us, I consented to go to Holland and bring back all the gold and jewels, which my misguided compatriots had deposited in the Dutch banks. Their consent to this reasonable course was gained at once on a statement of the conditions imposed by the governor, and they unanimously confided to me the necessary instructions for gaining access to their deposits."

"May I ask what the conditions were?" Dorothy inquired.

"Since you have asked me a direct question, Miss Grange, I shall give an equally direct answer, although I had intended to pass over this detail in your presence. The governor assured me that unless I brought back the exported gold and jewels within four weeks, with not one day's grace, my fiancée would be turned over to the least civilized of the troops, first to be outraged at their pleasure and then, provided she still lived, to be shot. Following her death, all of my friends were to be executed. If I refused to undertake the mission, the proceedings were to go forward as I have just outlined, with the addition that I should be imprisoned for life without the means of destroying myself. As I have said, a revolution brings out much. If I consented to undertake the mission, and carried it through successfully, we were all to be set free.

"In putting the alternatives before my friends, I committed a serious blunder. I did not tell my fiancée of the governor's conditions. My associates—those whose wealth was to be sac- rificed to the public treasury—prevailed upon me, against my intuitive judgment, to keep the true reason for my mission from my fiancée. They said that it would only make her unhappy to learn the truth, and that it would probably result in her self-destruction to save their worthless wealth. It was agreed that my fiancée should be told nothing of my projected mission to Holland.

"As a human favor, I requested the governor to inform my fiancée that our common messenger, the loyal guard, had confessed his misconduct, and that she need not expect any further messages from me through such channels. This the governor very generously consented to do. To remove all suspicion from my fiancée's mind, the governor skillfully conveyed this information in the form of a sharp reprimand to my fiancée, warning her not to attempt the corruption of another of the faithful guards.

"My mission to Holland was entirely successful, and I returned to the governor's office on the twenty-sixth day after leaving the prison. The gold and jewels, I may say, were taken over at the frontier by secret police directly responsible to the governor.

"Perhaps I should have stated explicitly before this point that up till the hour of my return to the governor's office I had been strongly opposed to the revolution and refused to take the larger view that the good of the majority is the good of all."

"It was clear enough," Kott sneered. "You had to lose your money before you found out that it wasn't worth keeping."

"Like other things I lost," Serbin answered quietly.

"Such as?" Arkol encouraged.

"My respect for the natural man."

"Including the workers, I suppose?" Kott insinuated.

"Including the workers," Serbin agreed. "That is rather a remarkable question for you to ask, Kott. If you do not believe the natural worker capable of improvement, why are you squandering your great talents on trying to better nature?"

Kott saw himself cornered. "Go on," he said gruffly. "I merely wanted to warn these Americans that you are not a counter-revolutionist, in spite of your aristocratic connections."

Serbin nodded. "It is very important that Doctor Chase include no false impressions in his report. As I was saying, my mistaken loyalty to the old order never wavered during all my stay in prison. My awakening was sudden. I realized once and for all that corruption in high places is the evil that must be eradicated if human society is not to retrograde to barbarism. In that realization I naturally became one of the proletariat and allied myself with their cause.

"Having informed the governor that my mission had been successful to the last gold piece and the last emerald, I asked to be permitted to see my fiancée.

"The governor demurred. On being pressed to give a reason for his refusal the governor told me that my fiancée had told him expressly that she never wished to see me again, and that my presence would be most distasteful to her.

"Naturally I suspected the governor of double-dealing, and I was not deceived."

Serbin paused in his narrative to apologize to Dorothy for what was to follow.

"I was extremely young at the time, Miss Grange, so perhaps my insight into the character of women was not as keen as I had imagined it to be. Nevertheless, after what had passed between us, I believed it impossible for my fiancée to credit a slander against me without the most searching investigation. However, I may be doing her an injustice. She may, in fact, have done all in her power to sift the evidence, and the fact that she reached a false conclusion may have been due to youthful inexperience rather than to malicious jealousy.

"I learned from the governor that he had told my fiancée his own version of my mission to Holland, and that she had believed it. According to the governor, my message to her by the guard had ceased because of an intrigue I was carrying or with a woman of the people whom I was receiving in my cell. This infraction of the strictest prison rule was made possible, the governor declared, because I had corrupted my guard with the last of my personal valuables, a ruby signet ring, which I had concealed upon my person. My fiancée, to her great credit, stoutly refused to believe this canard until confronted with my alleged mistress. The woman was vivacious, physically attractive, sophisticated and intellectually brilliant. She had but little difficulty in convincing my fiancée of my infidelity. This in itself might not have induced my fiancée to take the course she did. It, however, was but the first detail in the governor's campaign.

"The governor then informed my fiancée that I had gone on a mission to Holland to recover the wealth of the aristocrats. This of course was the truth. But the governor added that I had betrayed my friends to the highest authorities on the promise that if I would go to Holland, accompanied by spies who were to see that I did not break my word, and turn over ninety percent of the hidden wealth to the spies, I should be permitted to escape to England or America, where no spies would be sent to follow me, with the remaining ten percent—a very comfortable fortune. To increase the plausibility of his story, the governor added that I had betrayed my friends into giving me the necessary instructions for withdrawing their deposits on the assumption that they would be set free when their wealth was turned over to the treasury of the people.

"Unfortunately, the governor added, in explaining this transaction to my fiancée, he was powerless to intervene. The execution of all my friends, including the father and mother of my fiancée, had been ordered by the supreme council. The concealment of gold was a capital offense, and the council had decided to make an example of this flagrant violation of the law. For my alleged loyalty to the new government I was to receive the ten percent reward I have already mentioned. My mistress was to join me in England or America at the earliest possible moment. In reply to my fiancée's request to be allowed to intercede in person for her parents, the governor informed her that they had already been executed. I have no reason to doubt the accuracy of this statement. Some days after my return from Holland, I learned that all of my friends, whose hoardings I had been sent to recover, were shot two hours after I left. My fiancée alone was spared.

"All this the governor told me in the privacy of his office, naturally without witnesses. Two guards, however, were on duty outside the door. I realized the folly of an attack on the governor's person. Moreover the conduct of my fiancée in believing what she had believed of me was a strong additional argument against violence. I asked what had become of her.

"The governor's answer convinced me that I shall never understand a woman's nature. After a melancholy depression lasting ten or twelve days, my fiancée sent word to the governor that she desired an audience. It was granted. She wished the governor to advise her how she might become a free citizeness of the new order so that she might be free to devote her life to making me suffer for my treachery. The governor suggested that she could solve both her problems at once by becoming his mistress, which she did.

"When I heard this, I expressed my eagerness to become a useful worker under the new regime. My desire to be one of the people was born then. I had failed completely to understand the one human being of all others of my own social order, which I should have understood, and I was anxious to see whether the other half of humanity was more comprehensible.

"The governor regretfully informed me that my conversion was too late. The central council had already ordered my execution and he, as governor of the prison, must see that it was carried out forthwith. My offense, it appeared, consisted in accepting a bribe, namely ten percent of the hoarded wealth, for performing a public service, which should have been done gratis as a matter of duty.

"The guards were summoned, and I was marched to the place of execution, a dark passageway ending in an abrupt flight of rickety steps into the mortuary pit. As usual in such circumstances, I was to be allowed to reach the top of the steps before receiving the volley from behind.

"Halfway down the passage I shouted to the men behind me. 'Comrades! Take me to the central council before you execute me. I have information of the highest value to lay before the council. If I am shot now, this information will be lost to the state. The loss in money alone will be tremendous.' They halted. I knew I was reprieved for the moment. Their dull wits were no match for my trained intelligence. I was led before the council. In five minutes I had prevailed upon the sagacious councillors to institute a search of the governor's quarters at the prison. Incriminating evidence was speedily uncovered, and within three hours all the aristocrats' wealth, which the governor and his accomplices had looted and earmarked for their own, with the intention of escaping with it over the frontier, was unearthed.

"Full citizenship, which I have cherished ever since, was granted to me immediately. Ten days later I was elected mayor of the city by popular acclaim. My first official act was to order the execution of the governor as a warning to all servants of the people to keep their trust."

"And your fiancée?" Dorothy asked.

"Pardon me, I had forgotten her," Serbin answered indifferently. "When the guards appeared at the governor's residence to arrest him and take him before the council, they found him with his mistress. They had been drinking, and both, especially his mistress, were heavily intoxicated. Hearing that he was to be arrested on a charge of misappropriating public funds, the governor sobered. It came out at the trial that he suspected one of his own spies of having betrayed him. It seems that he had grown quite attached to the physical charms of his mistress, and he was reluctant to leave them behind for others to enjoy. Before the arresting officer could interfere, the governor shot and killed his mistress."

"I think you are rather hard on her," Dorothy said softly.

"You mistake me, Miss Grange. I ceased to have any feeling regarding my fiancée, tender or harsh, the moment I learned that she had ceased to believe me a human being. Or rather—" qualified with a bitter smile, "the moment she showed me that I was more human than I had ever imagined myself to be."

"So this was the origin of the fifty year plan in genetics?" Chase remarked. "Excuse my obtuseness if I don't quite see the connection."

"The connection," Serbin agreed readily, "is perhaps not evident to anyone but myself. Indeed I failed to grasp the lesson of my own experiences for many months after I ordered the governor's execution. I resigned from the high office of mayor immediately after the execution. Such talent as I had was not political, and I easily convinced my more skillful confreres that I could render the state a greater service by returning to my scientific work. They generously allowed me to undertake biological explorations in Asia and Africa, and any other part of the world where I might hope to find useful material. Much of my eighteen months' exploring was done by myself, without even a guide. I made it my duty to become acquainted with all types of workers wherever I went—that is, where there were human workers—in an endeavor to understand their psychology."

"And did you?" Kott inquired skeptically.

"The fifty year plan is the answer. Contrasted with some of those whom I had studied during and immediately after the revolution, I found the workers everywhere more promising as possible builders of a sane and happy society than the effete nobility and the indifferent bourgeoisie. The new order must be built on the solid rock of nature. The lowly are unspoiled; on them we must build, avoiding the fatal mistake that has ruined every attempt the human race has yet made to rear a decent social order."

"And what may that mistake be?" Chase asked.

"The delusion that labor is noble. Brute labor is brutalizing and fit only for brutes. It must be overcome. Human work must be joyous, free."

"No doubt," Chase remarked. "Still, somebody's got to do it. Your scheme is to breed a race that will like what you call brute labor, and leave the rest of us free to loaf like gods on the rosy clouds of a crazy dream. Well, it won't work."

"It will!" Serbin cried. "I have proved that it will work. Those who relieve us of drudgery will revel in their tasks—"

"Rot," said Chase tersely.

"Let me convince you. I can explain it so that any mind not closed to reason must assent to the benign reasonableness of our plan."

"Explanations won't help my report," Chase retorted. "That's all I'm interested in—that, and our passports. The facts are sufficient, and I have more than enough now. But while we are talking of explanations, I have one for you to consider when we are gone. Has it never occurred to you that your whole fifty year plan is merely your personal gesture of contempt for the rest of us? Because the world treated you badly, you are going to get back at it with an insult that is just a bit too subtle for the very men you want to insult to grasp. They think your idea is great. I'll wager that not one of them will see the point of what you are doing. You know exactly what kind of a slap in the face you are handing them. They don't. It doesn't even hit them; it fans the air clear over their heads. I'm not psychological enough to credit you with doing all this stuff 'for the good of humanity' as a blind rationalization of your real motive. You understand what you are doing and why you are doing it—to get even. Why don't you grow up, or wake up, before you fall down and break your neck? Now, if it is not too much trouble, please get us our passports. Now."

Serbin turned to Dorothy. "Doctor Chase is speaking for you, too?"

"Yes."

"Then," said Serbin, "I shall say no more, Arkol, will you please telephone to my office and ask my secretary to send the passports here? They are already made out in full."

In the uncomfortable silence that followed, Arkol sat glaring at Serbin with murderous hate in his eyes, while Kott openly showed his disgust by an extraordinary series of satirical grimaces. Serbin appeared unaware of his collaborators' displeasure. When the passports arrived, Serbin handed them to Chase and Dorothy.

"The earliest steamer leaves in approximately forty-eight hours. Tickets will be furnished to you at the dock. We shall make all the necessary arrangements for your comfort. Until your boat leaves, I shall be happy to show you anything of interest, so far as time permits." He sighed. "Thank you for your patience. I regret that things have ended as they have."

Dorothy was conscience-stricken, and Chase fidgeted uncomfortably.

"Perhaps before I go I can be of some use in laying out the work for the serums. It is really quite simple."

Arkol brightened. "You think you can remember the details for A, P, and S?"

"I haven't tried," Dorothy confessed, perhaps too hastily. Seeing her slip, she pulled herself up short. "There were so many interruptions today I simply could not concentrate. But with Gog to help me tomorrow, I should have better luck. Will you please see that he is in the laboratory by six in the morning?"

"Certainly," Arkol agreed, seizing the opportunity to cooperate. "Perhaps you would like to put in a few hours this evening?"

"Will Gog be there?" Dorothy asked. She was more concerned for Gog's welfare than for her own, and she had a haunting fear that Gog might be mistreated in her absence.

"Of course, if you wish."

"Then," said Dorothy, ignoring a warning glance from Chase, "I should like to begin immediately after dinner. As I usually work for long stretches at a time when once I start, I shall ask you to see that I am not interrupted. You promised, you remember, that you would allow me to work in my own way, provided I produced results."

"I remember," Arkol said, eyeing her narrowly.

"Then I must ask that the armed guards be removed. I cannot concentrate with a bayonet or a machine gun at my back."

"But Gog—"Arkol began.

"Well?" Dorothy asked. "I will be responsible for him."

"But you do not understand," Kott burst out. "He may escape, and he is priceless."

"Gog won't run away," Dorothy promised quietly. "If he is not in my laboratory at six o'clock tomorrow morning, you may treat me as you did Lena.

"But, Dorothy," Chase expostulated, "you don't know what risks you may be taking. Why—"

"There are no risks," she insisted. "I understand Gog better than any of you, and I have said I will be responsible. If you like," she said to Chase, "you can sit in the laboratory while I work. But you must be quiet and I insist that the guards be removed. Gog must be treated as a decent human being. Unless he is free to enter and leave the building as he pleases, I refuse to work. That is final."

Serbin eyed her coolly. "I shall give the necessary orders," he said. "And I give you my word—which I have never broken to you, by the way—that the guards will be instructed not to interfere with Gog, no matter what he may do. Is that satisfactory?"

"Quite," she answered firmly.

"Thank you, Miss Grange," Serbin bowed. "Do you know, you have reminded me of my fiancée ever since that day I first saw you at the Admiral's luncheon?"

"Do I?"

"Irresistibly," he smiled. "That is why I cannot resist you. Anything you ask within my power to bestow is yours. Doctor Chase, I know, will not be jealous. He, not I, will share your watch. I really believe Miss Grange that your generous decision will accomplish all we have hoped from your visit. My plea has not fallen on barren soil. From the bottom of my heart I thank you."

If Chase disliked the ironical tone of Serbin's thanks, he disliked the sly expression of Arkol's face even more. Kott also seemed to be having difficulty in keeping a straight face. Chase wished he had a revolver, but could think of no way of asking for one without disrupting the cordial diplomatic relations, which seemed to have been established. He wished the coming forty-eight hours were past, for good or ill. Arkol added his appreciations to Serbin's as they strolled toward the dining hall for an early dinner.

CHAPTER TWENTY
Trapped

FOR SEVEN HOURS DOROTHY HAD WORKED rapidly and for the most part in silence. An occasional brief instruction to Gog reached Chase where he sat watchfully in the back of the laboratory.   Gog rarely replied; when he did it was in monosyllables. It was now exactly one o'clock in the morning. Dorothy looked up and called softly to Chase. When he joined her she asked Gog to leave the room for a few moments.   Gog shuffled off without replying.

"You are sure there are no guards about?" she began.

"Positive. The last time I took a stroll I walked clear round the building. If there are guards anywhere they must be on the roof. Serbin seems to have kept his word."

"He doesn't lie—that way."

"But he lies, just the same."

Dorothy agreed. "Why did he give me everything I asked for, do you suppose?"

"I've been trying to figure it out all night. We shall probably know by breakfast time."

"If not sooner," she agreed, lowering her voice. "Have you still got it?" she whispered.

He nodded. "They won't get it away from me. I have it all planned how to smash the box if I am searched."

"I wish I had never brought it," she confessed. "But I dared not leave it where they might have stolen it or tricked me out of it. Even the bank wasn't safe. My order to give it up could have been too easily forged. Hang onto it."

"I'll do my best," he promised.

Dorothy changed the subject. "You are sure about the guards?" Chase nodded, and Dorothy continued, "Can't we make a bolt for it?"

"How?" he demanded.

"I don't know, but I staged this night session in the hope that we might be able to get away and take Gog with us. He is not going to be left behind for them to torture. Did you see his face when he went out a moment ago?"

"I noticed it," Chase replied guardedly.

"We've got to do something, and do it now. Can't you think of a plan?"

Chase considered. "From what I've seen of the country, we haven't a ghost of a chance. All the roads are patrolled by armed troops. Besides, I couldn't find my way to the frontier in broad daylight. It must be a good three hundred miles to the nearest safe territory. And how could we ever cross the border? It must be heavily patrolled."

"It sounds pretty desperate," Dorothy admitted. "Still, we must try."

"Why?" he demanded.

She flung her arms around him. "Can't you see? They don't intend that you shall ever get out alive to make your report. You have guessed too much."

"Perhaps," he admitted. "We may as well face the facts. If your suspicions are justified, I rather imagine I shall be officially reported as a victim of the plague. They may even back up their report by sending back the evidence to the United States."

"You think you will be deliberately exposed to infection?"

"I shouldn't wonder. It could all be done very plausibly and without my knowledge. Or yours, either."

"If you go that way, I will too. I know how."

"You had better," he advised.

"Then you have guessed what they really want of me?"

"No," he replied evasively. "But being a slave to Arkol all your life would be worse than putting a natural end to everything."

"I believe you know more than you are willing to tell me. I shan't press you. Your word is sufficient. But can't we do something? If we lose out, we shall only have thrown away a few hours. And if we win, we shall have all our lives before us."

"Yes, but what are we to do?"

"Have you thought of Gog? He will do anything for me. Why not get him to show us the way to the frontier? I noticed Serbin's car parked under the trees by the dining hall as we left this evening."

"Probably it is locked."

"No. I noticed the keys."

"Very well. Do you want to try it?"

"Yes," she said decisively. "We can depend on Gog. You are a good driver. Our passports may get us over the frontier. Come on."

They found Gog outside the main entrance sniffing curiously at the night air. At the sound of Dorothy's voice he started. Before she spoke he had been standing erect and tall, a splendid figure of confidence and strength. Hearing her voice, he suddenly slouched into a different being, abjectly humble and ashamed in her presence. She explained what she wanted of him in a few crisp sentences.

"Will you show us the way?"

Gog bowed his head in shame.

"No," he answered.

Dorothy recoiled as if she had been struck.

"Not after all I have done for you?" she asked reproachfully. "It may mean my own life and the life of the man I love."

"No," Gog repeated with a groan that seemed to tear his mighty chest.

"Why not?" she insisted.

"There is no petrol in the car," he burst out. "Serbin left the car under the trees to tempt Doctor Chase. There are armed guards in the trees."

For a moment Dorothy was speechless. "Gog, are you telling me the truth?"

"Yes," he groaned. "They would have shot him as he entered the car. And then—"

"And then what?" she queried as Gog refused to go on.

"I will not tell you."

"That's right, Gog," Chase said. "You don't know what they planned next, do you?"

"No," Gog replied with a gasp of relief.

Dorothy dropped the inquiry. "What is to be done?"

"Keep cool heads," Chase replied. "We are no worse off than we were ten minutes ago. Rather better, if anything. What about some sleep? We shall need all our wits."

Gog coughed. "They asked me to tell Doctor Chase that Serbin's car was under the trees."

"And you did not?" Chase encouraged. "Why not?"

Gog bowed his head. "I told you that night on the boat."

Chase glanced at Dorothy. From her face he could not be sure whether she understood. Her next words removed his doubt.

"Thanks, Gog," she said. "His life is more precious to me than my own."

Gog seemed to be having a terrific struggle with his own mind. At last he reached a decision.

"Come with me," he said to Chase.

"Come on, Dorothy," Chase said. "We can trust him with anything."

"No," said Gog, motioning Dorothy back. "Go on with your work. Doctor Chase alone."

"Shall I?" Chase hesitated.

"Of course," she answered lightly, to avoid hurting Gog's hypersensitive feelings. "Gog knows more about this than we do. And I would rather trust his judgment than my own." She turned to go back into the laboratory.

"Excuse me," Gog muttered to Chase, turning to follow Dorothy. "I forgot something."

Chase nervously stood his ground, wondering whether he should follow, or more wisely stay where he was. To follow would be to show that he distrusted Gog. He stayed where he was, and presently Gog emerged carrying a large flashlight.

"We shall need this," he said huskily. "I must show you something." He set off at a long stride into the darkness.

The pace Gog set was so rapid that Chase was soon winded, and conversation was impossible. In considerably less than an hour Chase judged that they must have covered four miles.

"Wait a minute," he panted, "till I get my breath."

Gog stopped. "We must hurry," he said. "There are only four hours more of darkness."

"All right," said Chase. "How far is it there and back?"

"Twenty miles."

"How long will it take me to look at what you want me to see?"

"One look."

"Go ahead," Chase ordered. "Set the pace. I can do five miles an hour and keep it up. That will give us plenty of time to get back before daylight."

Gog avoided the highways. The path he had followed so far had led through open woods. Now he branched off to the right, and the growth became more dense. Chase judged that they were headed for one of the bamboo jungles he had seen from a distance on his tour with Serbin and Kott. Presently Gog plunged into the bamboo jungle, threading his way through the gigantic clumps with unerring tread, as if he knew every step of the way. Chase could not have found his way back alone, even in broad daylight. His sense of direction was hopelessly confused; he could only trust that Dorothy was right in her estimate of Gog.

They had gone about eight miles when Gog suddenly halted. So far he had not used his flashlight in the impenetrable darkness, and Chase had kept up with Gog solely by following the soft padding of his feet on the damp and decaying twigs and leaves. Now he heard Gog speaking.

"We are alone," he sighed in a husky whisper.

"Yes," Chase agreed. "And I have not the slightest idea how to find my way out of this jungle."

"If I betray you," Gog said, "no one will ever know."

"No," Chase agreed. "No one will ever know."

For some moments there was a palpitating silence, broken only by the soft fall of an occasional droplet from the needle tip of some bamboo leaf drenched in the night dew.

"You remember what I said to you on the boat?"

"Every word. You told me you loved Dorothy."

"I do."

"So do I," Chase replied.

"As much as I do?" Gog asked.

"How do I know? I believe nobody could love her more than I do." Gog sighed heavily, profoundly. "If I betray you," he repeated, "no one will ever know."

"No one," Chase echoed.

"I will not betray you," Gog said without emotion.

"I never thought for a moment that you would."

"Why not?" Gog asked with pathetic eagerness.

Chase gave him the answer he was secretly hoping to hear. "Because Dorothy thinks you are incapable of doing anything of which you would be ashamed."

Gog received this in silence. The silence was again broken by a despairing sigh.

"Will you betray me?"

"Good God, no, man. How could I?"

"By telling her."

"You misunderstood me. I meant that it would be impossible for any human being to betray you after what you just said."

"You will not tell her?"

"What don't you want me to tell her?"

"What you have guessed."

"I swear, Gog, I will never tell her."

"But she will see your report."

"My report will be seen by officers of the government only. It will never be published. Dorothy I am sure will never even hear of the part you mean."

"It must be published," Gog sighed.

"In a disguised form, perhaps," Chase admitted. "Look here, Gog, if it will ease your mind, I give you my word that I will suppress everything that might give Dorothy even the remotest hint of what you don't want her to know."

"You swear?"

"I do."

"And will you swear never to tell her that I showed you what I must show you soon?"

"I swear. But need you show me?"

"Perhaps not. But if I do, you will understand what I may be driven to do better than if you had not seen with your own eyes. It will make you believe your own report." Gog suddenly switched on the flashlight full in Chase's eyes. "I see you are telling the truth," he said, switching off the light. "We must hurry. It is still two miles farther on."

The bamboo jungle grew steadily denser, till all of a sudden it opened out in a broad clearing. Across the littered space of the clearing, Chase made out the dim massiveness of what looked like a fortification in the darkness.

"One of nearly two hundred," Gog whispered. "I have the key to the gate of this one."

Chase followed him across the clearing to a steel gate in the concrete wall. Gog fumbled in his clothes for the key. "The gate is locked at night, after the inmates have been herded in from the jungle. Guards are not needed at night; they will return an hour before daylight." He had swung open the gate. Chase followed him into a dim courtyard, of spacious proportions, in which open sheds with low roofs sloping inward from the high concrete walls were barely visible through the darkness. A faint, familiar crackling caused Chase to look up. Blue coronas of electricity bristled along the top of the wall from three high-tension wires.

"A prison?" Chase whispered.

"Their sleeping quarters," Gog answered in a husky whisper. "They sleep soundly. Follow me. I will show you one."

The shed, which Gog selected, was on the farther side of the courtyard. As they crept toward it, Chase heard the sound of slow, regular breathing. Gog stopped. The sleeper coughed huskily, and Chase started. The cough might have been Gog's. While his nerves were still on edge, Gog suddenly switched the flashlight on for a second and off again. The blinding light photographed every detail of the sleeper's posture forever on Chase's memory.

"Did you see?" Gog whispered.

"Yes."

Gog took his arm in silence and led him back to the gate. He locked the gate and started back through the jungle without a word. Nothing passed within them till they were within a mile of the laboratory. It was still dark. Chase was almost exhausted, although Gog showed no sign of fatigue.

"Let us rest a minute," Chase said. "I can make better time if I get my wind. We shall be back before daylight."

Gog halted and waited patiently. Still he said nothing. Everything, so far as he was concerned, had been said when he switched off the flashlight. Chase was fussing with his clothes. Finally he found what he wanted.

"Gog," he said, "I promised a man who believed in me to take back a report of the fifty year plan to America. If I should die of plague before I take the steamer, the report will be buried with me."

"Are you ill?" Gog asked anxiously. "Can you breathe freely?"

"I am all right so far. But I can take no chances." He handed Gog a small leather tobacco pouch. "This contains what I have written of my report. It is short but full enough. Most of it was written after I left you that last night on the steamer. I knew everything then. Now, I will trust you to keep this for me till I am safely aboard again, or until I ask you to give it back to me. If I do not return to America, you must get this across the frontier somehow, and see that it is mailed from the other side to Admiral Simpson. You know his city; that will be sufficient for an address. If you cannot get it mailed across the frontier, destroy it. Never give it up, and never let it be taken from you. And you must tell nobody that I have given you this."

"Not even her?" Gog asked, taking the leather pouch.

"Not even Dorothy. You promise?"

"I promise," he replied, stuffing the pouch into a trouser pocket. "No man living shall take this from me. And if I must, I shall mail it for you, or destroy it and myself. We must hurry. It'll soon be light."

They reached the entrance to the laboratory half an hour before dawn. Everything was ominously peaceful. Chase had expected to be met by one or other of the 'fifty-year boys', as he had dubbed Arkol, Serbin, and Kott in his somewhat contemptuous mental picture of them and their grandiose plan. His departure with Gog must have been observed, he told himself, by some spy or another concealed in the vicinity of the entrance. He had accepted Gog's invitation as the lesser of two dangers. The night, at any rate, had passed safely for Dorothy; the day could be faced with some assurance now that Gog's probable conduct was beyond suspicion.

The dead silence and the total absence of guards were more alarming than the most hostile reception Chase could have imagined. He tried the door. It was locked.

"Have you a key?" he asked Gog.

"No."

"Then how do we get in?"

"Serbin has the key."

Chase considered. "Can you force the lock?"

For answer, Gog put his massive shoulder to the steel door. Fortunately the door opened inward. It was a strong door with a good lock, but Gog forced it. Possibly the thought of Dorothy at the mercy of his masters increased his strength, but even without this urge Gog's strength was equal to that of any door and lock, which would have defied a battering ram.

The noise of the door being forced had penetrated the laboratory where Dorothy was at work. In alarm she fled down the passageway to the door to see what was happening.

"You are all right?" Chase asked calmly.

"Yes. What's happened?"

"The door was locked. Gog forced it."

Dorothy looked at the door. Then she looked at Gog.

"I did not lock the door," she said. "Why didn't you ring the bell?"

Gog answered. "The bell rings in Mr. Serbin's office."

"And he, presumably, is in bed. What are we to say about the door?"

"Brazen it out," Chase advised. "Some spy saw Gog and me leave, and locked the door on you to keep us out. They gave you their word that there would be no guards. This breaks the spirit if not the letter of their promise. If they ask us anything about it, we must deny all knowledge of how it could have happened. This is our story, and we stick to it: none of us left your laboratory all night, and we did not consider it our business to investigate any noises we heard. We did hear a peculiar noise about half an hour before daybreak, but I said it was probably an early worker delivering supplies at the entrance. You agree?"

Dorothy nodded. "What else can we do?"

"Nothing that I see. Gog, you will remember?"

"I will remember," he promised.

They returned to the laboratory, to find themselves confronted by Serbin.

CHAPTER TWENTY-ONE
First Degree

SERBIN IGNORED CHASE AND DOROTHY FOR the moment, addressing himself to Gog.

"So you did not care for what we gave you?" he demanded with caustic sarcasm.

Gog hung his head in shame. "I could not," he confessed with a humble glance at Dorothy.

Serbin ignored Gog's attempt at an explanation and turned to Dorothy.

"You have finished your work, Miss Grange?"

"I've barely started," she replied evenly.

"Then why have you abandoned it?"

"But I haven't," Dorothy protested. "We heard an unusual noise in the passageway, and went to investigate. Someone has broken the lock and forced the door."

"And what did you expect to find?" Serbin demanded coldly.

Chase spoke up unconcernedly. "I thought someone was delivering supplies for the laboratory."

"If you had ever heard Gog forcing a steel door," Serbin replied grimly, "you would not have made your very natural mistake. I happened to come in here just as Gog must have put his shoulder to the steel, and I recognized the sound immediately. Now, perhaps, you will admit the wisdom of our giving Gog an armed escort when he is cooperating with our bacteriologists. By the way," he added after a thoughtful pause, "it has just occurred to me that, as the door was forced, Gog must have been on the outside. Did he go out first, lock the door after him, and then break his way in?" Serbin smiled contemptuously. "In spite of what Miss Grange has done for him, I still believe Gog was born stupid and will die stupid. Now, Doctor Chase, how do you explain Gog's remarkable stupidity in the matter of that door."

"Easily enough," Chase retorted coolly. "Gog and I had been taking a walk. When we returned, we found the door locked. As you had given your word that all the guards would be withdrawn while Miss Grange was working, I naturally wondered what might be happening in the laboratory when I found the door had been locked. If some spying guard did not lock the door, who did? I consider my action in ordering Gog to force the door fully justified by both the ethics and the common sense of the situation."

"Before going into the ethics," Serbin replied, "I may answer your question as to who locked the door. I locked it myself. When the night watchman—not in any sense a guard, by the way—reported that you had disappeared in the darkness with Gog, I was alarmed. Miss Grange, I knew would be justly perturbed if she should discover herself alone at night in an open building. Fortunately the night watchman happened to be passing that way on his regular rounds when you and Gog disappeared. He waited a full two hours for you to return, keeping his eye on the entrance to prevent any guards or other undesirables from gaining unauthorized entry. When you failed to return within a reasonable time, I took the only sane course to protect Miss Grange, and locked the door. Why did you not ring when you returned?"

"I did not wish to disturb your rest," Chase answered ironically. "Gog told me the bell rang in your office, and I knew you would be dozing there in case of emergencies."

Serbin acknowledged Chase's consideration with a bow. "Do you wish to discuss the ethics of this—and other phases of your investigation—now?"

"Not particularly," Chase admitted indifferently. "Just at present I am more interested in breakfast. Miss Grange is too, I imagine, after working all night. Is it too early for coffee?"

"Much too early," Serbin replied with a cruel smile.

"Then what time is breakfast?" Dorothy demanded. "I need regular meals when I am working."

"Breakfast will be served when you make up your mind to tell us the truth," he answered her. "Not before."

"What do you mean?"

"Exactly what I say. You will neither sleep nor eat till you tell us what you have been concealing from us ever since Professor Brown's death."

She received this threat with a short, contemptuous laugh. "Do you believe I would have been foolish enough to trust myself in this country, with which the United States has no treaties that can protect its citizens, if I had anything you want and I am unwilling to let you have?"

"You are a very impetuous young woman," Serbin replied with evident double meaning. "I am more and more reminded of my fiancée."

"Oh, bother your fiancée!" Dorothy burst out. "I'm going to the kitchens myself to see if I can find anything at this unholy hour. I'm starving."

"Pardon me, Miss Grange, you are not starving. But you may starve before we have concluded our investigation, unless you take the sensible course of making a clean breast of everything." He shrugged his shoulders. "However, it is your own affair. If you will not talk, you can help us in other, equally effective, ways."

"We can talk about that later. Come on," she said to Chase, "help me find something to eat."

Serbin watched them with a satirical smile. When Chase tried to open the door leading into the passageway to the office and found it locked, Serbin spoke. "I carry the key in my pocket. The outer door that Gog forced is now guarded. As Doctor Chase broke the spirit of his agreement to keep you company during your work, Miss Grange, I concluded that you no longer wished to have our agreement with you observed."

They ignored this unnecessary equivocation.

"Gog," Chase called back, "please open this door for us."

"Stand where you are," Serbin commanded.

Gog hesitated. For a second or two he seemed to be on the point of going to his friends' assistance. Then he caught the look in Serbin's eyes.

"No," he answered, and stood where he was.

"Gog," Dorothy entreated, "won't you please open this door for me?"

Serbin did not bother to give an order. The battle over Gog's loyalty was not even in doubt, so far as he was concerned. "No," Gog repeated.

Dorothy changed her tactics. "All right, then, let's talk and get it over. Then perhaps we can return to common sense."

"I knew you would be reasonable, Miss Grange, when you realized exactly where you stand. And," he added with a contemptuous glance at Gog, "where your cleverest pupil stands." Joining them, he unlocked the door. "Let us go into Mr. Arkol's office. He will doubtless be waiting for us."

They looked back at Gog. Dorothy's look held only disappointment and reproach; Chase's anxious wonder. Gog had not moved. His blazing eyes burned into them as if he were trying desperately to convey some message, which he dared not speak. Seeing that they failed to understand his meaning, he slumped into an attitude of utter dejection.

"Cheer up, Gog," Dorothy called. "It wasn't your fault. You couldn't help it."

Her words sent a shudder through his huge frame, and for a moment Chase thought he was about to revert to the madness that had racked him on the steamer. But the trembling passed instantly, and whether accidentally or intentionally, Gog's doubled right fist smote the pocket containing Chase's report. He nudged Dorothy, and answered her inquiring look with a reassuring nod.

"Gog," Serbin called back, "make the usual disposition of yesterday's volunteers." For Dorothy's benefit he added a note of explanation. "I gave that order in English, Miss Grange, so that you might appreciate the extreme urgency of your work. The serum, which Mr. Arkol prepared in America, is worse than worthless. All of yesterday's volunteers died within ten hours of inoculation."

"I am not surprised," she said.

"Indeed?" he caught her up eagerly. "This is most interesting. You knew that the serum was worthless?"

"Nothing of the kind. When it was competently prepared it was very promising. You saw for yourself what it did in Gog's case."

"From which I gather that you suspect Commissioner Arkol of being incompetent?"

"I did not say so."

Further discussion of Arkol's competence as a pathologist was dropped. It could not well have been continued, for they had entered the office, to find Arkol and Kott waiting to receive them.

A conspicuous detail of the reception at once caught Dorothy's eyes and her nose. A steaming coffee urn and two large trays with the remains of two liberal breakfasts signified that Kott and Arkol at any rate were well fortified for the coming discussion.

"Everything as it should be," Chase commented with mock approval. "I understand this is quite a common feature of such sessions as this."

Arkol beamed. "Scientifically exact, as usual, Doctor Chase. We do not practice this refinement as a rule, but thought it might make you feel at home. Lena suggested it to us. Her experiences in your prisons were not without their value."

"As it happens," Chase replied. "We are not hungry now. The sight of all this dramatic scenery has killed our appetites. Suppose one of you gets on with what you want to ask us? Please stick to the point; I don't understand subtleties. If you are looking for information you may get it if you ask plain questions."

Arkol glanced at Serbin. "Shall I begin?" Serbin nodded, and Arkol continued, addressing himself to Chase.

"Who is your employer?"

"The United States Department of Agriculture."

"They are financing your investigation?"

"They gave me a leave of absence."

"Who gave you your instructions?"

"Nobody in particular. There was a popular demand for an impartial investigation, by an American, of your fifty year plan in genetics. You know as well as I do the reason for that demand. Your government invited me to undertake the investigation."

"Thank you, Doctor Chase," Arkol purred. "That is all. Mr. Serbin, would you care to ask any questions?"

Serbin wasted no words. "Who made out the questions, which were asked from the door or the gallery of the various lecture halls, during Mr. Kott's tour of the United States?"

"I did," Chase replied without a moment's hesitation.

"You thought Mr. Kott and I would be too dull to suspect that the questions were inspired?"

"No," Chase lied on the inspiration of the moment.

Serbin acknowledged the implied compliment with a satirical bow. "Who induced you to have those questions asked?"

"Nobody. It was my own idea."

"Rather a costly idea," Serbin remarked dryly. "The men who asked the questions followed us from city to city. Who paid their travelling expenses?"

"Themselves, of course."

"I fail to see the obviousness of it. Why 'of course'?"

Chase was equal to it. In fact he had rehearsed his reply mentally a dozen times in preparation for just such an emergency, anticipating that some day he might be called upon to explain the blunders of the secret service.

"It is rather a long story," he began, "but if you knew the American character as well as I do, you would anticipate every word. First let me acknowledge that I had no scientific belief in your plan from the very first moment I heard it explained."

"Explained?" Kott cut in indignantly. "Do you expect us to believe that? Who explained our plan to you?"

"You did," Chase retorted.

"I—" Kott exploded. "You are lying. When?"

Before satisfying Kott's pardonable curiosity, Chase disposed of the insult. He turned to Serbin.

"Make that man apologize for calling me a liar."

"He meant nothing by it," Serbin answered indifferently.

"All right," Chase replied. "Until he apologizes you get nothing out of me. That goes whether you shoot me or put me in jail."

The bluff worked. Serbin nodded to Kott.

"I withdraw the offensive word," Kott grinned. "Now please tell us when and where I explained the fifty year plan to you. And remember," he added menacingly, "that my word is as good as yours. No slick invention without facts to back it up will get by."

Chase smiled. "I might be back on a Hundred and Thirty-Fifth Street. However, to answer your question. You explained the plan to me in Mr. Serbin's presence, in my office behind the glass houses. Remember? You remarked that the janitor had done a sloppy job on my office window. Your enthusiasm, Mr. Kott, told me everything I needed to confirm the suspicions I gathered from Mr. Serbin's more temperate statement. What both of you said about brute labor and the rest was enough for any geneticist to see through the whole plan at a glance. You may remember that I told you I thought the plan crazy. I still do."

Between rage and injured self-love, Kott was speechless. Serbin also seemed to have been unprepared for Chase's defiant frankness. Returning to the attack, he changed its direction.

"If you knew from the first the nature of our plan, why did you go to the trouble of preparing those questions for Mr. Kott to answer on the lecture tour?"

"If Mr. Kott will not interrupt again, I shall tell you. Both of you begged me to help you to recruit 'young talent, virile talent' for the plan. Well, it so happens that I know a good deal about the kind of young fellow who would jump at a job in these times, and I did not want him to get stung. There are several thousand more like me at home, and many of the older ones have considerable idle capital—owing to the last depression. It did not take much persuading to talk them into financing my regiment of hecklers. That's exactly what they were. Some paid their own expenses; others, the young ones particularly, had their way paid by the older fellows who stayed at home and read Kott's speeches in the papers."

"All this still seems unnecessary to me," Serbin objected, "and insufficient to explain the questions. If you knew everything before we left your office, as you claim, why did you not publish your conclusion then?"

"Excuse me if I seem to be sarcastic, because I am not," Chase replied. "You are so sold on your fifty year plan that you cannot see how crazy it really is. Why, it is so completely silly that I would not have had the nerve to put out a draft of it over my own signature. Remember, I am a public servant, an employee of the government, and if I go about advertising that I will swallow every half-baked scheme for bettering the workers, and the human race in general that every nut tries to sell me, I'll lose my job so quick it will make my head swim. Yours is not the only crazy scheme I have been asked to endorse. Sponsors for some of the others would have paid me enough for my signature to make me independent for life. I turned them down because they were nuts and because I value my own reputation.

"Now, to answer your question once and for all. I saw that your bid for our young fellows was tempting and skillfully disguised. But I could not expose the common red brick beneath the gold skin without losing my own reputation as a geneticist with some common sense. So I decided the only way to show the young fellows what they were going up against was to let Mr. Kott himself tell them. Hence the questions."

Arkol's anger at Chase's estimate of the fifty year plan exploded in an eruption of personal abuse. When Serbin finally succeeded in calming his outraged colleague, Arkol confined his remarks to a single, withering prophecy.

"Before this investigation ends," he declared with venomous emphasis, "you will be glad to admit that the fifty year plan is not the crazy dream you say it is."

"In the meantime," Chase retorted, "I must reserve judgment on the sanity of your bizarre schemes for the betterment of the human race. Are there any more questions?"

"Just one," Serbin answered. "According to your own account you were convinced of the worthlessness of the fifty year plan long before you left America. Why did you come here at all?"

"For two reasons. First, the questions at Kott's lectures were a failure. The students were so interested in what Mr. Kott had to say on economics and world problems that they paid little attention to his unguarded replies when he lost his temper—as he often did. Not that I blame him," Chase hastened to add, seeing Kott squirm, "some of the questions were unpardonably rude. The worst of all were the spontaneous ones with which I had nothing to do."

"Are you making a fool of me?" Kott shouted, jumping to his feet.

"No," Chase answered, giving him a hard stare to interpret as he pleased. "If you will stop shouting I can go on." Kott subsided, and Chase continued. "The questions having miscarried, I was more or less bound to come here to get incontrovertible first-hand evidence."

"Have you got it?" Serbin interposed quietly.

"I told you yesterday that I had, and I have seen nothing since then to make me change my mind. My second reason for coming here was to enjoy Miss Grange's company. We became engaged before we left America. Any more questions?"

Serbin asked each of the others whether they were satisfied. Both nodded, and Serbin delivered the decision.

"Would you care for breakfast now, Doctor Chase?"

Chase repressed the sigh of relief, which was about to escape.

"Thanks. I could go a good order of ham and eggs with toast and plenty of coffee. What about it, Dorothy?"

She rose with alacrity. "Will I? Show me the dining room."

Serbin politely raised a detaining hand.

"Pardon me, Miss Grange, but my question was not addressed to you. If you will answer our questions as satisfactorily as Doctor Chase has, you may go to breakfast with him. We shall not detain you long. Pray be seated."

Dorothy slowly resumed her seat. Before Serbin put the truth to words, she guessed its import.

"Your testimony will be of more importance to us than your fiancée's. We shall not question him further, because we do not wish to waste your time and his. He has made up his mind to tell us nothing but preposterous fables. You agree?" he asked his colleagues. They nodded emphatically. Then Serbin resumed, "We may continue with Miss Grange. A guard will show you to breakfast, Doctor Chase."

"Thanks, but I prefer to wait for Miss Grange."

"As you wish," Serbin replied indifferently.

Dorothy's examination began.

CHAPTER TWENTY-TWO
Second Degree

ARKOL LED OFF IN DOROTHY'S GRILLING. "Let me put some facts before you, Miss Grange, in order that you may fully appreciate the importance of the questions I shall ask you presently." Conscious of his own swelling importance, Arkol paused impressively. "You were present, Miss Grange, when

Admiral Simpson asked me to examine a certain slide under the microscope. You remember?"

"Perfectly."

"And you doubtless will recall that Admiral Simpson accused me of being responsible for what was on that slide—the first made from Gog after his inoculation?"

Dorothy nodded. "You need not be so explicit. I remember every detail of what happened."

Arkol leaned toward her. "Then you remember that Admiral Simpson accused me of having infected Gog with my 'dirty instruments.' It was an insult!" he shouted in her face, making her jump out of her chair. "Sit down. Do you consider me a careless bungler incapable of sterilizing my instruments?"

"You are one of the most expert technicians I have ever seen," she replied calmly.

"Then what do you infer from that slide?"

"What I guessed at the time. The bacteria on it that none of us recognized were new."

"Yes," Arkol snapped impatiently. "But how did they get on the slide?"

"Naturally, of course."

"Professor Brown did not contaminate the culture to incriminate me?"

"Why should he have done so?"

"Because he was extremely angry at me for inoculating Gog without his supervision."

"Well," Dorothy replied, "Professor Brown may have been as angry as you say he was, but no matter how angry he was, he would never have done a dirty trick like that. If I remember rightly, I told you so at the time."

"Not exactly in words, Miss Grange. However, that is of no immediate importance. I ask you again, how did those bacteria get on the slide? You say 'naturally.' That is not a sufficient answer."

Dorothy eyed him coldly.

"Why do you bully me to tell you what you know already?"

Arkol smiled craftily. "How do you know that I know?"

"Because you and Mr. Serbin tried to steal the slide."

"Ah," said Arkol. "I shall come back to that presently. Now, if Admiral Simpson was not above blackening my character by producing that slide after I had left the United States, would it not be the most natural thing in the world for me to attempt to gain possession of it?"

"Not at all. Your defense against Admiral Simpson was watertight, as the Admiral himself admitted. My testimony would have been worthless in any court. I could not swear that the safe had not been opened."

Arkol felt that he was doing famously, better even than he had expected. He rubbed his hands together in joyous anticipation of his next question.

"Forgetting my alleged attempt to steal the slide, for a moment, let us go back to that evening when Gog smashed the window and saved you from an imaginary attack at the hands of Mr. Serbin and myself. Do you know, Miss Grange, that your extraordinary actions after the watchman—Johnson, I think his name was—left us with the wreckage were the immediate cause of your presence here and now in this office?"

"I'm afraid I don't understand."

"Let me explain," he purred. "You remarked that Mr. Serbin did not seem to be particularly 'put out' by Gog's very efficient destruction of the slide, which you were to have photographed for us. And Mr. Serbin startled you by returning the remark. Miss Grange, we knew then for a certainty that you had substituted another slide for the one with Gog's culture. Why did you make the substitution after you had promised to let us have a photograph of the original?"

"I don't know what you are talking about."

"Come, come now, Miss Grange. You are an extremely intelligent young woman. Please do not attempt to duplicate Doctor Chase's performance. It was a failure, as you saw. You do know what I am talking about, and you know the answer. Let's have it."

Dorothy considered, and was lost—or saved, she could not tell which from Arkol's expressionless face. She decided to tell the truth.

"I made the substitution because I did not want you to have a photograph of the slide."

"Why not?" Arkol prompted softly.

"I give you my word that I cannot give a satisfactory reason."

"Give any reason," Arkol encouraged.

"Professor Brown distrusted you."

"I know that," Arkol admitted with mock sadness. "Unjustly. But what has that to do with the slide?"

"Everything. Professor Brown left his unfinished scientific work to me. I know he would not have wished you to have a photograph of that slide."

"Loyalty," Arkol mused, "often gets us into trouble. Do you happen to know why Professor Brown did not want us to have the slide—or would have refused us a photograph?"

"As I have told you, he distrusted you."

"Yes, but why? What form did his distrust take?"

"Every form, after you broke the regulations by inoculating Gog, and after Professor Brown had followed the course of Gog's illness on account of the inoculation."

"Please be more explicit."

"Very well, I shall. He suspected you of looking for new and deadly forms of bacteria for use in bacterial warfare. He believed that your story of looking for an effective inoculation against the pulmonary diseases ravaging the people of Gog's tribe was a myth to disguise your true purpose. You were looking for some disease that would resist all inoculation, and you were going to tryout his serums—the best known—on a victim whom you had deliberately infected with a disease unknown to civilized peoples. Have I made myself clear?"

"Clearer than you realize," Arkol replied with a satisfied smile. "So Professor Brown willed you all of his unfinished scientific work? Most interesting. Let us leave this for a moment. Do you believe, Miss Grange, that our fifty year plan is of a military nature?"

"I have no means of forming an opinion."

"Thank you," Arkol bowed. "Your answers, Miss Grange, have been entirely satisfactory. Quite unlike Doctor Chase's. May I compliment you on your straightforward truthfulness?"

"It isn't necessary," she said.

"Then, before putting my most important question, I shall go back and give you my reasons for insisting on an answer—as I shall insist with all the urgency at my command. First, let me say that I already know the true answer to my question from what you have told me. I give you the reasons for my question merely as a matter of courtesy, and to induce you to tell the truth of your own free will. It is unpleasant to make a witness tell the truth against his— or her—will, as Mr. Serbin doubtless knows from his rich and varied experiences in our revolution. Please listen closely to what I have to say. It concerns you vitally.

"Professor Brown was wholly mistaken in his surmises regarding our fifty year plan. In its present phase at least, and probably for seventy years to come, the plan is precisely what we have repeatedly declared it to be—a means of lightening the burden of human labor. Gog's people are the solution, provided we can conquer their ruthless enemy, disease.

"The remarkable history of Gog's case was a wholly unforeseen revelation to us. Let me be frank. We were not seeking to destroy merely one enemy when we inoculated Gog with Professor Brown's serum, but a teeming host. If you wish, you can examine for yourself the cultures, which we have made from the blood and mucus of men of Gog's people. Those cultures teem with bacteria new to science; many are just on the threshold of visibility in the highest powered microscopes, and we can only guess at those below the threshold from their devastating effects. That not all of these are virulent is obvious. Many no doubt are beneficial, and necessary to the balance of health. Otherwise no living creature could survive such a swarming invasion.

"For long we have suspected the existence of these beneficial bacteria, controlling or destroying the harmful ones, much as bacteriophage is assumed to do in the normal human body. But owing to the multitude to be examined—there had been nothing like it in the history of human pathology—we have made absolutely no progress in identifying the beneficial bacteria. Consequently we cannot tell in any particular experiment whether we are going to kill or cure. Without some reasonable clue we may experiment by hit and miss for a century before we find a single fact of medical value to Gog's unhappy people. Can you be indifferent to their helpless suffering?"

Dorothy made no reply, and Arkol continued.

"When Gog survived his phenomenal fever, we knew that we had blundered onto a clue of the highest practical significance. Brown's serum had created the ideal condition for the destruction of the harmful bacteria and the survival of the beneficial. The astounding awakening of his intelligence—under your sympathetic care—was even more significant. The poisons, the waste products from the ceaseless warfare going on in his body, had been completely burned out of his system, leaving his brain clear and his mind free to function normally. Think of the possibilities! If we can control the intelligence as well as the health of our potential workers, we shall at last be able to live like men and not like weary beasts."

"Who shall?" Chase interrupted.

"The whole human race—all of us."

"Oh," said Chase. "I thought for a moment you had forgotten the workers. Pardon my interruption; I see you haven't. Go on. What else did you learn from Gog?"

"Isn't what I have told you enough?"

"If so," Chase replied, "I fail to see it."

"Then let me put it so that you can see it plainly. When I saw the surviving bacteria on the slide, which Brown made, I was amazed. I had studied thousands of slides made under the same conditions, and all of them teemed with unknown bacteria. The single unknown variety on Brown's slide was conclusive proof that his serum had destoyed all but the most beneficial—the one that had saved Gog's life and awakened his mind."

"Maybe so," Chase remarked. "I am no pathologist. I'm not even a bacteriologist."

Arkol appealed to Dorothy. "As an expert you should know that my hypothesis is not unreasonable?"

"I'm afraid I'm not expert enough to have an opinion."

"An evasive answer," Arkol retorted angrily. "You know as well as I do that my hypothesis fits the facts of Gog's case."

"My scientific training has not gone as far as yours," she replied with a touch of irony; "so you must not be impatient if I lag behind you in theorizing. I only know what Professor Brown taught me."

"But that was enough to convince you that Admiral Simpson's charge of incompetence against me was groundless?"

"I knew all along that the new bacteria on the slide must have come from Gog's body."

"Ah," Arkol purred. "Now we can return to what we left a moment ago. So Professor Brown bequeathed all of his unfinished scientific business to you, did he?"

"I have told you that he did."

"The nature of that new bacterium certainly comes under the head of unfinished business. And so, does Professor Brown's curious delusion that our fifty year plan is a scheme to annihilate our enemies by new and unanswerable warfare. Now what would an intelligent young woman, highly trained in bacteriology, devotedly loyal to the memory of her great teacher, and determined to carry out his wishes as a sacred duty, make of such a remarkable pair of bequests?"

"I am sure I don't know," Dorothy replied when Arkol paused suggestively for an answer.

"But you are the young woman in question, Miss Grange."

"Am I? The picture is too flattering. I am neither silly nor sentimental."

Arkol continued to enjoy himself. "Perhaps I am not very skillful as an artist. Let me tell you what my imaginary young lady would do. She would do everything in her power to justify her benefactor's generosity and his confidence in her. And how would she go about doing this?" Arkol tried to look modest.

"I confess, Miss Grange, that I was not shrewd enough to guess. Mr. Serbin—so he tells me—got the answer before he left the office of the pesthouse that evening when Gog smashed the window and leapt in to protect your honor. And almost immediately after Mr. Serbin guessed why you had substituted the slide, he decided that you must be invited to visit this laboratory. That, my dear Miss Grange, is the real reason why you are here at this moment. But I must let Mr. Serbin have the honor of telling you how our imaginary young lady would go about honoring

Professor Brown's memory.   Mr. Serbin, will you take the witness?"

Serbin lost no time in devious subtleties.   "Miss Grange," he said, "your probable reactions to what Mr. Arkol has aptly called Professor Brown's 'remarkable pair of bequests' is obvious to any amateur in psychology.   Knowing your generous and loyal nature as I do, I have no hesitation in asserting the following deductions as facts.

"First, you determined to carry on Professor Brown's quarrel with Mr. Arkol.   You have never trusted Mr. Arkol, and you have been inclined to share Professor Brown's suspicions.   I do not mean," Serbin stated emphatically, "that you were convinced that our plan is concerned with bacterial warfare.   Your training has been soundly scientific, and you do not jump to conclusions that can be tested against facts.   Nevertheless you did share Professor Brown's feeling that our plan is open to grave suspicion of harm to human society.

"Second, you realized from the moment you heard of the new bacteria that they had originated in Gog's body and not on Mr. Arkol's instruments.   You have practically told us so yourself, and innumerable trivial but significant incidents in America confirm what I say.   Your excellent training, and your estimate of Mr. Arkol's technical ability could lead you to no other conclusion.

"Third, putting these two together, you decided that the only way of testing Professor Brown's hypothesis was to identify the new bacterium by comparing it with others obtained from cultures made from Gog's people.   Gog himself had been thoroughly cleansed of the suspicious infection.   Therefore you became Mr. Arkol's assistant, to have abundant opportunities of investigating the disease at first hand.   It is plain that you would also have reasonably good chances of discovering whether we were cultivating the bacteria for military purposes.

"Fourth, with commendable scientific caution, you brought that slide with you for purposes of comparison with others you hoped to make in Mr. Arkol's laboratory," Serbin turned to Arkol.   "You may resume the examination."

"Before you begin," Dorothy interrupted, "I must protest at the absurd nonsense you have been putting into my mouth—or mind, as I certainly never imagined such rubbish."

Arkol enjoyed her heightened color with evident relish for some moments before putting his next question.

"Where is that slide now, Miss Grange?"

She laughed shortly. "Really, all this is so silly I can't give a sensible answer. Don't you remember that Gog ground the slide to powder when he twisted the platform of the microscope all out of shape?"

Arkol sighed wearily. "Let us not go over all that ground again. Mr. Serbin, I must return the witness to your more experienced hands."

"You deny possession of the slide?" Serbin asked.

"I know nothing whatever about it, except what I have already told you."

Serbin in his turn sighed. "Please answer yes or no to the next question. Is the slide in your possession?"

"No."

"Is it concealed in your effects—in your clothes, your luggage—anything you brought with you?"

"No."

"You can not tell me where it is?"

"No."

"Then," said Serbin, "let me tell *you* where it is. Doctor Chase has it on his person."

Chase hung back his head and roared with laughter. Arkol and Kott reddened with rage: there was something too genuine about the quality of Chase's laugh to be comfortable. Had they all been making fools of themselves? Chase continued to roar.

"Oh, this is too rich," he whooped. "The greatest wild goose chase in history ends in a mare's nest. What an egg, oh, what an egg!"

Serbin waited patiently for him to subside. When Chase at last coughed himself out of breath, Serbin returned with deadly calm to the attack.

"Did Miss Grange ever give you the slide to keep for her?"

"Hell, no," Chase shouted. "Can't you fellows think of a single sensible question to ask?"

"Give us time," Serbin smiled. "We shall come to the sensible questions presently. Did Miss Grange ever give you anything to keep for her?"

"I'll say she did."

"What?" Serbin demanded.

"Since you insist on knowing, I'll tell you. She gave me her love, and I intend to keep it."

"Was that all?" Serbin asked contemptuously.

"Isn't that plenty?"

"Not having shared Miss Grange's bounty, I cannot say. Do you think you will be able to keep it?"

"Go ahead," Chase retorted. "I can't hit you. You've got too many friends in the passageway. What else do you want to know?"

"Nothing, if you will give me the slide now, without causing me to ask more useless questions. You are determined to evade the truth. I know you have the slide on your person, because your effects have been thoroughly searched by experts. So, for that matter, have Miss Grange's—as an entirely unnecessary precaution, perhaps. I think it is obvious that Miss Grange entrusted the slide to your care. You are her fiancée; you would be less likely than she to be questioned by the ordinary police officer, and you, being a man, could more easily dispose of the slide or destroy it in an emergency than she might."

During this rather acute analysis of Serbin's Dorothy kept her eyes on the floor, not as if she were guiltily apprehensive, but as if she were bored. Arkol and Kott, keenly scrutinizing her face, detected no symptoms of uneasiness. When Chase next spoke, she glanced up briefly, but that was all.

"I admit the soundness of your logic," Chase remarked to Serbin. "But I deny your hypotheses. If I know anything about reasoning, nothing follows from anything you have said."

"Perhaps not," Serbin agreed. "To be brief, I shall ask you, for the last time, to hand me the slide."

Chase flung out his hands.

"I haven't got it."

"Then where is it?"

"Search *me,*" Chase retorted indifferently. "For all I know, there never was any slide, I never heard of it till you and Mr. Arkol told me all about it a little while ago."

Kott took it upon himself to explain that 'search me' was American slang for 'I have not the slightest idea,' or 'damned if I know,' or something of the sort, expressing ignorance and in-difference. Serbin thanked him for the information.

"I prefer, however," he said, "to take Mr. Chase's invitation literally. I shall have him searched. Mr. Arkol, will you telephone for a competent agent?"

While Arkol was telephoning, Dorothy rose. Evidently, from her suffused cheeks, she was overcome by modesty. "May I wait in the laboratory till the search is over?" she asked Serbin.

"Certainly, Miss Grange. You will doubtless find Gog there to entertain you."

"Thanks," she said, and slipped from the office, without so much as a glance in Chase's direction.

CHAPTER TWENTY-THREE
Third Degree

AS SERBIN HAD PREDICTED, DOROTHY FOUND Gog in the laboratory. The assistants she had instructed were busily engaged in preparing serums, but Gog was not helping them. He sat slouched over Dorothy's worktable, fingering the pieces of apparatus she had touched. When she entered, his back was toward her. For some seconds she watched him, to see what he was doing, and her eyes filled with tears. Gliding swiftly toward him, she called softly. His head shot round, revealing a face with misery and shame stamped indelibly on its repulsive ugliness.

"Come away," she whispered, "where we shan't be overheard."

Without a word he rose and shuffled before her to a steel grill in the south wall. Unlocking it, he motioned her to enter. He followed, and locked the grill behind him.

"This way," he said in his husky whisper, leading her across a white-tiled floor to the far corner of a spotlessly clean hall that might have been a vast surgical operating room. The air reeked of disinfectants.

"This is where they are inoculated," he said. "The dead are in there, waiting to be burned." He indicated a solid steel door in the south wall.

"Yesterday's volunteers?"

"Yes," he replied, bowing his head. "My own people. I betrayed them."

"They drove you to it," she soothed. "Gog," she went on rapidly, "will you do something for me?"

"Anything."

"I am in desperate trouble. The man I had hoped to marry may be unable to clear himself of suspicion. I don't know what they will do to him if he can't clear himself, but I dread the very worst. He will never return to America. They will find some way of making it all seem natural, and I shall have nothing to accuse them of."

"No," Gog said. "You will have nothing."

"You know, then?"

"Everything."

"Is he to be executed?"

"No. But he will never return to America."

"They told you?"

"They tell me nothing. I read it in their faces."

"And so have I. They will do anything to stop him from reporting on what he has seen. If he dies, I die. But I will not die without a fight—it isn't natural. You must help us to escape."

"How?"

"Come back with me to the office. They will be ready for me now. You must act instantly. Knock all three of them unconscious before they have time to shout. By the way, where are the guards this morning?"

"Outside. There are no volunteers today, and I am trusted to obey when I do not have to help with them."

"I see. When you have knocked them out, we shall lock them in the office. Then, somehow, we must get hold of a car and drive to the frontier. You can show us the way. It is our only chance. We have our passports. If we lose—well, I would rather die in the open, under the sky. Will you do this?"

"Will you answer me a question?"

"What is it?"

"Did Arkol ever tell you that I loved you?"

"Yes, he did."

"I do."

"Then you will help me?"

"Do you love me?"

"I think you are one of the finest men I ever knew."

"But you do not love me?" Gog sighed. "I knew it, but I wanted to hear the words from your own lips."

"Gog, what I feel for you is better than the love Arkol meant."

"And what I feel for you is better," he sighed. "Do you wish to go to the office now?"

"Yes," she said. "We must hurry."

In response to her knock on the door, Serbin's voice called out, "Come in." Chase was putting on his coat. The professional searcher had already left. Dorothy nudged Gog.

"Now," she said.

Serbin looked up as they entered.

"Thank you, Miss Grange, for bringing Gog back with you. I was just about to send for him. You will be relieved to know that Doctor Chase had nothing on him but his clothes. Gog, will you close the door, and lock it?"

Before Dorothy could recover from the shock of Serbin's announcement, he was already well started on the next lap of his inquiry. Completely bewildered by Gog's inactivity, and almost at the fainting point, Dorothy listened as in a fever dream to what Serbin was saying. Why did not Gog do what he had promised? But had he promised? She could not remember. Now or never was the time to attack. Why didn't he attack, instead of slouching there listening to what Serbin was saying?

"I shall not keep you much longer," Serbin said to Chase. "You have satisfied us that you do not have possession of the slide. But Miss Grange, I am convinced, entrusted it to you for safekeeping. It follows that you must have delegated her trust to a third party. Who could that third party be? You know only the persons in this room. I trust my colleagues sufficiently to eliminate them. They could have no possible motive for deception."

Dorothy woke from her troubled dream at the sound of her own name.

"Miss Grange, will you submit to a search?" she heard Serbin saying.

"Gladly," she said, the blood bounding through her veins again.

"Thank you, Miss Grange. The obvious sincerity of your reply, not to say its eagerness eliminates you. The slide is not on your person. Nor is it in your effects."

"Then," she said defiantly, "perhaps you will believe what we have been trying to tell you—only you wouldn't let us. The slide isn't here. We may as well have breakfast, it seems to me."

"Presently, Miss Grange." He turned to Gog. "Give me the slide."

Gog reached his hand into his trouser pocket and tossed Chase's pouch into Serbin's lap.

"As I thought," Serbin remarked, opening the pouch. He glanced at Chase's report and tossed it aside. The small wooden box, which Dorothy had confided to Chase, was easily opened with a penknife. Arkol applauded; Kott smirked. Serbin handed Arkol the slide. "You may now continue your extremely important researches, Commissioner."

Kott was all effusive admiration.

"How did you guess it?" he bubbled.

"It was obvious. Doctor Chase became fast friends with Gog on the steamer. Last night they went for a long walk together, Doctor Chase has always disliked us. Need I say more?"

Dorothy was on the point of collapse. Gog either did not see her frantic signals, or he saw and ignored them. Chase tried to brazen it out.

"Well, that's that. What's next?"

"Mr. Kott has something he wishes to say," Serbin replied. "It concerns Miss Grange particularly, as you, Doctor Chase, have eliminated yourself from our further consideration. Your unsuccessful attempt to commit sabotage on the fifty year plan in genetics has rendered you liable to sentence of death. However, we have no wish to exact the extreme penalty, as you are a foreigner, and we think it only courteous to the United States to waive our rights in this matter and commute your sentence to imprisonment."

"For how long?" Dorothy stammered.

"One day," Serbin replied. "The sentence, you see, is a purely nominal one. Doctor Chase will be free to leave the country twenty-four hours after this inquiry ends."

"I am sure our government will be grateful to you," Dorothy said fervently. "Please don't think too badly of us. We really understand nothing of your plan, and we came here with a lot of prejudices. Perhaps Doctor Chase can do all that is necessary by simply reporting that in his opinion working and climatic conditions here are unsuitable for young Americans."

Serbin turned to Chase. "Will you do that for us?"

"Tell me first where I am to serve out my one day sentence."

"We shall not subject you to the indignities of a common prison," Serbin replied with dignity. "The sentence was imposed upon you merely as a proper gesture to the respect, which is due our government. You will be permitted to spend the twenty-four hours pleasantly enough investigating living conditions in one of our workers' camps. Perhaps you will take a more charitable view of our great project after a first-hand investigation of conditions as they are, and not as you have imagined them to be."

"Perhaps," Chase agreed. "But which particular camp have you in mind?"

"As you showed great interest in it yesterday, we shall permit you to spend the twenty-four hours in that camp where you met Gog with his volunteers."

"Thanks," said Chase. "Everything is clear. May Miss Grange share my term—if she wishes?"

"I regret that it is impossible," Serbin replied. "Women are not allowed in the camps. Mr. Kott is anxious to speak."

Kott explained in unnecessary detail the techniques of artificial fertilization whereby the females of Gog's people were enabled to bear offspring with the desirable traits of a common father who might, in the normal course of his activities, father thousands. By brilliant discoveries under Director Serbin's leadership the productivity of the females had been speeded up by causing them to bear twins, triplets, or quadruplets, and to accomplish these marvels of fecundity in less than two thirds the unimproved, natural time.

"The possibilities are unlimited," Kott enthused.

"Disgustingly so, I should imagine," Chase remarked. "Just think of all the cannon fodder you could raise that way."

"We have given the point our earnest consideration," Kott acknowledged with a smirk. "Of course only the lowest grade workers would be permitted to sacrifice themselves in the national defense. But the least intelligent often are the strongest. You see the possibilities?"

"You needn't elaborate."

"Then," said Kott, "I shall continue with the larger aspects of the plan. As geneticist in charge of the program in animal breeding, I have been entrusted with the problem of making our new workers self-sustaining. The artificial breeding is only a preliminary expedient, a means to an end. And what is that end?" he demanded rhetorically.

"You needn't tell us," Chase interrupted, with a quick glance at Dorothy.

"Oh, but I must," Kott insisted. "Otherwise you will miss the main point of the present investigation. These artificially bred workers, magnificent as they are in all other respects except their susceptibility to disease, are as barren as mules. Either from lack of desire or from incompetence, they obstinately refuse to multiply. Only in the rarest instances does one of them manifest an attraction to another of the opposite sex, and even in these rare instances the union is invariably without issue. We had hoped for better success by mating the desirable males with the original females, but here again we were frustrated. The males looked with aversion on the females."

Kott seemed unaware that Gog was following his remarks with blazing eyes and short breath. Dorothy however noticed it, hopefully. Carried away by his own conceit, Kott proceeded to the nub of his lecture.

"You will realize," he smirked, "how gratified we were when the finest of all the males we have so far produced showed unmistakable signs of love. His splendid resistance, his brilliant intelligence, and his immunity to the diseases, which devastate his people, all mark him as the progenitor, the Adam, if I may put it so, of a new and higher race of workers. So now," he concluded archly, "if the predestined Eve is not too coy, we shall encourage our friend Gog to enter his paradise, and once more bring heaven to earth."

Dorothy tried not to understand. But it was all too plain what Kott meant.

"You have overlooked one detail," she said.

"And what may that be?" Serbin asked. "I myself have observed no oversight."

"Gog may refuse," Dorothy answered.

Serbin demurred. "Pray do not take his apparent indifference of last night as a fair indication of his feelings. Gog had a certain delicacy so long as his rival had a prior claim."

"Why not say outright what you mean?" Chase asked contemptuously. "If you think Dorothy will survive my death in your rotten camp to go through with this, you are just a fool. She will be dead before I am."

"I think not," Serbin contradicted coldly. "Miss Grange is an extremely healthy young woman. We shall take all the necessary precautions that she does not destroy herself. Besides, you forget, Doctor Chase, that Miss Grange has a very real affection for her partner in this epoch-making experiment. However, she need not undertake it if she will give Commissioner Arkol full instructions for preparing Professor Brown's serums A, P, and S. Without this knowledge he may blunder for years in his search for immunity. With it, he could probably duplicate our success with Gog in a week." He turned to Dorothy. "As an additional inducement we shall suspend Doctor Chase's sentence of imprisonment indefinitely, if you will write out for Mr. Arkol the necessary instructions, and stay here a few days to verify their accuracy."

Dorothy was about to assent eagerly, when she caught the look in Chase's eyes.

"I would do it if I could," she said. "But, as I told Mr. Arkol, the technique is extremely complicated, and I have no hope of ever remembering it. Oh," she cried, "I wish now that I had never destroyed the notes."

"Undoubtedly," Arkol sneered.

"Under the circumstances," Serbin remarked, "I see nothing to do but to proceed to the alternative. Gog is our last hope."

"You are overlooking Gog's feelings in the matter," Chase remarked. "He may be more human than you think."

"Not more than half human, at the most," Kott smirked.

"He is more human than any of you!" Dorothy flashed.

Arkol sneered at Chase. "Is that your opinion too? You seem to have overestimated Gog's attachment to yourself."

"I agree with Dorothy," Chase answered firmly. "Gog is more decent than any of you. And I still have perfect confidence in him."

"You too, Miss Grange?" Arkol asked.

"Yes," she said. "Gog is decent."

Arkol decided to give his streak of oriental cruelty the tidbit it had been hungering for.

"Let us put your partner's decency to the test," he sneered. "Your partner may be more decent than we are. If so, the credit is his mother's. She was a gorilla. Gog, take her. She is yours."

Gog leapt to his feet. With one hand he grasped the back of Dorothy's dress, while with the other he unlocked the door. She was too terrified to scream, and Chase, when he tried to interfere found himself knocked breathless by a violent kick in the chest and pitched into the corridor, slap into Dorothy's lap. He heard a confusion of derisive laughter, a slammed door, and shouts of terror. The shouts were drowned in a crash of splintering furniture and shattered glass, and gradually they subsided in moans.

The door of the office opened again as Chase got to his feet and Dorothy scrambled up beside him in the corridor. Behind the huge figure of Gog looming in the doorway, Chase caught a dazed glimpse of the complete wreckage of the furniture. Arkol, Serbin, and Kott lay groaning on the floor. The clothing had been stripped from the upper parts of their bodies, and there was a red welt on the left arm of each. Chase became aware that Gog was speaking.

"Look," he said, exhibiting something in his hand, which he wished Chase to see. "Look," he repeated, as Chase failed to take in what he saw. Dorothy, however, was staring in horrified fascination at what Gog held in his hand.

"You inoculated them?" she gasped.

"Yes, with the virus from yesterday's dead. I waited till there was no doubt of their meaning. They are not fit to live." He turned back into the office.

"Listen," he commanded. "You three will be dead in less than ten hours. The infection is the most virulent of all."

Serbin sat up. He faced Gog with the old, superior smile on his lips.

"Ten hours? Eight minutes!"

While Gog stared at him in fascinated silence Serbin reached into his back pocket, extracted what looked like a silver cigarette case, opened it, and tossed each of his terror stricken companions one of the long, white capsules, which it contained.

"Your life insurance, gentlemen," he scoffed. "To your continued good health." He swallowed his own capsule. Arkol hesitated. A glance at the swollen blister on his arm where Gog had inoculated him ended his indecision, and he swallowed his capsule.

"What about you—*father?*" Gog jeered at Kott.

Kott wept, but he swallowed his poison.

Gog burst into a roar of harsh, triumphant laughter. It was the first time they had ever heard him laugh.

"You cowards," he shouted. "You intellectual fools. You will be dead in less than eight minutes. What Arkol said about my mother is the truth. Last night I showed her to Doctor Chase. But her son, and all of my brothers, all of my people whose mothers are like mine, have more courage and more cunning than you cowardly intellectuals. I inoculated you with distilled water! Now you fools have committed suicide because the three of you together lack the courage of a louse or the common sense of a gorilla."

Serbin alone smiled as he lost consciousness.

Gog escorted them to the frontier. The passports, which Serbin had made out, never dreaming that they would be presented, were honored without question. They decided to clear out at once, and not risk waiting the few hours more for the steamer. Within five hours of Serbin's exit they were in neutral territory.

They tried to take Gog with them, but he refused.

"The others need me now that the plan has failed. The government will never go on with it. The brains that bred it are cold. I shall take the healthy back to the place nature gave them. Good-bye, and forget me."

"Never!" they cried. "We shall see you again, when all this has been forgotten."

THE END

If you've enjoyed this book, you will not want to miss these terrific titles…

ARMCHAIR SCI-FI & HORROR DOUBLE NOVELS, $12.95 each

D-41   **FULL CYCLE** by Clifford D. Simak
          IT WAS THE DAY OF THE ROBOT by Frank Belknap Long

D-42   **THIS CROWDED EARTH** by Robert Bloch
          REIGN OF THE TELEPUPPETS by Daniel Galouye

D-43   **THE CRISPIN AFFAIR** by Jack Sharkey
          THE RED HELL OF JUPITER by Paul Ernst

D-44   **PLANET OF DREAD** by Dwight V. Swain
          WE THE MACHINE by Gerald Vance

D-45   **THE STAR HUNTER** by Edmond Hamilton
          THE ALIEN by Raymond F. Jones

D-46   **WORLD OF IF** by Rog Phillips
          SLAVE RAIDERS FROM MERCURY by Don Wilcox

D-47   **THE ULTIMATE PERIL** by Robert Abernathy
          PLANET OF SHAME by Bruce Elliot

D-48   **THE FLYING EYES** by J. Hunter Holly
          SOME FABULOUS YONDER by Phillip Jose Farmer

D-49   **THE COSMIC BUNGLERS** by Geoff St. Reynard
          THE BUTTONED SKY by Geoff St. Reynard

D-50   **TYRANTS OF TIME** by Milton Lesser
          PARIAH PLANET by Murray Leinster

ARMCHAIR SCIENCE FICTION CLASSICS, $12.95 each

C-13   **SUNKEN WORLD**
          by Stanton A. Coblentz

C-14   **THE LAST VIAL**
          by Sam McClatchie, M. D.

C-15   **WE WHO SURVIVED (THE FIFTH ICE AGE)**
          by Sterling Noel

ARMCHAIR MASTERS OF SCIENCE FICTION SERIES, $16.95 each

MS-5   **MASTERS OF SCIENCE FICTION, Vol. Five**
          Winston K. Marks—Test Colony and other tales

MS-6   **MASTERS OF SCIENCE FICTION, Vol. Six**
          Fritz Leiber—Deadly Moon and other tales

If you've enjoyed this book, you will not want to miss these terrific titles…

ARMCHAIR SCI-FI & HORROR DOUBLE NOVELS, $12.95 each

D-51   **A GOD NAMED SMITH** by Henry Slesar
WORLDS OF THE IMPERIUM by Keith Laumer

D-52   **CRAIG'S BOOK** by Don Wilcox
EDGE OF THE KNIFE by H. Beam Piper

D-53   **THE SHINING CITY** by Rena M. Vale
THE RED PLANET by Russ Winterbotham

D-54   **THE MAN WHO LIVED TWICE** by Rog Phillips
VALLEY OF THE CROEN by Lee Tarbell

D-55   **OPERATION DISASTER** by Milton Lesser
LAND OF THE DAMNED by Berkeley Livingston

D-56   **CAPTIVE OF THE CENTAURIANESS** by Poul Anderson
A PRINCESS OF MARS by Edgar Rice Burroughs

D-57   **THE NON-STATISTICAL MAN** by Raymond F. Jones
MISSION FROM MARS by Rick Conroy

D-58   **INTRUDERS FROM THE STARS** by Ross Rocklynne
FLIGHT OF THE STARLING by Chester S. Geier

D-59   **COSMIC SABOTEUR** by Frank M. Robinson
LOOK TO THE STARS by Willard Hawkins

D-60   **THE MOON IS HELL!** by John W. Campbell, Jr.
THE GREEN WORLD by Hal Clement

ARMCHAIR SCIENCE FICTION CLASSICS, $12.95 each

C-16   **THE SHAVER MYSTERY, Book Three**
by Richard S. Shaver

C-17   **THE PLANET STRAPPERS**
by Raymond Z. Gallun

C-18   **THE FOURTH "R"**
by George O. Smith

ARMCHAIR SCI-FI & HORROR GEMS SERIES, $12.95 each

G-5   **SCIENCE FICTION GEMS, Vol. Three**
C. M. Kornbluth and others

G-6   **HORROR GEMS, Vol. Three**
August Derleth and others

If you've enjoyed this book, you will not want to miss these terrific titles...

ARMCHAIR SCI-FI & HORROR DOUBLE NOVELS, $12.95 each

D-61   **THE MAN WHO STOPPED AT NOTHING** by Paul W. Fairman
           TEN FROM INFINITY by Ivar Jorgensen

D-62   **WORLDS WITHIN** by Rog Phillips
           THE SLAVE by C.M. Kornbluth

D-63   **SECRET OF THE BLACK PLANET** by Milton Lesser
           THE OUTCASTS OF SOLAR III by Emmett McDowell

D-64   **WEB OF THE WORLDS** by Harry Harrison and Katherine MacLean
           RULE GOLDEN by Damon Knight

D-65   **TEN TO THE STARS** by Raymond Z. Gallun
           THE CONQUERORS by David H. Keller, M. D.

D-66   **THE HORDE FROM INFINITY** by Dwight V. Swain
           THE DAY THE EARTH FROZE by Gerald Hatch

D-67   **THE WAR OF THE WORLDS** by H. G. Wells
           THE TIME MACHINE by H. G. Wells

D-68   **STARCOMBERS** by Edmond Hamilton
           THE YEAR WHEN STARDUST FELL by Raymond F. Jones

D-69   **HOCUS-POCUS UNIVERSE** by Jack Williamson
           QUEEN OF THE PANTHER WORLD by Berkeley Livingston

D-70   **BATTERING RAMS OF SPACE** by Don Wilcox
           DOOMSDAY WING by George H. Smith

ARMCHAIR SCIENCE FICTION CLASSICS, $12.95 each

C-19   **EMPIRE OF JEGGA**
           by David V. Reed

C-20   **THE TOMORROW PEOPLE**
           by Judith Merril

C-21   **THE MAN FROM YESTERDAY**
           by Howard Browne as by Lee Francis

C-22   **THE TIME TRADERS**
           by Andre Norton

C-23   **ISLANDS OF SPACE**
           by John W. Campbell

C-24   **THE GALAXY PRIMES**
           by E. E. "Doc" Smith

If you've enjoyed this book, you will not want to miss these terrific titles…

ARMCHAIR SCI-FI & HORROR DOUBLE NOVELS, $12.95 each

D-91   **THE TIME TRAP** by Henry Kuttner
THE LUNAR LICHEN by Hal Clement

D-92   **SARGASSO OF LOST STARSHIPS** by Poul Anderson
THE ICE QUEEN by Don Wilcox

D-93   **THE PRINCE OF SPACE** by Jack Williamson
POWER by Harl Vincent

D-94   **PLANET OF NO RETURN** by Howard Browne
THE ANNIHILATOR COMES by Ed Earl Repp

D-95   **THE SINISTER INVASION** by Edmond Hamilton
OPERATION TERROR by Murray Leinster

D-96   **TRANSIENT** by Ward Moore
THE WORLD-MOVER by George O. Smith

D-97   **FORTY DAYS HAS SEPTEMBER** by Milton Lesser
THE DEVIL'S PLANET by David Wright O'Brien

D-98   **THE CYBERENE** by Rog Phillips
BADGE OF INFAMY by Lester del Rey

D-99   **THE JUSTICE OF MARTIN BRAND** by Raymond A. Palmer
BRING BACK MY BRAIN by Dwight V. Swain

D-100   **WIDE-OPEN PLANET** by L. Sprague de Camp
AND THEN THE TOWN TOOK OFF by Richard Wilson

ARMCHAIR SCIENCE FICTION CLASSICS, $12.95 each

C-31   **THE GOLDEN GUARDSMEN**
by S. J. Byrne

C-32   **ONE AGAINST THE MOON**
by Donald A. Wollheim

C-33   **HIDDEN CITY**
by Chester S. Geier

ARMCHAIR SCI-FI & HORROR GEMS SERIES, $12.95 each

G-9   **SCIENCE FICTION GEMS, Vol. Five**
Clifford D. Simak and others

G-10   **HORROR GEMS, Vol. Five**
E. Hoffman Price and others